ANGEL

ANGEL

NICOLE "COCO" MARROW

AND

LAURA HAYDEN

A TOM DOHERTY ASSOCIATES BOOK

NEW YORK

ANGEL

Copyright © 2011 by Ice Touring, Inc.

A Forge Book
Published by Tom Doherty Associates, LLC
175 Fifth Avenue
New York, NY 10010

www.tor-forge.com

Forge® is a registered trademark of Tom Doherty Associates, LLC

ISBN 978-0-7653-2709-3 (hardcover)
ISBN 978-0-7653-3023-9 (trade paperback)

First Edition: September 2011

Printed in the United States of America

0 9 8 7 6 5 4 3 2 1

To my mom, Tina, and sister, Kristy,
for believing in me and believing in ghosts.

Your support and our belief inspired this book.

Love, Coco

ANGEL

1

CoastalEast Air Flight Number 617

The woman's body convulsed. She woke with a gasp. It was as if she suddenly recalled why and how to breathe. The screech of roaring engines at full thrust thrummed in her ears. The noise was so loud it made her body vibrate in a similar pulsating rhythm.

A second later, a different shiver coursed through her. She couldn't think. Couldn't remember . . .

Even trying to remember was like moving through a fog. Nothing was visible. Nothing made sense.

The overwhelming wall of sound seemed to take her over, as if her body was in the grip of its rhythm.

She clenched the arms of . . . what? A chair?

Where am I?

She opened her eyes, slowly focusing on the blue panel directly ahead of her: a small flat-screen television that featured a tiny icon of an airplane pictured against a map of the East Coast of the United States.

What's that?

The screen changed, the map now showing a larger airplane over a jagged blob tagged with "LGA."

I'm . . . on a plane?

A male voice from an intercom tried to cut through the shrieking engine noise. "Ladies and gentleman, the pilot has informed me that we've been cleared to land. Please turn off and stow all portable—"

The plane bucked and the passengers groaned en masse.

Where am I going?

"—electronic equipment. We apologize for the turbulence."

Where have I been?

"Please return to your seats, make sure your seatback is in an upright position, and—"

The plane pitched sharply to the right and dropped a good fifty feet. She gripped the arms of the chair and fought the small wave of nausea that seized her stomach. The other passengers reacted with universal sounds of alarm including groans and more than a few screams.

What's happening?

The flight attendant's voice lost its cultured polish. He swore "Oh, shit . . ." into the uncovered microphone. Then the sound cut off.

What was happening?

Now the attendant barked into the mike, "Fasten your seatbelts, now!"

The seatbelt?

She unpried a hand from the chair arm long enough to reach down to discover the safety strap was already pulled tightly across her lap. Nevertheless, she tugged the free end of the belt harder.

If tight was good, tighter must be better.

She glanced to her right at the sleeping man seated next to her. Slumped against the window, he was evidently the sort of seasoned traveler who didn't let a little turbulence disturb a good nap. At least he wore his seatbelt.

Was he a stranger? Did she know him? Were they traveling together? Questions pounded at her, slamming into the blank wall of her memory.

I don't even remember getting on this pla—

The aircraft lurched again, resulting in another chorus of screams from the passengers. Two young men on the other end of her row laughed and raised their arms as if riding on a roller coaster.

And yet neither the rough ride nor the noise woke the dozing man next to her.

Glancing past him, she looked through the small window, expecting to see rain lashing the glass, or bolts of lightning slicing through angry clouds . . . anything that could be considered an unfortunate but logical cause of the plane's erratic movements. But she saw nothing unusual. She looked down at Manhattan, where the tops of very tall buildings clawed a cloudless blue sky like fingers searching for a handhold.

It was at that moment when she realized that the small window at the end of her row was actually part of an exit door. She stared blankly at the instructions on how to open the door in case of emergency, but her mind was too confused to absorb much detail. The directives and graphics printed there mostly boiled down to open door, throw it aside, and get the hell out.

If the situation warranted it, she would do just that.

The plane shuddered again, this time with such violence that several unbelted passengers slammed into the ceiling. Her mind supplied the sound of breaking bones but she couldn't have heard anything over the now-unsteady roaring of the engines. Several of the overhead bins burst open. Their contents spilled out, flying around and striking unsuspecting victims.

Shouts of concern or surprise transformed to screams of pain and fear.

The man next to her awoke. "What th' hell?"

She had no time to answer. Another sharp motion slammed her to the left, then to the right, and then, God help her, turned them all upside down.

The sound of screeching metal, screaming people, and explosions replaced the engine roar.

Suddenly, whole chunks of the airplane tore loose as they slammed into something hard. The plane bounced, maybe even cartwheeled several times, before settling upside down.

Something hit her hard on the head, then blackness.

She must have passed out for a moment.

When she awoke, she heard no screams, no panicked pleas for rescue by man or by God. Either the explosions had affected her hearing or everyone else was dead.

She was afraid to look around to see which it was.

But she had to do something.

As she hung from her seat, her fear and panic shrank into one small, highly condensed knot in her stomach. Something deep inside told her that she wouldn't have a choice of fight or flight.

If she wanted to live, she'd have to do both.

Bracing herself, she took a good look at the wreckage of the plane she still couldn't remember boarding.

She took stock of her options for escape. Where the right wing had been attached to the fuselage, there was now a great gaping hole. She could see flashes of daylight through it. But it was ringed with tangled metal and sparking wires. The smoke boiled through the opening, rapidly filling the cabin. Despite the decreasing light, she could see that the seats just one row ahead of her had been torn away.

Then she smelled burning. The smoke reeked of plastics and wiring . . . and the unmistakable stench of burning flesh.

She looked forward.

The first-class section was engulfed by an inferno. And then the sound of water rushing in, along with a great wave of burning fuel washing down the center of the plane, racing toward her. But not here yet, not yet . . .

"Hell! Time to move!"

She reached over the bloody body of the man who had been sitting next to her, trying to ignore that fact that most of his face was now missing.

Before she could reach the exit-door handle, the plane shifted with a groan of metal on metal.

She clutched the arms of her seat. At least she was no longer hanging upside down. She was on her side, with a gaping hole in the plane threatening to drown her.

The ragged hole dipped so close to the water's edge that oily waves lapped into the plane.

The metal of the remaining fuselage groaned under the stress. She could see cracks forming in the plastic and metal sides of the jet. It was breaking up under the pressure, and sinking fast. *No time for the door,* she thought.

She coughed, struggling to breathe, somehow aware that there were toxins in the smoke. Between that and the rising water, she had to react.

Now.

Using her legs to brace herself, she released her seatbelt. It took all her control to stay in place and not plunge into the smoldering water, filled with broken pieces of airplane, luggage, and people. She had one, maybe two chances to swing herself toward the gap in the metal before the smoke, the fire, or the water killed her.

Using strength and dexterity she had no idea she possessed, she took a deep breath and launched herself toward the gap just as the plane shuddered once more and rolled over again.

As she struggled through the hole, her shoulder hit something hard, slowing her momentum. But she managed to continue forward, propelling herself like a world-class caver through the tangle of conduits, wires, and cables that lined her escape route.

Her progress jerked to a complete stop when something wrapped around her ankle and held her fast—a deadly tether anchoring her to the plane. It was almost as if the plane were refusing to allow her to leave, but insisted she perish along with the rest of the victims.

Refusing to give in to her rising panic, she reached back, groping blindly through the murky water in hopes of reaching the snare. Somehow she had to find a way to get loose, so that she could surface.

The loop bit even harder into her ankle as the plane shifted once more. The sinking plane seemed determined to drag her down with it. Rather than paralyzing her with fear, the revelation pushed her into overdrive.

Fear or hesitation would kill her.

Once she touched the cable twisted around her foot, she realized it was metal, not something she could easily saw through or break. The only thing she could do was to try to untwist the cable by maneuvering herself.

Her first turn was in the wrong direction and the cable grew even tighter. She turned the opposite way. With each revolution, the noose loosened. Finally, just as her lungs threatened to burst, the cable released and she was able to push herself free.

She swam for the surface and her last hope of survival.

Breaking through the waves, she was rewarded not with clean air, but with more inky black smoke.

She coughed and gasped for breath, battling the minefield of burning debris, razor-sharp pieces of metal, the contents of a hundred suitcases, and the broken bodies of those who had once owned those items.

She strained to hear the sounds of fellow survivors yelling for help. But she heard nothing other than the groan of metal from the airplane that threatened to disappear completely beneath the water's surface.

As water filled the inside of the airplane, the small currents it created gently tugged at her.

Not again, she thought.

With a few hard kicks, she moved far enough away from the plane to escape the pull. When she turned around, she found herself mesmerized by the sight of the sinking plane. Any sane woman would have tried to put as much distance as she could between herself and the plane.

But something in the back of her mind insisted that she watch. Even worse, her brain insisted on analyzing the mechanics of the situation.

Water filled the fuselage even farther. The intact wing rose up in the air as the water-logged broken wing caused the plane to submerge sideways into the water.

She squinted through the smoke and spotted the outline of New York City.

We went into the river. The Hudson, I guess.

Time to get out.

She rolled over and kicked harder, pushing herself farther away from the plane. But in the process, she bumped into a metal suitcase, mostly intact, that bobbed on the water's surface. Grabbing the suitcase by its broken handle, she attempted to pull it close and take advantage of its buoyancy, but it was slick with oil and difficult to hold.

Something else floated nearby, obscured by the smoke. She swam toward the object, recoiling only when she realized it was the body of a man, floating facedown.

Rest in peace, she thought automatically.

A light breeze stirred the smoke that clung to the water, creating clear patches, allowing her to see more. More destruction, more bodies, more random objects floating in the water—a child's doll, a ball cap in perfect condition, a mangled pillow, a shoe . . .

. . . a seat cushion, which could also double as a flotation device.

She took a stroke forward and grabbed it.

With the cushion strapped in place, she pushed herself through the water with scissor kicks, trying to ignore the increasing number of bodies and body parts that blocked her way.

Small sounds started to creep into her consciousness—sirens in the distance, voices that seemed miles away. And something closer—a small burbling sound. It sounded almost human. She stopped, trying to determine where the noise was coming from. Behind her? Swinging around, she took another look at the items she'd passed by. She spotted the doll, now floating precariously close to the airplane, directly beneath the sinking wing.

It was wearing a blue outfit.

She peered at it. *Did that thing just move?* Or was she just seeing the results of the toy being buffeted by the occasional wave? Then she spotted one little hand moving, the fingers flexing as if trying to latch onto safety.

A baby . . . ?

The plane lurched with a moan of failing metal and some of the cables that held the broken wing aloft snapped. Now it swung loosely, as if waiting for the last support to fail before tumbling free. If it fell, it would land directly on the baby.

One more innocent victim . . .

Not if I can help it.

She began to swim hard and fast toward the child, abandoning the cushion when she realized it was slowing her down. The airplane continued to sink, sliding faster into the water, dragging other debris along with it. Even if the wing didn't separate from the airplane, it would be mere seconds before the undertow sucked the baby beneath the water's surface.

She swam harder, dodging debris.

Twenty feet, ten feet, five feet . . .

Too late. The wing shifted in the water, pulling at the small bundle and dragging him under the water.

Taking a deep breath, she dove beneath the surface, letting the moving water drag her down. She reached out, her fingers grazing the child's chilled flesh. Then she grabbed the torn jumpsuit he wore and pulled him close.

With a strength she shouldn't still possess, she fought against the current and pushed to the surface. Once they broke through, she kept the baby's face above the water as she swam away from the churning, boiling spot where the plane had once floated.

Searching her memories, she tried to recall if she knew how to give artificial respiration to a child, but the baby made that moot by opening his mouth and releasing a weak mew of a cry.

"It's all right, sweetheart." The sound of her own voice startled her, as if she'd never heard it before. How could that be?

She kissed the baby on the forehead as she cradled him close to her side above the waves. "You're safe now."

The baby responded with a strangled cry that sounded more pained than upset.

Then his cry turned into a coughing barrage as he tried to breathe. To further complicate things, she realized each rip in the child's little jumpsuit exposed a bleeding injury. Some cuts looked small, others looked threatening.

No time to lose, she thought.

"Hang on, kid."

The sounds of sirens and voices grew closer and the smoke dissipated. She shielded her eyes from the sudden, brilliant sunshine and saw something large and dark closing in on their position.

A voice shouted, "We're coming. Hang in there."

The baby stopped coughing and, perhaps, even breathing.

"Hurry! The baby . . . I think he's stopped breathing. Hurry!"

There was a large splash and someone swam toward her with powerful strokes. "I'm coming." It was a man's voice. A strong voice.

Then the rescuer reached her. As he approached, he called out, "Are you okay? Are you hurt?"

"No, but the baby is. I think he stopped breathing."

The man reached for the baby, but she had a difficult time releasing the child. Cramping muscles, she told herself, not a reluctance to let go.

He knows what he's doing. He can help. Let him take this responsibility, she whispered to herself.

After he gently extricated the baby from her arms, he cradled the baby in the crook of his arm. The man's relief seemed as strong as hers when the child moved and cried out.

"I'm so sorry, kiddo," he crooned. "I know it hurts. But I'm glad you're breathing."

"Me, too."

He turned to her. "You hurt, too?"

"No, I'm glad he's breathing."

The man managed a smile, then glanced beyond her. "Looks like our ride is here."

She turned in the water and was startled to see a ferry boat floating a short distance away. A handful of people stood at the rail in the bow, gawking.

"A commuter ferry?"

"We were the closest boat. Can you swim that far or do you need help?"

"I can swim." She proved it by doing so.

The man glided alongside her, saying quiet words of reassurance as he held the child's head out of the water.

"The baby's too young to understand you," she said between strokes.

"He can understand the tone. Right, kiddo? I could be reciting the Gettysburg Address to him and it wouldn't matter so long as it sounded reassuring."

"I guess . . ."

He managed a watery smile. "Just watch. 'Four score and eight years ago—'"

"Seven."

"Huh?"

"'Four score and seven years ago.'"

He smiled at the baby. "I hope you grow up to be as smart at she is. 'Four score and *seven* years ago, our fathers brought forth on this continent . . .'"

When they reached the boat, the gawkers turned into helpers with outstretched arms.

She was dragged aboard the boat like some strange fishing catch. She sat up, dripping and gasping, safe at last.

The ferry passengers crowded around her. She owed them her life for the timely rescue, she supposed.

But their insistence on patting her as if their gestures were reassuring was more than a bit irritating.

Why do they have to touch me?

She hid her surprise when her rescuer held out the baby. "I suspect he'd rather have you hold him right now."

She looked at him and then at the baby and made no moves. "Why? You're doing a fine job."

The look of astonishment on the man's face confused her for a moment, then she suddenly understood. "Oh . . . I'm not his mother."

Something twisted in her gut and a sharp pain sliced through her head from one temple to the other. "At least I don't think I am."

The man's concern deepened. "Think? You don't know?"

She opened her mouth to speak, but nothing came out. Thoughts and images whirled in her mind like a merry-go-round revolving at warp speed.

She didn't remember getting on the plane.

She didn't remember where she'd been.

She didn't remember anything until a few moments before the crash occurred.

This wasn't her child. Was it?

After a moment of empty-handed soul-searching, she added, "I don't really know." She reached blindly behind her and found a chair. The people standing around her helped her sit.

Her rescuer's expression softened. "I think we need to get you two to shore and to some medical attention." He knelt down to her level. "What's your name?"

She drew in a long breath as if she could draw in knowledge at the same time. But the question stumped her.

What was her name?

She knew what color the sky was. She knew the Gettysburg Address well enough to correct an error.

But a simple question like *What is your name?*

She didn't have a clue.

She expelled the breath that she finally realized she was holding. "I-I don't know. I don't know who I am."

2

Ten minutes earlier

Dante Kearns dredged up a friendly smile and pointed the camera at his quarry. "So, how long have you captained the *Admiral Calvin Baumgartner*?"

The ferry's captain, who had begrudgingly introduced himself as Kerwin Grant, stared straight ahead, his hand resting on the wheel. "Eight years."

"I bet you've got some great stories to tell, right?"

"Yep."

Silence.

Great. The talkative type. "Could you tell me one, Captain Grant?"

The man's impressive mustache twitched slightly. "Nope."

Dante tried to keep his pleasant expression in place. "Why not?"

The man turned and stared into the lens. "I'm tolerating you in my wheelhouse only because my boss says I have to. Don't push it."

Dante raised one hand in mock surrender. "I'm not going to get in your way, sir."

Grant curled his lip in a growl. "You're already in my way."

Dante shifted back a few inches, hoping to demonstrate how he would neither block any view nor touch any of the controls. *Anything to get on Captain Ahab's good side.*

"Look . . . sir, I'm just trying to do my job." *If you even* have *a good side.*

"Me, too."

"Just give me a good sound bite, a bit of footage of you at the wheel, doing your job, and I'll get out of your hair and your wheelhouse."

The man stiffened. "You want a sound bite? Well, try this." Grant turned toward Dante. He drew in a deep breath and made a hand gesture that would have to be blurred or excised in the final cut. "This is what I think about you and your moronic *Twenty-FourSeven* Internet crap that masquerades as news."

Dante bristled. "It's the twenty-first century and we're beyond two-dimensional—"

Grant dismissed him by slicing through the air with one callused hand. "You're nothing more than a bunch of motherfucking . . ." His voice trailed away and his ruddy face drained to a pasty white. "Oh, shit."

Dante straightened. He thought, *Reporter causes captain's heart attack. Ferry runs aground. Film at eleven.* "Are you all right, sir?"

"Shut the hell up." The captain picked up his microphone. "All hands, all hands. This is not a drill. I repeat, this is not a drill. We got another one. Prepare for—"

An explosion blasted the boat, the percussion making the glass rattle and the deck list momentarily to one side. Dante almost dropped his camera. Once he regained his footing, he spun around to peer out the wheelhouse window behind him. That's when he saw the source of the captain's concern.

An airplane had just finished tumbling end-over-end down the Hudson, leaving behind broken, burning chunks of metal in its wake. The fuselage lay in three main pieces, and the center portion was floating for the moment. Its two broken wings were probably the only thing keeping the main cabin afloat. One wing stretched out on the water's surface and the other stuck straight up, acting as a counterbalance.

The captain continued barking orders into the microphone. "Prepare all emergency equipment—all lifeboats, all life-saving paraphernalia, all medical supplies. Secure all passengers inside the main cabin and brace them for impact if there are more explosions. All ahead full."

Dante used the camera to get a better look at the carnage. He zoomed in but the spilled jet fuel flamed up, filling the lens with inky black smoke.

No way in hell anyone survived that.

Nonetheless, this was going to be the lead story on every news Web site, every television, and every newspaper. And here he stood, in the wheelhouse of what might be the first rescue ship to reach the disaster.

"This is Dante Kearns, on board the *Admiral Calvin Baumgartner,* a ferryboat operated by City Waterways. The captain has just given the order to all hands, altering their usual mission of commuter transport. We've just witnessed a passenger jet crash-landing on the Hudson River." He focused on the bit of the airplane's tail that had broken off completely and was bobbing on the surface several yards downriver. He zoomed in on the logo, a globe lapped by stylized waves, now replaced with real ones, making the tail bob erratically.

"It appears to be a CoastalEast flight but we can't determine what flight or what equipment. We have no idea the number of passengers and crew on board. We don't know how many of them—if any—may have survived."

He swung the camera around to focus on Captain Grant, who was still barking into his microphone.

"This is the *Admiral Calvin Baumgartner* to the U.S. Coast Guard. A passenger jet has just crash-landed in the Hudson near Fifty-sixth Street. We are responding in rescue. There is fire and spilled fuel. I repeat: A passenger jet has crashed into the Hudson. We are the closest vessel to the main wreckage and we are responding."

A tinny voice answered him. *"Admiral Baumgartner,* this is the Coast Guard. We copy. We will alert all necessary responding units."

Dante shot a last bit of footage while standing in the wheelhouse door. He slipped out before Grant could stop him. Tripping down the metal staircase, he managed to keep upright as a choppy wave hit the bow. They'd picked up speed, something the ferry boat wasn't necessarily designed for. Deckhands stood at the rail with jackets, boat hooks, and binoculars, scanning the wreck site.

"See anyone yet?" Dante yelled above the engines roaring at full throttle.

"Not yet," one crew member replied. "But honestly? No way anybody survived that. No way in hell."

As they moved closer to the wreckage, Dante realized that the current in the river was causing the remains to drift downriver, spreading the carnage and the burning fuel. If there were any survivors, they could be practically anywhere. Plus, the growing flames and smoke were going to make any rescue that much more difficult.

The boat slowed as it came closer, minimizing the wake so that they wouldn't churn up any oily water. The captain's voice emanated from the deck speakers. "I see something. I think there's something or someone moving off the starboard bow."

The crew rushed to the starboard side and Dante followed them, only to be blocked by a rather large young man who planted himself in the way. "No one but crew permitted on deck."

"Are you kidding?"

Gargantuan looked like he'd never kidded anyone in his life. Maybe pounded them into the ground, but never kidded them.

Dante tried to smile. "I'm with TwentyFourSeven." When the name failed to elicit a response, Dante switched tactics. "C'mon, man, I'm only doing my job."

The man's stern expression never changed. "Me, too. You. Stay."

Unable to see what was happening on the other side of the boat, Dante turned his attention to what his limited view afforded him. Using his camera, he methodically searched the floating debris, spotting and identifying pieces of insulation, seat cushions, and suitcases—some broken, some intact.

At least he tried to convince himself that the things he saw had always been inanimate. But he knew full well many of the unidentified floating masses were bodies.

In his head, he was composing the voice-over that would accompany the footage, drawing words from the horrific images.

Is this "wanton" destruction or "capricious" destruction? Which word is better?

He knew not to voice his thoughts. He'd be thought coldhearted. In reality, compiling a mental monologue was a defensive technique he'd used since college to distance and distract himself from the shocking sights that often existed on the other side of his camera lens. It was the journalist's creed. Someone had to keep a cool head and a keen eye in order to preserve a factual history of events.

But once he put the camera down, he no longer had a barrier

between him and the disaster in front of him. He knew that without his journalistic barrier, his heart broke just like anyone else's upon witnessing such devastation.

A series of small blasts rocked the wreckage and the main fuselage began to sink, its broken wing dipping closer to the water's level. Dante didn't want to contemplate what might happen if the wing broke off. It was probably the only thing keeping the cabin from sinking completely.

That's when Dante saw movement. Someone struggling in the water.

A survivor?

Impossible.

He used the camera to zoom in on something light-colored, bobbing in the water. A person?

My God, someone survived.

"A survivor!" he yelled, trying to get the attention of the deckhands on the other side of the ship. "We got a survivor."

No one appeared to hear him.

At that moment, his self-protection procedures failed. Using the camera to see the victim more clearly, he couldn't subdue the voice inside of him that screamed for him to stop shooting footage and *Do. Something. Now!*

He watched as the survivor—a woman—stopped swimming and swiveled around in the water to peer behind her.

"No, don't look back!" he yelled. "Keep swimming! This way!" He waved his free arm as if she could possibly overlook the fact that he was standing on the deck of a big-ass boat headed straight at her. It wasn't like he thought she'd turn into a pillar of salt if she looked back, but the sight of the sinking plane might overwhelm her. Demoralize her.

Make her give up . . .

"Survivor on port side!" he screamed, drowned out by another small explosion. The ferryboat's engines rumbled and they began to move, but away from the sinking plane.

"No, no, don't go," he yelled.

He watched in dread as the woman began to swim back toward the sinking plane. Was she crazy? Confused? She needed help. Now.

He pulled the camera down, the horror no longer neatly framed in the viewfinder, but laid out in front of him. There was only one thing he could do.

He wedged his camera into a nearby deck chair, weighing it down with his camera bag, trying to point it in the general direction of the wreck.

Stuffing his wallet into the bag, he kicked off his shoes and grabbed a lifesaver ring. Then, ignoring the voice inside his head that told him his job was to report the news from an impartial angle, not interact with it, he jumped over the railing and into the churning waters below.

Although he hadn't been in a body of water larger than a hot tub in the last five years, memories of his misspent youth as a high-school lifeguard struggled to the surface. Luckily, the waters were cold but not freezing—after all it was May.

His first few strokes were uncoordinated and ineffective, but it didn't take long before he found a rhythm he could use to move forward despite the wake caused by the boat and the fetid waters, fouled by jet fuel and debris.

And bodies.

Ignore the bodies, he told himself. *You can't help them. Help the living.*

As he swam, he kept his head up, trying to keep his face out of the fouled water and hoping to spot her again amid the watery field of flotsam. Finally, he found the woman, now swimming back away from the sinking wreckage.

"We're coming," he shouted. "Hang in there."

Please be okay, please be okay, please be okay, he chanted with each stroke.

Her voice carried over the water. "Hurry! The baby . . . I think he's stopped breathing." She released an anguished cry. "Hurry!"

Oh my God . . . a baby?

He dug into the water harder, faster. He tried to respond to her but an oily wave hit him in the face. Swiping away the slime with one hand, he managed to shout, "I'm coming."

It took what seemed like an eternity for him to reach her. As he closed in on her position, he asked, "Are you okay? Are you hurt?"

Before she could answer, he heard shouts behind him. Maybe someone on the ship saw splashing around in the river. Then again, maybe they were headed off to rescue someone else. Panic coursed through him, giving him an added boost of energy which he used to bat away a floating chunk of something in his path.

Some*thing,* not some*body,* self-protective instincts reminded him. "Are you okay? Are you hurt?"

The woman's voice seemed weaker. "No, but the baby is."

Dante pushed himself, covering the last few yards with only a couple of strokes. The bedraggled woman held the baby close to her chest with one hand as she treaded water.

"I think he stopped breathing," she said between coughs, her own breath sounding labored.

He reached out for the baby while searching through his memories and trying to remember if he'd ever learned how to do CPR on an infant.

Slow, shallow puffs . . .

"Let me help," he said gently. *I know what I'm doing. I can help. Let me take the responsibility.*

The woman seemed confused, unable to release her child. It was evident she was caught between warring emotions—"Let someone help" versus "Who is this stranger who wants to take my baby from me?"

She finally released the child and he shifted the limp bundle into the crook of his arm.

Slow, shallow puffs, he reminded himself.

But before he could position the tiny blue-clad bundle, the baby opened his eyes and emitted a tiny cry.

Thank God, he's breathing.

Paternal instincts kicked in. Actually, more like the instincts of an uncle with six nieces and nephews, all under the age of five.

"I'm so sorry, kiddo," he said, using the same voice that had calmed his youngest nephew, affectionately known as Colin the Colic. "I know it hurts. But I'm glad you're breathing."

"Me, too," the woman said in a strained whisper.

There were two victims here, he reminded himself. The child and his mother. Maybe a third if he couldn't get them back to a boat soon. He turned to the woman. "You hurt, too?"

She managed a smile that didn't quite reach her pained eyes. "No, I'm glad he's breathing."

Now, how in the hell am I going to get both of you back to the boat? He looked behind him, expecting to see the *Admiral Calvin Baumgartner* long gone, but to his relief, it was chugging their direction. Someone *had* finally seen them.

He didn't have to fake his grin when he nodded toward the ferry. "Looks like our ride is here."

She followed his gaze, but her expression didn't change at first. Then realization kicked in and relief flooded her face.

"A commuter ferry?"

"What can I say? We were the closest boat." He judged the distance between them and the edge of the debris field and pointed to a chunk of insulation at that edge. "Can you swim as far as that big white floating . . . thing or do you need help?"

"I can swim," she said with an odd air of resolution.

To his surprise, her stroke was relatively strong, at least for some-one who had just survived an airline crash that should have killed her. It certainly seemed to have killed everyone else on board.

Except this little guy.

Later, Dante couldn't recall what he said to the baby. It was just the sort of things you chatter about to fill the silence, to remind the child that he wasn't alone, that someone was there who cared.

He did the same with the woman. He chitchatted as they swam, anything to distract her from her injuries and what had to be hor-rific memories of the crash. But what surprised him the most was that her answers were prompt and on subject. Between her mental clarity and her physical condition, she seemed to have survived with only minor problems.

Then again, he wasn't a doctor, just a reporter who gave up the story of his life to enter said story.

Neither of them commented when they pushed past a dead body or the pieces of floating debris in their way that turned out to be parts of bodies. Those observations were bad enough. They didn't need to talk about them.

When they reached the ferry, the gawkers along the rail turned into helpers with outstretched arms. They pulled the woman up and then helped to brace Dante as he climbed up the ladder, one rung at the time, carrying his precious passenger.

Once on deck, the circle of rescuers erupted in applause, but Dante ignored them and held out the baby to its mother. "I sus-pect he'd rather have you hold him right now."

She looked at him as if he'd grown a purple horn right in the middle of his forehead. "Why? You're doing a fine job."

Dante gaped at her and immediately took back his assessment of her mental state.

She looked equally surprised, then her expression faded. "Oh . . .

I'm not his mother." She paused as if suddenly realizing that she was in pain. "At least I don't think I am."

"Think? You don't know?"

She opened her mouth to speak, but nothing came out. The crowd surged around her, helping her to sit. One of the passengers, a motherly type, reached out for the baby.

"Let me. I'm a peds nurse. I need to check him for injuries."

He gave this woman a once-over. She looked like someone who knew what she was doing, so he reluctantly gave up the child.

After a moment of obvious bewilderment, the woman from the plane finally spoke in a soft voice. "I don't really know."

He tried to smile, to assure her that this sort of confusion was a normal thing after surviving a trauma such as this. "I think we need to get you two to shore and to some medical attention." He knelt beside her. "What's your name?"

She remained silent for several seconds before expelling the breath that she probably didn't realize she was holding. "I-I don't know. I don't know who I am."

He maintained his smile. "That's okay. That's not unusual after an accident. Everything'll come back to you soon."

She reached out as if she wanted to grab his arm, but pulled back just short of touching him. She couldn't disguise the panic in her face. "You sure?"

"Absolutely," he said in his most encouraging voice, hoping he wasn't lying.

One of the deckhands pulled Dante aside. "Captain wants to know if you saw any other survivors."

"Tell him no." Dante's stomach suddenly twisted. He'd worked hard to ignore the bodies floating in the water. But now the images were burning in his brain and he couldn't knock them loose.

So much death, so much destruction. He swayed a little at the thought.

Helping hands braced him. "You okay, sir? Here, sit." Someone wrapped a blanket around him because he was shaking. But it wasn't a chill; it was the memories—of the bodies, of the water slicked with oil and blood . . .

That's why he was shivering. Right?

By the time they approached the dock, he'd managed to work hard and push the memories to the back of his mind. He'd fought and won, regaining some semblance of control. It wasn't the first disaster he'd covered, he told himself. And it wouldn't be the last.

One of the female deckhands brought him his shoes, camera, and bag. As he stared at the camera, he wondered how long he could stall before reviewing the footage. Maybe he could send in the raw footage and let someone else edit it. He wasn't sure he wanted to see the whole thing again.

In any case, he needed to send in his footage.

Dante looked up to realize the young deckhand was still standing next to him.

"Don't look in the bag right now," the young woman said in a quiet voice. "Captain Grant ordered me to destroy your camera."

3

Dante opened his mouth to protest, but the young woman shook her head. "Don't worry. I talked him into letting me throw your memory card in the river instead." She placed her forefinger across her lips to silence him. "Ssh . . . and then I only pretended to toss it. It's in the side pocket."

At his expression of shock, she added, "The captain can be a real bastard sometimes. He lets his anger get the best of him. The crew and I . . . we kinda watch out for him."

"Th-thanks."

"No prob." She turned and took a step away, but halted. "I really like TwentyFourSeven," she whispered, loud enough only for Dante to hear. "If the captain figures out what I did and fires me, I sure would like a job working there."

"Uh . . . sure. But I don't think we have a company boat . . ."

She released an un-sailor-like giggle. "You do, but that's beside the point. Lucky for you, while you were in the river, I shot some footage for you." She nodded toward his camera bag and winked. "Consider it my audition reel."

Dante couldn't help but smile at her chutzpah. "You know the definition of luck, right?"

"When opportunity meets talent," she called over her shoulder. "That's what my dad always says."

"Your dad . . . ?"

"Captain Grant." She disappeared into a doorway.

Pushing away the blanket, Dante stood with a renewed sense of purpose. The young woman's confession cheered him more than he expected. Picking up his camera bag, he moved to the boat's railing and pulled out his Nikon. A situation like this called for still shots, not video. The paramedics bundled their two lone patients into an awaiting ambulance on the dock. Dante, getting back to business, took a couple of shots of the action.

After stowing his camera, he pushed his way through the throng of people that lined the gangway. Once he reached the dock, he stepped around the front of the ambulance. He tapped on the driver's side window. The man sitting behind the wheel looked somewhat familiar so Dante gave him a friendly if somewhat waterlogged smile.

"Hey, I know you, don't I?"

The driver looked straight ahead and spoke in a low voice, his lips barely moving. "Ten-car pileup on the bridge last month, caused by a blowhard politician. I was your unnamed source."

Dante searched his memory. "Komatsu, right?"

"Yep." The man made a show of checking his side-view mirror. A small grin tugged at his lips. "Sure was nice to watch the councilman be held responsible for what he did. Thanks for keeping my name out of it."

"Sure thing." Dante leaned in closer and lowered his voice. "Listen, I need a favor. I want to ride to the hospital with your patients."

Komatsu noticed Dante's wet clothes for the first time. "You hurt?" His eyes widened slightly in alarm. "Oh, man, you weren't on the plane, were you?"

A voice from the ship called out, "Don't talk to him. He's a god-damn reporter."

Dante glared at the captain who stood at the railing and answered him, "A goddamn reporter who helped the survivors that none of your crack crew managed to spot." He belatedly hoped his deckhand/wannabe-camera-operator didn't take offense at his comment.

The ambulance driver shook his head. "Sorry, dude. Officially? No room. Unofficially? I don't want anybody making a connection between you and me. Not after all the heads that rolled last month. I need to stay unnamed and unidentified."

"Okay. I understand. At least tell me where you're headed."

The driver scanned the dock as if afraid he was going to be overheard and then he finally whispered, "St. James. That's the primary ER for survivors. Not that there are many."

"Thanks."

Spinning on his heel, Dante headed for his car. He managed to maneuver out of the parking lot just in time to fall in behind the departing ambulance. To speed things up, he slapped a portable light bubble onto the roof of his car. He'd won it a couple of months ago from one of New York's finest who couldn't play poker worth crap.

Of course, if any cop caught him with the light, there'd be hell to pay, not to mention "impersonating an officer" charges to sidestep. So he'd told himself he'd only use it during extreme situations.

Like this one.

The ambulance cut a swift path through traffic. Dante kept pace, tucking in behind the bigger vehicle and literally drafting it.

While he drove, he speed-dialed. His brother Bryant picked up on the third ring.

"I don't have time for this, Hellboy. We're expecting a rush of patients because of the big crash."

"Then let me be the bearer of bad news. You're only getting two. Everybody else is dead."

There was a moment of silence. Dante knew it wasn't a matter of his brother deciding to believe him or not, but Bryant merely digesting the news.

"Shit. Should I even bother asking you why you know this?"

"I was there. On the river doing a piece on a ferryboat captain. We pulled out a woman and a child. There's nobody else."

"You sure?"

"I was there," he repeated. "It was bad. Real bad." He hesitated before adding the next part. His brother would learn soon enough. "I'm the one who spotted the survivors and jumped in."

"Of course you did." Bryant's sigh reminded Dante of the sort of response their father usually made when the brothers were young. "You're just as apt to make the news as report it, these days."

"Hey, don't blame me. The councilman swung first."

"I know. I saw the footage. So what do you need?"

"I want into the hospital. I know you're holding a tight rein on the media, but that's not why I want inside. I got a stake in this. I need to know that the woman and the baby are okay."

His brother remained silent for a moment as if debating with himself. Finally he spoke. "No photos. No video."

"Not without your express permission." To Dante's surprise, he realized he meant it.

Bryant continued. "You stay in the background. No calling attention to yourself. No breaking visitor rules, no bribing nurses, no sneaking around. No interviewing fami—"

"I get it. I get it. I agree."

"Okay, I'll put you on the cleared list." Bryant paused. "So what would you have done if they'd taken her to a different hospital?"

Dante dodged a potential snarl of taxis by swerving and then accelerated to close the distance between his car and the ambulance. "I would've phoned you anyway, hoping you could call in a favor or two with the head of security at whatever other hospital they ended up in."

His brother snorted in laughter. "Sorry, bro. There's no Benevolent Order of Healthcare Security Heads with a secret handshake or something like that."

"Really? So I shouldn't ask about that so-called security conference you go to every year?" Dante rocketed through a red light. "Does Norah know anything about this?" It was an idle threat and they both knew it. Norah usually knew more about her husband's world than Bryant did, himself.

His brother sighed. "Very funny. Just don't screw up when you get here. Or I'll throw you out myself." He hung up.

When the ambulance made the final turn at the St. James Emergency Room sign, Dante passed it by and flew into the closest parking lot. He skidded into an open spot and pawed through the various parking passes he had stashed under the seat. Pulling out the one marked CHAPLAIN, he slapped it on his dashboard. He even remembered to remove the police bubble from the roof. He'd actually tried to play police chaplain once before, but that had failed miserably when a real police chaplain showed up.

There was already a phalanx of security guarding the entrance.

Instead of flashing his press credentials, Dante pulled out his driver's license. "I have business in the hospital. My brother should have my name on the pass-thru list."

The guard glanced at Dante's face, then at the picture on his license. When the man registered on the last name, he cracked a small smile. "You the one he calls 'Hellboy'?"

Dante nodded, trying not to grimace. "With affection, of course." As he passed through the checkpoint, he stopped and called back, "And for future reference? He'll answer if you call him Bear." *Then probably punch you out, but he'll answer out of habit . . .*

Although Dante had chanced a dozen moving violations and traffic citations to get to the hospital, once there, it was a case of hurry up and wait. First, he cooled his heels waiting for the emergency room staff to decide to admit the woman for observation. The baby had been taken to neonatal intensive care immediately on arrival.

While he waited, he used his cell to send the raw footage to Victor Smithfield, his assignment editor at TwentyFourSeven. It was likely that other news outlets were already flogging footage from security cameras that happened to be aimed in the right direction. So even if he was a bit late with his potentially award-winning video, it was from a unique perspective that no other reporter could have had. Hopefully the deckhand's footage might be passable and, if the gods were smiling, would finish up what he'd started.

Then again, a Yamashita Pro25e was a pretty sophisticated piece of video equipment, not exactly a point, shoot, and upload to You-Tube handheld.

He'd just completed the upload when an orderly stuck his head through the doorway. "Mr. Kearns? She's going upstairs."

Dante nodded his thanks, stowed his stuff, and trudged upstairs to sit in a different waiting room with the same uncomfortable plastic chairs. The only consolation was that Bryant's security gauntlet had successfully kept all the other media types at bay. That meant Dante only had to share the waiting room with one weepy family waiting to hear if their grandfather would pull through his latest heart attack. That is—six weepy adults and one kid trying not to giggle as he tweeted.

After a half hour, listening to the occasional bursts of emotion from the opposite side of the room, Dante stood and stretched. He might have promised to not bribe any nurses, but Bryant hadn't said anything about not trying to charm them.

Dante's first attempt fell flat. The nurse behind the ward counter pegged him immediately as a reporter. In honor of that, she used only four-letter words to send him back to the waiting room, slightly singed.

Luckily, a shift change an hour later resulted in a charge nurse who was less inclined to shoot first. Maybe it helped that he used a different tactic.

"Uh, excuse me, ma'am?" He balanced his expression between polite and charming and anguished. "I was wondering if there was any update on a patient. I haven't heard anything in a while." He added a faked cough which turned into a real one. Life imitating art.

"Are you all right, sir?"

He nodded as he cleared his throat. "I'm okay. I think I swallowed some of the river water. The Hudson isn't the cleanest river in the best of times, but add jet fuel and debris and—" Another real cough interrupted his artful explanation. *Damn,* he thought, *I guess I did swallow some of that swill.*

The nurse wore a look of appropriate concern. "You were in the river?" She noticed his still-damp clothes and her concern stiffened into something more alarming. "You weren't in the plane, were you?"

He shook his head. "No, ma'am. First responder."

"Oh." The nurse relaxed visibly and shot him a friendlier smile.

"Have you seen the coverage?" She thumbed over her shoulder to the television behind her. "They're calling her a hero for the way she saved that child."

Dante watched the screen, recognizing his footage of the woman in the river as she stopped, turned around, and headed back toward the sinking plane. He then saw what he'd missed after propping up his camera and prepping to jump in.

The woman hadn't just gone back for the baby; she'd done so despite the overhead threat from the broken wing. It was pointing down toward the water like a guillotine's blade, ready to slash through victims—big and small. A dark blur—motion on the deck—obscured the view. When the camera refocused, it showed that seconds after she retrieved the baby, the broken wing detached itself and plunged down into the water.

It would have killed anyone in its path.

Then Dante watched his brownish blur launch from the railing, and becoming a splashing blur in the water. Although he remembered the incident as taking forever, in reality, it only took a few seconds for him to reach her, take the child, and start swimming back toward the boat. The footage ended there.

The nurse turned back from the screen to study him. "That's you? The one swimming with her?"

Dante shrugged. "Yeah. I was the only one who spotted her."

The nurse tilted her head in thought, then gave him a resolute nod. "Then I think I can spare you a minute or two to visit her. Here." She handed him a plastic badge. "Put that on and follow me." As she rounded the counter, she added, "But you can't stay long."

"Yes, ma'am." He followed the nurse down the hallway until she stopped by a doorway.

"She's in here. You've got two minutes."

"Thanks. Um . . . one more thing: Do you know anything about the baby's condition?"

The nurse grinned. "He's quite the little scrapper. I talked to the NICU about fifteen minutes ago. They said he had a broken leg, but other than that his breathing is good and his heart rate's strong. He's going to be fine."

"Thanks."

She pointed to the door. "Two minutes. I'll be timing you."

Dante stepped into the room and stopped next to the woman's hospital bed. He looked down on her peaceful, sleeping face.

So much for getting more information for a follow-up story.

The nurse stayed at the door, either keeping an eye on him, or playing lookout. He wasn't sure.

Looking past the patient's collection of minor cuts and bruises, he noted she was basically pleasant looking with an open, intelligent face framed by blond hair. Someone had even taken the time to comb away most of the tangles. Even though injured and asleep, she looked conditioned, as if she either ran often or hit the gym a couple times a week.

"She couldn't remember her name," he said softly.

The nurse spoke from the doorway. "I know. That's one of the reasons why the doctors are holding her for observation. But that's not unusual for people like her who've been in a traumatic situation. A good night's sleep and I bet she'll remember everything tomorrow."

He thought about the look of panic on the woman's face when she'd admitted she didn't know her name.

"I sure hope you're right."

She remembered. Screams. Fire. Water.

Water . . . she thought. "Water."

"Here you go."

She opened her eyes and tried to focus on the blurry shape

looming in front of her. Parting her lips, she accepted the straw and sucked greedily. Half of the cool water trickled down her throat and the other half spilled from the corner of her mouth.

"Not too much." The flow of water was suddenly cut off. "Slow down."

Her eyesight sharpened. The face that went with the voice turned out to be that of a female, maybe a nurse, dressed in blue scrubs. "That's better. Slow sips."

After several swallows, her thirst faded and her concern built. "Where am I?"

"St. James Hospital. Do you remember what happened?"

She nodded and the room spun a little. "I was in an airplane. It crashed. We landed in a river." She fought to keep control. "Everyone died."

"No, *you* survived. And you saved a baby. You're a hero."

"I don't feel like one."

"How do you feel?"

She shifted in the bed, finding it exceedingly uncomfortable. "Okay, I guess."

"Feel like answering a few questions?" The kindness in the nurse's eyes lit her otherwise no-nonsense features.

"Okay." Her voice sounded much stronger than her actual conviction.

"What's your name?"

Such a simple question. The answer should have flowed from her like—she winced—water. However, when she looked inside, she didn't meet resistance, but a void. Nothingness. It wasn't like she'd forgotten who she was, but as if she'd never known at all.

"Still a little hazy?" the nurse inquired.

"More than hazy. I don't remember anything. I don't *know* anything."

"Sure you do. You know what a hospital is." She reached down and plucked at the dingy top sheet. "You know what this is called, right?"

"A sheet."

The nurse nodded. "And you know that it should be white, instead of . . ." She studied the material for a moment. "What *do* you call this color? Off white? Eggshell? Verging on gray?"

"Threadbarely white?"

The nurse grinned. "See? You've even found your sense of humor. So it's not that you don't know anything, you simply don't remember your name. But you will. It'll come back to you. But, until then, we do need to call you . . . something."

"Jane Doe?"

"Trust me. You don't look like a plain Jane." The nurse nodded toward the silent television hanging from the ceiling in the corner of the room. "In fact, you've been the most popular person on television lately. The news media have already given you a name. And I think they did a good job, too."

"What?"

"They're calling you the Angel of the Hudson."

"Angel . . . ?" She repeated the name aloud. Nothing inside of her sparked in recognition. Then again, she wasn't repelled by the name, either.

"The ER even admitted you under that name: 'Angel Hudson.' That's so much better than Jane Doe, don't you think?"

Angel. The name was growing on her. She could at least answer to it. "Okay, I'll be Angel. Until we know better."

There was a knock at the doorway and a man in a white coat stepped into the room. "Hope I'm not interrupting anything." Rather than wait for an answer, he stepped into the room, retrieving the chart that hung at the end of the bed. "You are one very lucky young woman, Ms. . . . ?" He paused as if his silence would shake loose an answer.

She answered promptly. "Today, it's Angel of the Hudson. To-morrow, I'm not too sure."

"Pleased to meet you, Ms. Of-the-Hudson." His brief bark of laughter sounded forced, as if he didn't run across much humor in his line of work. "I'm Dr. Solano. And I'm pleased to say that you're in remarkably good physical shape, considering what you've been through." He consulted the chart. "No broken bones, no internal injuries. Just a few bumps and bruises. Nothing more than that." He paused and made eye contact with her for the first time. "So, how do you feel?"

How do I feel? When the nurse had asked, Angel had responded automatically. This time, she took a moment to think about it. "I feel . . . sore, a little, but mainly, I feel okay."

"Excellent." He nodded as if she'd provided the right answer. "Just as I hoped. So, let's see about that bruising." He shoved the chart toward the nurse who, swallowing back a reaction of surprise, caught it with both hands.

He performed a series of tests, checking Angel's reflexes, her eyesight, looking under her bandages, all while making noncommittal clucking sounds. Finally he turned to the nurse and rattled off an alphabet soup of initials, abbreviations, and numbers, which the woman duly transcribed into the record. After he finished, he graced Angel with a wide smile. "There, dear. That wasn't so bad, was it?"

The nurse almost choked.

Angel ignored his question and asked her own. "When will I get my memory back?"

He shrugged. "That's hard to say. Although we don't see any overt signs of swelling, nonetheless, your brain has suffered a trauma. It's going to take a while for everything to get back to normal. Just hang on. It'll all come back to you." He took the chart from the nurse long enough to scribble a signature on the top page. "Meanwhile, the airline is doing its best to figure out who you are."

"How?"

He glanced at the nurse, then shrugged again. "Process of elimination, I guess." He shot her a jaunty salute. "Take care and I'll see you tomorrow and we can talk about releasing you." He ran out the door, scurrying to the next bedside on his rounds.

Angel turned to the nurse. "I don't understand. Process of elimination?"

The nurse sighed. "They're recovering bodies from the Hudson and working to identify them. There were over two hundred people on the plane's manifest. They've recovered about half that many bodies. They're making progress."

A sudden flash of memory sucker-punched Angel: the somersaulting plane, the screams, the oil-slicked water . . .

Her rescue.

She fought to battle back the wave of unpleasant memories. "The baby . . . the baby isn't mine, is he?"

The nurse shook her head. "No. He's not yours. The airline said he was the only baby on board and he was traveling with his grandmother." The nurse replaced the chart at the foot of the bed. "You're not his grandmother. You're much too young for that."

Realization punched Angel in the gut. "How would I know? I . . . I don't even know what I look like." She reached up and tugged a strand of hair into her line of sight. It was light brown, or maybe dark blond. She couldn't tell.

"You're a blonde. And I thought your eyes were green," the nurse said, peering closer. "But right now, they almost look blue. Strange." The nurse rummaged around in the bathroom and came back with a handheld mirror. "Take a look, see what you think."

Angel took the mirror—and a stranger looked back at her in it.

That was so frightening she handed the mirror back before she even got a good look.

"How old am I?"

"I'd guess late twenties, maybe early thirties. It's hard to tell. Young, anyway. You're fit, too. That's for certain. Clear skin, clear eyes. You look like you exercise often. Considering what you did in the water, you definitely must swim a lot."

Although the woman now called Angel expected to find some solace in the nurse's description, it served only to depress her. How could she not even know what she looked like? Her stomach tightened and she pulled the thin sheet to her chin. "Why hasn't somebody come to claim me? You'd think someone would miss me."

The nurse cocked her head, then her face tightened. "You'd think . . ."

4

It took at least an hour for Angel to gather up enough courage to limp into the bathroom and examine the stranger in the mirror again. Her reflection wore a nice face, nothing spectacular, but with normal features—hazel eyes, a straight nose, and reasonably full lips. She had no discernible scars, clear vision requiring no glasses, and strong hands with short nails.

Average in every way.

A forgettable face, she decided.

She'd just crawled back into the hospital bed when there was another knock on her door.

"May we come in?" A woman and a man stepped into the room. The woman carried a briefcase and the man, a ready smile. They had an official air about them.

The man approached the bed. "Ma'am? I'm Lewis Marlowe. My

colleague Ms. Seymour and I are with CoastalEast Airlines." He placed two business cards on the tray table near the foot of the bed. "We just wanted to check in on you. How are you feeling?"

There was that question, once again. This time, she had a better prepared answer. "Not bad."

Marlowe came closer and graced her with a smile that made his average looks turn into something far more appealing. "If I may say, you're a very lucky woman and a brave one at that. We wanted to know if there was anything we could do to make you more comfortable."

"I'm not sure I feel lucky. It'd be nice to know who I am. Right now, everyone's calling me Angel and that's okay. But I'd really like to know my real name."

Marlowe maintained the perfect balance of compassion and professionalism. "We've spoken with the doctors and we're work-ing very hard at figuring that out. I know how . . . disconcerting it must feel to be missing those key memories." He reached over and touched her hand, causing her to shiver in a way that she really liked.

He continued. "I just wanted to assure you that we at Coastal-East are very concerned about your well-being. We pledge to do whatever necessary to make sure that you're taken care of."

"But may we offer a word of caution?" The woman stepped for-ward, stepping between Angel and the handsome man paying her attention.

Go away. I want to talk to him, instead, Angel thought instantly.

The woman continued, unaware of Angel's reaction. "At times like these, there are people who will try to take advantage of you. Fast-talking ambulance chasers, insurance adjusters." The woman made a sour-lemon face. "The media. All we ask is that you hold off from signing anything with anybody until you've talked to us."

To Angel's relief, Mr. Marlowe shifted back to the bed. "So far, the hospital has been able to limit media access, but the public is clamoring for more information. We thought that perhaps we ought to use that to *your* advantage."

"My advantage?" Somewhere in the back of Angel's slightly scrambled brains, a voice whispered that this was public-relations doubletalk. But it was hard to concentrate with such an attractive man standing so close to her.

When he smiled again, her heart sped up.

"To be honest, Angel? America loves to love people like you. People who prove themselves to be not only survivors, but heroic ones."

"Heroic?" she echoed.

He nodded and reached over, touching her hand once more. "America wants to meet you. You need someone in America to help identify you."

You're not just trotting me out to make CoastalEast look better to a doubtful public?

She stopped herself. *Where did that come from? He would never do something like that to me. He's a nice man. He cares about me.*

She pushed back the intrusive thoughts. "If you think that's the right thing to do, Mr. Marlowe."

"Lewis," he corrected.

She looked into his glorious brown eyes. "When, Lewis?"

Lewis Marlowe smiled, looking almost . . . triumphant. "Tomorrow morning. We'll hit all the news morning shows." He turned to his cohort in crime. "Ms. Seymour will help you learn what to expect, help you prepare your answers."

"You want me to rehearse?"

Ms. Seymour's smile stiffened slightly. "Of course not. We just want to make sure you're prepared. Press conferences can be a bit overwhelming. Shall we begin?"

"Aren't you staying, Lewis?" Angel asked wistfully, ignoring the woman. There was something about the man, a connection she felt with him that offered her courage and relief. She hadn't felt this good since . . . since . . . she couldn't remember.

He rewarded her with a grin that was nearly heart-stopping. "If that would make you happy, I'd be delighted. Now, shall we start?"

The usual flock of media poured into the conference room. Dante and his cameraman, Raul, had a prime position in the front of the crowd, thanks to an advance notice from Bryant.

Once they'd jockeyed for the best position, they waited.

And waited.

Finally, two white-coated medical types and almost a dozen suits—probably a mixture of hospital administration, airline representatives, and NTSB officials—filed into the room.

A balding man took his place at the podium. "Thank you for your time. My name is Ralph Maloney and I'm with the National Transportation Safety Board. We'd like to give you a brief update on the crash of CoastalEast Air Flight 617. As has been already reported, shortly after being cleared for landing at LaGuardia, the aircraft, a Boeing 737, developed engine trouble. The pilot attempted to land in the Hudson River but the airplane broke apart upon landing. Early this morning, we recovered both the flight data and cockpit voice recorders but have not analyzed that data. However, we do have eyewitness reports that describe a series of three explosions that occurred after the plane made its initial turn for approach. At this time, we cannot speculate as to the cause. Recovery dive teams are working today to bring up the aircraft remains, as well as searching for the bodies of the remaining passengers. The plane's manifest shows that there were two hundred thirty-seven passengers and seven crew members on board this flight. At this time, we have accounted for one hundred eighty-nine passengers. Most are pending identification. Family seeking the whereabouts of passengers on this flight should contact Coastal-East immediately. We will hold another press conference at six tonight to update you on our progress. I will now take a few questions."

The noise level in the crowded room rose as the various news organizations launched a volley of questions. The NTSB rep calmly chose which questions he wanted to answer.

"We can't speculate on the cause but at this time, from air traffic chatter, we believe the crew was in command of the plane and that there were no terrorists aboard. This was not a hijacking."

To the next questioner, he responded, "We've spoken briefly with the lone adult survivor but learned nothing of significance to reconstruct the accident."

Dante shouted the next question. "Can we get the names of the surviving passengers?"

The representative glanced at the clipboard in his hands. "We've been asked by the family of the child to withhold his name and are respecting their wishes. But we can tell you he was a two-month-old boy traveling with his grandmother. She did not survive. He has been reunited with his parents and is currently under observation for moderate injuries. His prognosis is excellent. The adult passenger . . . well, let me turn this over to her doctors."

The rep stepped back and a man wearing a white lab coat over a bright purple shirt approached the microphone. "My name is Dr. Miguel Solano, S-O-L-A-N-O, and I'm head of neurology at St. James with a side specialization in neuropsychology. The adult survivor is as yet unidentified."

He raised his hand to stem the fresh cascade of questions and comments including several journalists who called out, "The Angel of the Hudson!"

"Let me continue. She's a female, in her late twenties, or early thirties, currently suffering from amnesia. She's unable to recall her name or any other pertinent details about herself. In fact, we'd like the public's help in identifying her." He turned toward the door and signaled to someone with a quick nod.

The door opened and a pair of doctors escorted a woman into the room. Dante barely recognized her as the scrappy survivor he'd seen the day before. This woman appeared frail, timid, and completely unsure of herself. Her previously strong features paled beneath the onslaught of flash strobes and shouts.

The doctors helped her up to the dais and Solano put his arm around her waist, which seemed to make her even more uncomfortable.

"It's okay," he said off-microphone. "They only want to help." He turned to the audience of journalists and made the gesture to lower the noise which slowly abated.

"This is our 'Angel of the Hudson,' the heroic woman you've seen in the footage from TwentyFourSeven. Despite having freed herself from the sinking plane, we've all watched how she went back, risking her own life to rescue the baby."

There was a smattering of applause that gained power until it grew into a roar of support. Dante gaped in amazement as he watched his usually dour, detached cameraman shout, "Way to go, lady!"

After everyone calmed down, the doctor continued. "As I said before, she's having a bit of difficulty with her memory and we're hoping that someone watching this broadcast might be able to help us identify her. She's five-foot-five, with blond hair and hazel eyes, appears to be in her late twenties or early thirties, and has no visible scars beyond the minor injuries sustained in the crash." He reached into his coat pocket and pulled out a piece of paper. "We have a toll-free number, 800-555-1204, which you can call if you have any information as to her identity."

"How do you feel?" one reporter shouted at the woman.

Dante watched her cringe in response.

"Do you remember the crash?" another asked.

She bobbed her head. "It was terrible. So many people scream-ing."

A hush fell over the crowd and the only noise in the room was the clicking of cameras.

"There were so many people in pain." She looked up, tears streak-ing her pale cheeks. "The man sitting beside me had no face." She cocked her head as if listening to the echo of screams. "No, there was nothing I could do." She stiffened. "It's not my fault that I sur-vived."

A woman from the back of the room broke the silence. "How did you get out of the plane?"

"Fire. Fire on the water. And smoke." She began to hum a famil-iar tune.

The CNN reporter standing next to Dante whispered, "That's Deep Purple. She's humming 'Smoke on the Water.' This bitch is crazy."

Dante looked around, stunned at the rapid change in the audi-ence from roaring in applause to suddenly quiet and confused.

Angel turned around and grabbed the lapels of Solano's coat. "The baby. The baby is okay, isn't he?"

The doctor nodded and tried to soothe her. "He's fine. His par-ents are here and they're very appreciative of what you did."

She began to cry. "I thought he was a doll. A dirty, broken doll." She stopped and glanced over her shoulder as if noticing the cam-eras and microphones for the first time. "Me? I'm not dirty and broken. Why would you say such a thing? Why?"

Due to his front row position, Dante knew no one had made any such comment about her. Evidently, she was hallucinating.

Suddenly, she reached out blindly, latching onto a microphone which she tore from the stand and hurled toward the audience. It hit a camera and bounced away.

"That's a mean thing to say," she screamed.

Solano wrapped his arms around her. "No more press conference." He began to half-carry, half-drag her toward the door.

She screamed the entire way, shouting, "My name is Regan. No, it's Eve. Why are you calling me crazy? My name is . . . my name is . . ." The woman released a howl worthy of a wolf in heat.

Raul, Dante's cameraman, leaned over, his usual hard-faced expression back in place and whispered, "She's fucking nuts."

"Keep shooting the press conference," Dante ordered. "I'll be back." He didn't stay long enough to hear Raul's response. He headed out a side door, knowing that if he sprinted, he could reach the elevators before the doctor and his patient. Tucking his press badge into his coat pocket, he slid into place by the elevator bank before they approached.

Like a rolling stone, the entourage picked up other members as they headed toward the elevator—an additional nurse, at least two hospital admin suits, two security personnel, including Dante's brother. Bryant made serious eye contact with Dante as he chased along at the outskirts of the crowd.

Bryant's glare meant, *No way in hell are you getting on an elevator with this woman.*

Dante nodded and took a step, acknowledging his brother's silent order. Surrounded by people, she continued to sob and to pull away from everyone trying to touch or comfort her.

"Leave me alone," she screamed, jerking away when a nurse accidentally brushed against her. "I'm not crazy," she babbled. "I only want to know my name. Tell me my name." A moment later, she screamed, "That's not true."

As the entourage came closer, Dante couldn't stop himself from reaching out and touching Angel's arm. "It'll be okay."

Instead of shrieking or wrenching away, she paused to stare at him. Then the crowd of officials swarmed around her, pushing her into the awaiting elevator car. Bryant remained behind.

They both watched the doors close and could hear her renewed shouts until the car rose several floors away.

"Poor woman is nutzoid," Bryant said softly.

"She wasn't when I talked to her."

Bryant shrugged. "I haven't seen her string two coherent sentences together."

"Post-traumatic stress disorder?"

"Maybe. Or maybe she was nuts before the crash. Once they figure out who she is, maybe then they'll know. . . ."

As the men flanked her, almost force-marching her down the hallway, she chanted silently, *My name is Angel. My name is Angel.*

She had to do something, anything to drown the swarm of noise that filled her head. She realized the name was merely a placeholder, but she clung to it, nonetheless. It was both familiar and foreign to her. It was hers for the time being, and repeating it over and over again seemed to help keep some of the noise and confusion at bay.

When they reached the door to her hospital room, most of her unwanted entourage stayed outside and only Dr. Solano and a nurse helped her inside.

The doctor pasted on a phony smile. "Press conferences can be overwhelming. I'm so sorry we had to put you through that. But we needed to reach as many people as possible in hopes of finding out who you are." He helped her into the bed. "You'll feel better in no time at all."

She managed to nod. "Yes. I do feel a little bit better." It was no lie. The hundred-million-bee buzz in her brain had subsided to only a single raging hive.

He continued. "I understand why you're confused. Why you might even feel angry. Your reaction isn't unusual."

Her confusion had floated around her like an angry cloud. But now it turned into a solid, a lump of something unpleasant settling in her stomach.

Anger?

Hell, yeah, she was angry. They'd turned her misfortunes into some sort of freak show. Put her on display. Allowed cameras to capture and memorialize her confusion. She was probably now a laughingstock from coast to coast.

"You understand?" she said in a mocking tone. "Really? So how many times have you lost *your* memory? And been paraded in front of a media horde because of it?"

The doctor shot her the sort of tight smile one might give a misbehaving child. But she stared him down.

No confusion. No uncertainty.

"Explain to me why it was necessary to parade me in front of that media gauntlet like a prized piece of meat?"

The doctor's Texan roots began to uncurl from their hiding place. "Just calm down, honey. It won't help to get all riled up, now."

"Riled up," Angel mimicked. "Is that a medical term or did you bone up on homespun terminology just for little ol' me?"

The nurse flashed a quick grin, covering it immediately with her hand. The doctor stiffened, pivoted, and stalked out.

The nurse continued to help Angel get comfortable. "Making him mad won't really help," the nurse offered.

Angel felt the anger subside as if someone had opened a drain inside her. The nurse was right. Baiting the doctor served no real purpose other than . . .

"But it did make me feel better," she admitted.

The woman grinned. "I could tell. And you were right. He could have said no to the airline representatives. They're the ones who pushed the hospital to show off the miraculous survivor in good condition. Dr. Solano could have insisted that they show a picture of you instead. But he didn't." She leaned closer. "Between you and me? He deserved everything you threw at him."

The nurse finished fussing with the sheets and turned to the blinds, tilting them so that the room darkened. "Why don't you try to get a nap? Who knows? Maybe something good will come out of all this. Maybe someone will identify you and you'll be reunited with your family."

The door closed in a lazy arc after the nurse left. Angel turned on her side and stared at the shadows that the blinds cast on the wall. From her viewpoint, the vertical stripes looked horizontal, mimicking prison bars.

But the real prison was the one in her head. The one that kept her memories chained up, refusing to release them.

Why can't I remember me?

5

Angel's cuts and bruises healed quickly but the hole in her memories refused to close up. She spent the next three days watching bad television, eating bad food, and wondering what she was going to do if she didn't get her memories back. Did she have a life somewhere out there to return to? If so, why hadn't someone seen her picture and claimed her? If she was on her own, what was she going to do if she couldn't remember where to begin living again? Part of her wanted to get out of the hospital at all costs, even if she had nowhere to go. The other part secretly preferred this temporary, cloistered life.

But she wasn't completely alone.

First, there was the usual assortment of medical professionals who poked and prodded her hourly. Plus, Lewis Marlowe and his partner either visited or called at least once a day to give her an update of the latest tips they'd received on the "Who's Angel?" hot line. They also reported on their efforts to identify the bodies and to whittle down the passenger manifest to a short list—their "process of elimination."

At first, Angel had looked forward to the contact, if for no other reason than for a small moment of human companionship that didn't involve cold stethoscopes or impersonal conversations. But each time after the two reps departed, she was left with an unsettled, almost uncomfortable feeling. Although Ms. Seymour was polite on the surface, she seemed upset—perhaps even jealous of Lewis's friendly demeanor.

I wonder why . . .

The rattle of the food cart interrupted her thoughts. A moment later, Angel's favorite nurse, Kalli, brought in a lunch tray that consisted of a cellophane-wrapped collection of plastic plates and bowls. Angel climbed out of bed and moved over to the chair by the window. She pulled the bed tray over to act as a table.

The nurse mustered up a half smile when she placed the food tray on the table. "Today for your dining pleasure, we have brown stuff, gray stuff, white stuff, and today, the Jell-O is"—she whisked away the napkin to reveal the gelatin cup—"green!"

Angel stared at the tray and its lumpy, unidentifiable foods. "Oh. Boy. Green. My favorite flavor."

The nurse grinned at the weak attempt at humor.

Angel unwrapped the cup of lime gelatin and attacked it with a plastic spoon, knowing from experience that this was the only tasty part of the meal. "Delicious."

"Okay, so we're not known for our cuisine," Kalli said, her expression warming. "Just our healing abilities."

Angel held out her left arm, pointing with the plastic cutlery at her fading bruises. "I'm healed already," she said around a mouthful of Jell-O. "When are they going to let me go?"

"Go where? Until you know who you are, this is the safest place for you." Kalli paused. "By the way, you-know-who is here, waiting for visiting hours to start."

"Again? He's already been here once already."

Kalli laughed. "Maybe he's smitten with you."

Angel tried not to choke. "Oh puh-leze. Him? No, thank you."

Kalli glanced toward the door as if worried she'd be overheard. "He is sorta creepy in a Dick Dickly sort of way."

"Dick Dickly?"

"You know what I mean. Perfect hair, perfect teeth, perfect tan. Just a bit too perfect to be real. Like a plastic anchorman on TV." She held up an imaginary microphone and she adopted an artificial smile. "This is Dick Dickly with the news."

The description was eerily accurate.

Kalli tapped the edge of Angel's food tray. "But judging from the fast-food bags he's carrying, it looks as if he might have brought you a real lunch so maybe you don't want to try to choke down any more of this. At least not yet." She grimaced at the tray. "It's not like your food's warm. It'll be just as cold and congealed later as it is now."

"True."

"So shall I let him in a few minutes early?"

Angel replaced her empty Jell-O cup on the tray table and rolled it aside. "As long as you run him out a few minutes early, too."

Kalli headed toward the door, stopped just short of leaving, and turned around and faced Angel. "You say that now, but you never seem to want him to leave."

A moment later, Lewis Marlowe slipped into the room. "Good morning!" he boomed. Then he made a show of glancing at his watch. "Or should I say 'good afternoon'?" He didn't wait for a response. "I hoped I'd get here early enough to save you from another dose of hospital food." He held up a large fast-food bag. "I didn't know what you liked so I got a little of everything."

She had told herself she wouldn't smile, but she couldn't help it. After all, he was being thoughtful. And she was sure she missed the taste of real food—even the fast-food version of it, although she couldn't remember it. Maybe it'd spark an appetite in her. "That's okay. I don't know what I like, either."

He laughed, pulled up a chair, and began to empty out the bag on the tray table. It was a junk-food lover's bonanza of items from fries to sloppy burgers to fruit fritters oozing cherry glop from one end. "Dig in," he commanded once he laid out his haul.

Although Angel hadn't been hungry, she suddenly felt ravenous. She chose a burger, unwrapped it, and began to eat.

"Isn't that the best burger you've ever eaten?"

She nodded instead of speaking, finding herself totally enraptured with the taste and texture of the sandwich. After the brown and white hospital food, it was a feast. And before the hospital food, her life was a blank.

"There is nothing better than watching someone enjoying a gift, don't you think?" He selected a boxed burger for himself, pulled out the sandwich, and took a big bite.

She nodded, her enthusiasm and her hunger increasing exponentially as she chewed. She ate fast, following the first burger with a second one, as well as a sleeve of fries.

"I love a woman with an appetite," he said between bites. "There's nothing worse than watching a lady pick through a salad as if she was afraid there might be an extra calorie hiding behind a piece of celery. My partner does that. Some days, I'm afraid a stiff wind will carry her off."

"Where is Ms. Seymour?"

"She's been reassigned because she's completed her job."

Angel stiffened a bit. If his partner had completed the job, did that mean what she thought it meant? She dropped her burger on the paper. "Then you've identified . . ." She couldn't finish her sentence, her stomach seizing with anticipation . . . and perhaps a bit of terror.

"Every last passenger," he said, his grin increasing. "Including you." He reached into his briefcase and pulled out a single piece of paper. "I'm very pleased to meet you . . . Miss Angela Sands."

Angela Sands.

No drumroll. No crashing cymbals.

Nothing. The name didn't mean anything to her.

"Angela. Sands," she echoed, testing the names for familiarity. There was no hint of recognition beyond what had to have been the accidental coincidence between Angel and Angela.

Shouldn't there be fireworks?

Something to signal that the great mystery of her identity had been solved?

She pushed away the tray table and stood. Shouldn't there be a floodgate opening in her mind? Why weren't Angela Sands's memories thundering through her brain?

Instead, there was nothing. No sparks. No sense of awareness. No . . . nothing.

"What do you know about me?" she said.

His grin dimmed a watt or two. "Not as much as we'd like to know." He tapped the paper. "On May fifteenth, you booked a round-trip ticket on CoastalEast via an online Internet booking site. Departure was for Tuesday May seventeenth from LaGuardia, bound for Los Angeles, LAX. Our records show that you did indeed take that flight. Then you returned to New York on May nineteenth."

"What else?" she asked, trying to catch her breath as she sat down on the edge of the bed.

His expression waivered. "Not much more. You gave your address as the Hotel Jefferson in midtown." He stood up and retrieved the briefcase he'd placed at the end of her bed. "We checked with them. Evidently, you'd been staying there for four weeks. You checked out the morning of your flight to Los Angeles."

"Do they know anything about me?"

"We can't really get any hard data from them without a court order."

"Hard data?"

"How you made your reservation, how you paid, what personal information you gave them. We showed them your picture but nobody recognized you. Then again, it's a pretty big hotel so maybe it's not surprising that no one really remembered what Angela Sands looked like."

He reached over and patted her hand. "I know how disconcerting this must be. To learn who you are, but not much more than that. But it's a start, right?"

"Do I have any family? Is anybody missing me?"

His expression faltered. "I . . . I don't know. We can't find anything, even now that we know your name."

"So you know my name and nothing else." She tried to rein in her emotions, but the dam broke under the weight of her disappointment. Everything she'd held inside spilled out in great gulping sobs. As she cried, Lewis moved closer to the bed and sat down next to her, cradling her hand in his.

"But we did learn one thing."

"What?" she said, trying to stop this sudden explosion of emotion.

"You're *Miss* Angela Sands. 'Miss' as in unmarried. And do you know how refreshing it is to see a modern-day woman willing to flaunt today's convention of hiding one's marital status?" He paused, then his plastic smile wavered into something a bit more realistic. "It makes it easier for me."

"Huh?"

"These past few days, I've found myself very much . . . attracted

63

to you. It's crazy, I know, but I can't help it. You're a beautiful damsel in distress and I think you've come to see me as a knight, ready to ride to your rescue."

Angel . . . no, she had to think of herself as Angela. Whatever name she used, she was confused by his little confession. And yet, something inside her warmed to his overture of affection.

"I swear, Angela, I'm going to do everything I can to help you rediscover yourself. I won't leave your side. We'll go through this, together. I promise. You won't be alone."

When he reached over and hugged her, she found herself hugging back, holding him as if he was her last lifeline. Maybe he was. He was the only person who truly understood the feelings that swamped her self-control. What she needed, what she craved was comfort. Male comfort.

When he kissed her, she was neither surprised nor repelled. She wanted consolation. She desperately needed something, someone to care for her.

She wanted him. Needed him.

Angela pulled him closer. Something tightened in her chest and then the sensation dipped lower. She wanted satisfaction, love, companionship . . .

She wanted sex. Right now. Right here.

He stroked her back and arms as they kissed. Together, they leaned back until he rested completely on the bed, lying beside her, almost on top of her.

"Oh, God," he groaned in her ear. "You don't know how much I've wanted to do this. Seeing you lying there. Helpless, confused. Knowing I could be the man to awaken the woman within you."

He cupped her face with his hand, then trailed it down her neck and farther down to the valley between her breasts.

"Such perfection," he groaned, squeezing her breast, then pulling her gown back at the shoulder to expose her even more. "Tell me you want me," he demanded as he began clawing at his jacket, stripping it off and flinging it onto the floor.

Straddling her, he jerked his tie loose and pawed at the buttons on his shirt, almost ripping them off in his enthusiasm.

"I want you," she answered.

What the hell are you doing? an inner voice screamed inside her brain. *You don't know this man. You don't want him. Hello? Dick Dickly? Remember?*

"Tell me how badly you need me," he groaned. His shirt fell open, revealing a surgical scar the full length of his chest.

She pulled him down to straddle her and began to kiss his scar. "The moment I saw you I knew I had to have you to myself. With me. In me . . ." She trailed her kisses down the scar until she reached a few inches above his waistline.

Inside her head, she screamed at herself to stop. But her hands, her mouth, her libido acted on their own accord.

His fingers trembled as he fumbled with his belt. "You don't know how bad I want you. Just the thought of you makes me hard." He unbuckled the belt and released the clasp at his waistband. He began to breathe heavily, but his panting turned quickly into gasps for breath.

Something was wrong.

But despite his distress, he continued to moan in pleasure. "I have to have you," he repeated, his voice escalating each time he said the words until he was finally screaming. He grabbed his chest.

"Don't stop," she said, reaching up for him, pulling him closer. "Please don't stop!"

In her mind, the words changed order and emphasis. *Don't. Please stop.*

Then suddenly, he was no longer straddling her but was spilled halfway out of the bed, his perfectly tanned face turning red, his features pinched in pain.

"Don't stop," he said in a strangled voice.

Something in Angela snapped. Her uncontainable libido evaporated as quickly as it had formed and her conscience regained control.

"Help!" she tried to shout, but her voice refused to cooperate.

The door burst open and Kalli ran in. "Angel, what's wr—" She spotted Lewis, who had completed his descent to the floor, and then looked at Angela. "Oh, my God. What was he doing to you?"

Angela couldn't speak, still caught in the throes of her emotional duality. She desperately wanted to explain how she couldn't control herself. How the inner woman was pleading "No," while another part of her was screaming "Yes."

Kalli whipped off the stethoscope she wore around her neck and listened to his heart. "He's having a heart attack. Hit that red panic button on the panel above you and for God's sake, put your gown back on."

Angela responded automatically to Kalli's orders, calling for help and then trying desperately to erase the evidence of her enormous lapse in judgment.

When she turned back, Kalli had zipped his pants. "I need a crash cart in Room 206," she bellowed at someone in the hallway.

The next five minutes were a blur.

Angela watched two doctors and three nurses work on Lewis, who was lying on the floor. She'd inched up to the head of the bed, trying to put as much distance as she could between herself and their new patient.

Guilt didn't eat at her; it devoured her. Her earlier overwhelming sense of desire dispersed completely as if it had never existed in the first place.

Had it?

Why had she responded so dramatically to his overture? It wasn't as if she even liked the man. Was she so starved for affection that any offer of companionship was sufficient to trigger the raging nymphomaniac in her?

Had she always been so . . . indiscriminating?

She made herself look at the man on the floor, struggling to hold on to the thin broken threads of his life.

Had she killed him because of her lack of self control?

It took three attempts to shock Lewis's heart back into a normal rhythm. Once they stabilized him, they brought in a gurney, loaded him up, and wheeled him away.

Angela didn't move from her huddled spot at the head of the bed until Kalli returned. When she entered the room, she closed the door behind her and marched to the bed.

"Did he attack you?"

Angela barely heard the woman. Her brain insisted on lingering in the past, reliving every moment of the last half hour in vivid detail. Her senses were on overload, threatening to blow a major circuit in her brain.

And yet, a secondary part of Angela looked at the scene with a surprising amount of dispassion. "No," she said.

"Are you sure? I know what I saw."

"He didn't attack me." Angela marveled at the control in her own voice.

"But you and I were just talking about him. If you ask me, you sure didn't sound like you were anxiously waiting for him to jump your bones."

"I wasn't. It just sorta . . . happened."

The nurse balanced a fist on each hip, elbows out. "You mean to tell me he said, 'Hey, babe, how about we do it, right here, right now,' and you agreed?" A look of pure confusion filled Kalli's face. "Dick Dickly, remember? The perfectly creepy man?"

"I don't know what to tell you. It seemed . . . right at the moment." As easily as her calm, detached control formed, it short-circuited, her world exploding into knife-edged shards. "I don't know what happened." Her voice dropped to a low, hoarse whisper. "One minute I was tolerating him, and the next we were kissing."

"C'mon, Angel. He didn't need to take his pants down to kiss you."

"Angela," she corrected.

The nurse straightened. "You're starting to remember?"

"No." Angela nodded toward the door through which they'd wheeled out Lewis on a gurney. "*He* told me. They figured out who I am. My name is Angela Sands."

Kalli's stance changed as her anger appeared to fade away. "And? What else?"

"Not much." She managed to relay what little information she'd learned.

After she finished, Kalli released a sigh.

"Okay. I'm going to chalk this up to a momentary lapse in judgment—for both of you. I'm pretty sure Mr. Smiley isn't going to feel like broadcasting the fact that he had a heart attack while trying to screw a recovering hospital patient. Judging from that scar on his chest, this isn't the first time he's had serious heart problems. He should have known what he was capable of . . . though he looks just like the kind of idiot who might combine Cialis with heart drugs like nitrates." She paused, then caught Angela in a glare that would wither a redwood tree. "You should have noticed, too, you know."

Angela pulled the sheet up to her chin, her mind swirling with responses.

"I know. It makes me worry about who I am. Who's to say that I'm not some sort of black widow? Or simply a slut? Or gullible or stupid or selfish or . . ." The air grew thick, and suddenly she had difficulty drawing in a deep breath.

Kalli stepped closer to the bed, lowering her voice. "If you don't calm down, I'm going to have to give you a sedative. You have to get control of yourself. Do you understand?"

Angela nodded, scooting farther down in the bed and curling into a ball. Closing her eyes, she began to chant to herself, *I'm not crazy, I'm not crazy, I'm not crazy. . . .*

Maybe if she said it enough times, she'd actually believe it.

6

The next morning, Kalli marched into Angela's room far too early and slammed open the blinds, letting brilliant sunshine flood into her room.

"Go away," Angela mumbled. She liked the darkness and the sense of protection it afforded.

"Nope. I've decided that part of your problem is that you're going stir-crazy. You need to get out. Get some fresh air."

"Leave me alone."

"Sorry. Doctor's orders."

Angela turned away from the glare coming through the uncovered window and pulled the thin pillow over her head. Moments later, it disappeared and Kalli's stern face swam into Angela's field of vision.

"You are getting up. Combing your hair. Putting on a robe.

And you'll be eating your breakfast in the solarium. The sunlight will do you good—vitamin D and all that."

Fifteen minutes later, Angela shuffled down the hallway in a hospital robe and operating-room slippers, following the nurse through a double set of doors and into a large sunlit room. A few patients were scattered throughout the space, eating from trays.

Kalli sat her down at a table in the far corner of the room and returned a moment later with a tray of food. "The hospital breakfast special. Rubbery eggs, soggy bacon, cold toast, and"—she nudged one bowl of unidentifiable mush—"a player to be named later." She crossed her arms like a stern schoolteacher. "Now eat it. And stay here for at least an hour to enjoy the sunshine. Understand? It's good for you."

"Yes, Sergeant." Angela touched her temple with two fingers in a mock salute and began to unpeel the plastic wrap from her meal.

Tasteless.

As she picked at her food, she couldn't help but remember the hamburgers Lewis had brought the day before. They'd tasted so very good. Of course, those memories led to more damning thoughts about Lewis and her behavior toward him. She'd spent most of the night trying to sort through her feelings and figure out exactly what had happened.

Had she become so starved for affection that she was willing to bed anyone just to experience a momentary sense of connection?

Her appetite vanished, replaced by an ache in her stomach that food wouldn't alleviate. She pushed away her tray and sat back in the chair, daring the sun to make her feel better about herself.

A gravelly voice spoke. "Pardon me, but is this seat taken?"

She opened her eyes and saw a man in a robe standing next to her. Glancing around, she realized the entire room was now empty except for the two of them. She sighed, not really wanting the company, but not quite sure how to rebuff the man. It was obvious he was trying to be polite.

She gave him a once-over. Judging from his striped robe, he was also a patient. Standing no more than five feet two, he was mostly on the pale and pudgy side. If she was attracted to "perfect" specimens like Lewis, then she was safe from this guy and, more importantly, he was safe from her.

The man offered her a nicotine-stained smile. "I know. Empty room, plenty of space. But I really hate eating by myself. Can I join you? Please?"

She surrendered, waving him toward the chair across from her. "Sure. Have a seat."

"Thanks!" He dropped into the chair and began to chow down as if the food had taste. He shoveled in several forkfuls before pausing long enough to wipe his mouth on his sleeve. "Sorry. I'm really very hungry. My name's Donnie D'Andrea. You?"

She drew in a deep breath. Maybe it was time to accept her fate and her name. "Angela. Angela Sands."

"Pleased to meetcha, Angela. Whatcha in for?" He laughed as if he'd made a great joke.

She shrugged and began to poke holes in the plastic wrap over the unidentified mush. "Not enough altitude."

He cocked his head as if trying to understand her. "Huh?" Then his eyes lit up. "Oh, hell, you're the chick from that plane. The one that went down in the Hudson." He sat up straighter. "I'm having breakfast with a celebrity. How cool is that?" He stuffed a pastry in his mouth. "And she's funny, too. 'Not enough altitude.' Good one."

She poked more holes in the plastic. "You know what they say. A good landing is any one you can walk away from. Or in my case, swim away from."

He snorted in laughter. "You're a regular Joan Rivers. Get it? Rivers?"

He guffawed. She couldn't help but smile at his reaction.

"I like you," he said around a mouthful of the breakfast sludge. "You're a funny broad." He eyed the pastry sitting on her tray. "You gonna eat that?"

Angela pushed the bread toward him. "Have at it, Donnie."

"I'm still a growing boy, you know." At the minimum, he was pushing forty and probably tipped the scales right at two hundred pounds.

She laughed. "Growing side to side, you mean."

They sat there for at least a half hour, slinging one-liners at each other, a good-natured competition to see who could come up with the worst—or maybe—best groaner.

It felt good to laugh, she decided. Better than good, it felt fantastic. In her eyes, Donnie went from being an odious intruder with bad table manners to a well-fed partner in comedic crime as they slung jokes and traded barbs back and forth. He was exactly what the doctor ordered: a distraction from her problems.

After the half hour, they grew silent as if both had run out of steam. Donnie had polished off his meal and hers, and now he sat back, hooking his hand in the waistband of his pants.

"So, Donnie, I never asked. What are *you* in for?"

He leaned forward. "Can you keep a secret?" Without waiting for an answer, he whispered, "I'm not. I come here to drum up business." His robe gapped and she realized he was wearing a suit beneath it. He reached into his breast pocket and pulled out a slightly wrinkled business card.

"Donald Q. D'Andrea, Esquire. I'm an attorney. I specialize in accident cases." He wiggled his bushy eyebrows. "Just like yours."

"An ambulance chaser?"

He shook his head. "I'm too smart for that. I come here, I steal a robe from the linen closet, and I mingle."

She glanced down at his food tray. "And on occasion, cadge a free meal?"

"Exactamundo. The cart's just sitting there. And no one bothers checking on a patient eating in the solarium. Sweet, eh?"

"Definitely."

"This way, I don't have to chase anybody. I just sit and wait for them to come to me." He rubbed his fingertips together. "So, why don't you let me see what I can do for you, eh, doll baby? You need a bulldog of a lawyer like me in order to rake CoastalEast over the coals. If you hire me, when I get through with them, you'll own the goddamn business. Fly anywhere you want to, anytime. Free."

She reached over and tweaked his pudgy cheeks. "You say the sweetest things. I've always wanted my own airline company."

"Gimme a buck for a retainer and I'm all yours."

She patted the torn pocket of her robe. "Sorry. Like you, I'm a bit short."

He wagged a finger at her. "Hey, no height jokes, okay? Then how about a kiss? That'll seal the deal. We'll call it services in lieu of cash."

She leaned over to kiss him and he grabbed her head between two paws and pushed his face into hers, his tongue sliding into her mouth. Her instant wave of revulsion faded and something else accepting grew in its place.

Once he was finished, he pulled back and wiped his face on his sleeve. "Man, you're a good kisser. I can't wait to bill you for my consultation fee." He looked around as if checking to see if anyone had seen them. "You got a roomie or did CoastalEast spring for a private room?"

She tickled him under the chin. "It's just me alone in that big hospital bed. I have room for you and six more dwar—"

"Excuse me, ma'am?"

A looming figure stood over them. Donnie went from pale to pasty. "Uh, hiya, Bryant. Long time no see, buddy."

The man standing next to them wore a dark blue blazer with a gold badge clipped to the breast pocket and the word "Security" stitched just below.

"That's Mr. Kearns to you, Donnie. I thought we already had our long talk about you bothering our patients." He glanced at the two empty trays. "And stealing our food."

Donnie jumped to his feet, his head just reaching the same level as the man's badge. "I didn't steal anything. She was sharing."

"Two trays?"

"She thought she was hungry. Turns out . . . not so much." He shot Angela an apologetic smile.

"Sitting near a creep like you would put any person off their feed." Kearns turned to the door and waved in another man dressed in a similar blazer. "Would you escort Mr. D'Andrea to the east door. There's a patrol car down there waiting for him."

Kearns reached down and plucked a piece of nonexistent lint from the lapel of Donnie's robe. "We're charging him with theft of hospital property."

Angela watched as Donnie tried to strip off the robe. But Kearns stopped him, shaking a finger in his face.

"That won't work. You also stole a tray of food." At Donnie's expression, he added, "And if you try to rid yourself of the evidence by tossing your cookies on my shoes, I'll personally march you over to the training wing and let the student nurses practice on you. I hear it's 'How to Give an Enema' day."

Angela covered her laughter by pressing her hand over her

mouth. Donnie gaped at her as if she'd betrayed him by finding his predicament funny.

Kearns pushed the attorney toward the second security man. "Get him out of here."

As the two men left, Angela could hear Donnie alternately pleading with and threatening his unwanted companion until he reached the hall. Either he'd realized it was fruitless to continue or the security guard had issued a warning that couldn't be ignored.

Or punched him in the mouth.

Kearns turned to Angela. "Ma'am, I hope you weren't taken in by his slick chatter. Donnie's not good enough to be called an ambulance chaser. At least they show some semblance of ambition. Donnie just wants to make promises in order to get a free meal or"—he added a discreet cough—"other services in exchange. In all honesty? I don't think he's ever been in a courtroom or ever made a settlement. I'm not sure he even passed the bar."

He paused, cocked his head, then his stern expression softened. "Will you allow me to escort you back to your room?"

There was something . . . familiar about him. His voice, his eyes. Something that told her she'd be safe with him. "Thanks. I'd like that."

He took her hand and tucked it under his arm, displaying manners that would probably make his mother proud.

Rather than feel as if she was being marched back to detention by the school cop, it didn't take long before she felt comfortable with him. As he escorted her, taking the long way around to her room, he spoke with surprising ease about his wife, his son, and his new baby daughter.

By time they reached her room, he'd pulled out his wallet to show her pictures of his kids. She already felt like she knew them all.

"Dora's beautiful," she gushed over the shot of a squinty-eyed baby girl with more cheeks than face. "How old is she there?"

"One day old. Here's what she looks like now, at three months." He pulled out another picture, this time of a much better-looking baby with her eyes open and her cheeks in check. She wore a frilly pink dress and had a white lace bow inexplicably stuck to her bald little head.

"You have a beautiful family, Mr. Kear . . . er . . . Bryant," she added, before he could correct her. They'd gotten on a first-name basis before they turned the first corner. "You and Norah must be very proud."

"Thank you. We are. Oh, and speaking of children: Tyler? The baby you saved? He's going home later today with his parents. I think they want to come visit you to tell you thanks. Would that be okay?"

She nodded.

Kearns stopped and gave her a critical once-over. "Are you okay, Angela? You look . . ." He blushed. "I shouldn't be trying to interpret your moods and I don't want to be insensitive. But if you need help, let someone know, okay? This may not be the finest hospital in New York, but we're good. We care."

He reached up and touched her cheek, then jerked his hand back as if her skin was scalding him. His blush spread from his throat to his hairline. "Sorry," he whispered. "I don't know what came over me." He shook his head as if to cast off unwanted thoughts. "Don't be afraid to ask for help. Okay?"

Bryant held open the door for Angela and she stepped inside. Following her, he took one half step into the room, then backed out. She reached out and snagged the sleeve of his jacket, suddenly overwhelmed by the need for his companionship.

Someone to sit and talk with, to laugh with, someone nice.

Someone like him . . .

"Please," she whispered.

Something in his eyes said he wanted the same thing. Then, the look faded away. He glanced down at her fingers clutching his sleeve, released a sigh, then gently lifted her hand to his lips for a quick kiss.

"Sorry. I'm very happily married. Good-bye, Angela."

The door closed behind him.

She stumbled over to the chair by the window, dropped down into it, and wiped away the tears that suddenly filled her eyes.

What's wrong with me? Am I crazy? Worse, am I an addict? A sex addict?

She put her head in her hands and sobbed.

7

"It's over."

Angela didn't recognize the man's voice, but the sentiment was unmistakable. And disturbing.

He continued. "I'm tired of you, of this idiotic domestic drudgery you jokingly call our marriage."

"What are you saying?"

It was a woman's voice and she sounded completely taken aback by the news. "You're leaving?"

"No. You're leaving me."

"B-but I don't understand."

"Of course you don't." He barked in laughter, evidently finding some twisted sense of amusement about her confusion. "How dense can one person be? I'm divorcing you. And, thanks to the prenup you were stupid enough to sign, it means you're leaving my *house*, my *world with exactly what you brought into this marriage. Zilch. Zip. Nada."*

Up to that point, the woman's reaction of fear and confusion to his declarations had met his expectations. Angela wasn't sure why she knew this. But she did. Just like she knew that the man always liked it when his wife cowered during one of his frequent tirades.

But this time, something changed.

The woman took a small but brash step, fanning a tiny flicker of courage into a thin flame. But in her excitement over her burgeoning spark of bravery, she made a strategic mistake.

"What prenup."

Angela realized immediately that the woman should have posed it as a question rather than make it a statement of fact. She'd tipped her hand, such as it was.

He caught on fast. "Why, you little bitch . . ."

Angela yelled a warning, but the woman in her dreams heard nothing. There was a blur and then the woman fell to the floor, bloodied by the man's fists. He stood over her writhing body. It was clear from the look on his face that he took great pleasure watching her beg for forgiveness.

For mercy . . .

"Stand up to him," Angela screamed. "Don't just lie there and let him win."

But the woman didn't rise. Her feeble attempt at rebellion, her brief struggle for independence had been thoroughly extinguished as quickly and easily as it had ignited.

"S-sweetheart, I'm s-sorry," she stuttered.

He reached down and grabbed her by the hair. "Don't worry, 'sweetheart.'" He said the endearment as if it was a supreme insult. He dragged her toward his desk. "You'll make up for your shortsightedness by signing the papers now."

Angela watched the word "No" form on the woman's lips, but then she obviously—and perhaps wisely—changed her mind. Then Angela saw something in the woman's eyes.

And she understood.

The woman hadn't given up. Somewhere deep inside of her the spark of challenge still lived. She would bide her time, promise him anything, string him along until she found the right opening. The right opportunity.

And then she'd escape.

The woman waited on the floor by the desk until he turned to the file cabinet. With his attention distracted, she scanned her surroundings, looking for a weapon.

His favorite statue sat on the corner of the polished mahogany desk, a bronze sculpture of a woman's naked torso. He'd fondle it while talking on the phone, wheeling his deals, conning his customers. He loved telling anyone who would listen how the artwork possessed the best attributes of a woman: all boob, no brain.

Shooting quickly to her feet, she grabbed the statue with both hands and swung as hard as she could. Right at the back of his head.

A chorus of screams exploded in Angela's ears—those of the attacker's, the victim's, and hers. And then there was the blood. So much blood.

When the woman looked down at the growing stain of red that blossomed on her shirt, she realized it wasn't her husband's blood.

It was hers.

Angela's throat closed. My blood.

She began to scream.

A voice thundered in her ears. "Angela, wake up!"

At first, she didn't understand that it was reality, hammering at the edges of her dreams. Confused, she roused enough to realize someone was shaking her.

"You've got to stop screaming, right now," the female voice demanded. "It's not real. It's just another nightmare."

Angela struggled against the hands that pinned her to the bed. She was panting, either out of fear or exertion—she wasn't sure which. She opened her eyes to the uncomfortable stab of light from the overhead fluorescent fixture, trying to focus on the face of the woman who loomed over her. It was someone she'd never seen before.

Her next scream died in her throat.

The woman in scrubs, presumably a nurse, rubbed her ear and winced. "Thank God. I didn't think you would ever shut up."

"Am I alive?" Angela whispered.

The nurse sighed. "Don't be stupid. You're here, aren't you?"

Angela reached out and clutched the woman's sleeve, crushing the material between her fingers. "No, I saw her die. I saw *me* die. See?" She used her free hand to pull at the neck of her gown and expose her chest. To her shock, there was only unblemished skin. No scars. Certainly no blood. "It's gone. I don't understand," she said, fear making her voice louder.

The nurse jerked her arm from Angela's grasp as if she wore a designer blouse rather than a set of wrinkled, faded scrubs. "For God's sake, get control of yourself."

"Please," Angela whispered. She closed her eyes even though she feared returning to that harsh reality. "Am I alive?" she whispered.

The nurse groaned in exasperation. "Yes, Angela, you're alive."

The images that had held Angela frozen in fear only seconds before suddenly evaporated like wisps of smoke in the harsh light. One second, she'd been both engrossed but horrified by the scenes in her head, presented in inglorious Technicolor. The next moment, there was nothing.

No images. No sounds. No memories.

And despite the absence of detail and her rapidly fading memory, Angela still knew that her dream had frightened her badly. She buried her face in her hands. "I remembered something about myself for a moment, but now it's gone."

The nurse began to straighten the sheets, tugging them without any consideration for the patient lying on them. "That's what you said last time."

Angela shifted, trying to free the material wrapped around her legs. "Last time?"

The woman glared at Angela as if she had just failed the world's simplest test. "You've woken up screaming three nights in a row, each time bawling something about being dead. Don't you remember? The first time you were screaming about dying in a fire. The second time you swore you were drowning in water. This time, the only thing I could make out was something about blood." She leaned closer, her voice growing more menacing. "Look. I'm tired of this. We're all tired of this. You're disturbing the other patients who are trying to sleep. If you do this again, I have orders to sedate you." Her faced hardened. "And trust me. I'll be glad to do it."

"I . . . I'm sorry. I won't . . ." Won't what? Promise she wouldn't go to sleep again? Promise that she wouldn't dream? Not have another nightmare? None of those things was under her control.

"I'm sorry," she whispered again, sinking back in the bed. The thin blanket she pulled to her chin offered little protection from the waves of anger rolling off the nurse. To further complicate things, foggy details of her dreams sat just beyond reach.

Dreams or maybe memories.

My memories?

The nurse stalked out, leaving the overhead lights on. It was an obvious power play, a deliberate attempt to remind Angela that she had inconvenienced a lot of people with her screams. Therefore, her comfort was of little concern to anyone.

Rather than get up and cross the chilly floor to switch off the lights, Angela rolled over, shielding her eyes from the harsh glare.

But she didn't fall asleep. She didn't dare.

Luckily, Mother Nature offered suitable distraction. The rumble of thunder danced in echoes through the city and a lightning storm turned its skyline into flashing silhouettes.

She watched, mesmerized, as the storm rose and then waned. Soon, the dark night gave way to a gray dawn, which turned into a gloomy, rainy morning.

Her mood remained dark.

At least the morning nurse was much kinder, apologizing for taking yet another vial of blood. After getting her sample, the woman brought in a breakfast tray then slipped out quickly as if not wanting to engage Angela in any further conversation.

I don't blame you. I wouldn't want to hang around the crazy woman, either.

Angela poked at her runny scrambled eggs while watching the fierce rain coat the window, blurring the world beyond. When someone knocked on the door, she couldn't bring herself to answer.

The door opened. "Miss Sands? May I come in?"

It was a foolish question to ask since the woman had already stepped into the room. It took Angela a moment or two to recognize the woman: Ms. No-First-Name Seymour from CoastalEast.

The woman displayed a warmed-over smile. "I just wanted to see how you were doing."

Angela shrugged. "Same as yesterday. It's still a blank." Something inside her demanded that she add, "How's Lew . . . er . . . Mr. Marlowe?"

The woman acknowledged the slip with a single twitch of her left eye. "The doctors say he's doing better. He's had heart trouble before, you know."

"So I heard." Angela cocked her head, trying to better read the woman's face. This wasn't a sympathy call. If this was meant to be an update on her identity, then Angela didn't want to waste any time with faked pleasantries. "Why are you here? You already found out who I am. I thought you folks were finished with me."

What little warmth the woman's smile possessed faded as she dropped into corporate-speak. "I can't imagine how you got that impression. We at CoastalEast still care about your well-being. In fact, that's why I'm here, this morning. I understand you talked with legal counsel, yesterday."

"Legal counsel?" Angela drew a blank and a chill fell over her. Was she now losing current memories as well?

"A lawyer by the name of"—Ms. Seymour consulted her clipboard, her left eye twitching again—"a Mr. Donald D'Andrea?"

Relief coursed through Angela, followed quickly by a wave of revulsion. The thought of the slimy little man turned Angela's touch of chill into a cryogenic deep-freeze. "Oh. Him. The pervert."

The representative seemed slightly relieved by Angela's assessment. "So, may I assume that you have not retained him to advise you in legal matters?"

"If you mean did I hire him to help me sue you, the answer is no."

Obviously relieved, Ms. Seymour dropped into the second chair and put her briefcase on the floor beside her. "All we want to do is make sure that you've received everything you need—medical help and any and all therapy, both physical and . . ." Her voice trailed off.

"Mental?"

Ms. Seymour blushed, bringing some color to her plain pale features. "The doctors report that there's been no significant progress in the efforts to recover your memories."

So far, the "efforts to recover" Angela's memories had consisted of three or four medical personnel coming to her each day, inquiring as to if she could remember anything new, yet.

"But they do say that your physical injuries seem to have healed nicely."

Angela tugged down her sleeves self-consciously until she realized that it was true; most of her bruises had faded to mild discolorations. But then revelation hit her, making her sit up straighter.

"With all due respect, why are my doctors discussing my medical condition with you, a stranger? Shouldn't they first talk to me? The patient? This seems quite a breach in standard medical ethics."

Ms. Seymour didn't appear to be bothered by Angela's challenge. "Normally, it would be, but since CoastalEast agreed to pick up the financial responsibility for your hospital stay, we have a right to know the costs involved. They are directly proportionate to your length of stay."

Angela sensed there was a more important message between the lines. "So what you are saying is . . . ?"

"That you're going to be released tomorrow."

"Released to where?"

The woman tried to wear a look of complete innocence, but her knotted hands gave away her guilt. "There." She pointed through the rain-slicked window. "The real world."

With no memories. No home. No means of support.

"I know what you're thinking, but trust me. I've taken care of that."

Ms. Seymour had deposited what Angela had assumed to be a briefcase by the chair. But it turned out to be a small suitcase.

She opened the case to reveal its contents. "Everything you need is here. I had to guess at your size, but I brought clothes and some basic personal products—you know, toothbrush, toothpaste, that sort of stuff. It'll be enough to get you started."

Her voice cracked under the weight of her lie. "It's a wonderful world out there, just waiting for you."

Before Angela could swallow back her shock and respond, the woman rose quickly.

"I wish you the very best of luck, Angela," she said over her shoulder as she escaped to the hallway.

Angela bit back the retort she wanted to hurl at the woman's departing backside. Instead, she spent the next hour worrying about her impending discharge from the hospital. Having no identity meant having no identification. No money. And what kind of life could she expect with no funding? "Out there" might be wonderful for some, but it was more than a scary proposition for her.

But that particular fear evaporated by midday when the doctor burst into the room without any warning.

"What in the hell did you take?"

Angela stared dumbfounded as he stormed across the room and slammed a metal chart on the end of the bed. It came perilously close to her feet.

"The drug you took. What was it?"

Her brain scrambled to comprehend his words. "Drug? I . . . I haven't taken anything." She hesitated. Maybe this was a trick. "I haven't taken anything other than what you people give me."

He stalked to the head of the bed, whipped out his stethoscope, and jammed it against her chest with little care. She tried to speak but he made a curt gesture that meant *Shut the hell up.*

After listening to her heart and lungs, he pulled out a penlight and stabbed her eyes with the bright light. "It was that goddamn ambulance chaser, wasn't it? Gave you something? Told you that you could prolong your stay, try to delay your release? Maybe create a situation that he could manipulate into a goddamn malpractice suit?"

She batted his hand out of her face, an action that surprised him . . . not to mention, her. That's when she realized that she wasn't just upset, she was angry. Damn angry. She hadn't been when he walked in, but now, a healthy blaze of righteous indignation filled her.

She stabbed him in the chest with her forefinger. "Listen to me, you quack. I have no connection with that odious little piece of shit other than having met him by accident. I wouldn't listen to him, much less hire him if he were the last attorney on earth. And for the record? I'm not stupid enough to take anything from him— not advice and certainly not any pills."

"Then explain this!" The doctor slammed open the medical chart. "Here. Elevated levels of an unidentified narcotic agent in patient's blood. The blood tests they did in the ER prove you were clean when you were admitted. So it's evident that someone, some confederate must have slipped you something while you were here. Probably in the last twenty-four hours." His face turned an ugly shade of red. "What'd you take? Some sort of new street drug?"

Anger roiled inside of her, but she resisted the urge to scream back. "I didn't take anything other than what your people have been giving me," she said between gritted teeth. She glared at him, praying she could keep her clenched fists at her sides. "Maybe *you're* the one who screwed up. Prescribed something you shouldn't have."

"Not on your life, lady. Not a high-profile case like yours."

"Oh, so you only screw up low-profile cases?"

"That's not what I mean."

She stabbed a finger at his white-jacketed chest. "I'm beginning to think I *do* need to talk to a lawyer—a real lawyer—about that potential malpractice suit." She watched a vein in the doctor's temple throb unevenly.

He moved closer to the bed. "You think you're some tough chick, don't you?"

She sat up in the bed, shifting so that she could meet him, stare to defiant stare. "What if I do?"

For one brief moment, the fire in his angry eyes transformed into something equally as personal, equally as strong. His face was only inches from hers and his lips parted as if he was going to sling yet another insult. But he said nothing.

He shifted closer. For one crazy moment, Angela wondered if he was going to slap her . . .

. . . or kiss her.

After a moment, he released a shuddery sigh filled with what appeared to be confusion, regret, and maybe, just maybe, a bit of desire. He took a step backward, snatched the chart, and stumbled toward the door. When he reached for the knob, he hesitated and turned around to face her.

A look of cold detachment replaced the unfathomable heat she'd seen moments earlier in his eyes.

"I'm discharging you tomorrow," he said in a hoarse voice. He swallowed hard as if tamping back an emotion that threatened to break free. "You're a liability, lady. And I don't need any liabilities in my life"—he corrected himself instantly—"my practice."

It was all she could do to keep herself from jumping out of the bed and launching herself at him.

"God, I could do you right here, right now. . . ."

For one heart-stopping moment, she thought he'd said the words aloud. That he'd allowed them to escape from the deep recesses of his hidden desire. But then she realized that she'd only heard them in her head.

But what she didn't know was whether they were her thoughts. Or his . . .

8

_____

"C'mon, Uncle D." Tucker, Dante's nephew, latched onto his leg, becoming an eight-year-old ankle monitor. "I demand a . . . a . . . What's that word?"

"Rematch. And no, I won fair and square and the only way I'll be able to do that again is if I cheat. And your momma will have my hide if I cheat. Remember what she says? Cheaters never . . . ?"

". . . prosper," Tucker supplied with a grimace. "I still don't know what that means."

"You will, some day."

"Hey, bro?" Dante's brother, Bryant, reached down into the ice chest at his feet and produced a fresh bottle of beer. "Wanna 'nother round?"

Dante shook his head. "Maybe later."

A voice from around his ankles chirped up. "Yes, he wants another round. Get him drunk, Dad, so that I can win the next game and beat his sorry hide."

Norah, Bryant's wife, stepped out of the kitchen door onto the backyard deck just in time to hear her son. "Are you trying to corrupt the morals of a minor, Dante?"

She carried her youngest in one arm and balanced a bowl of potato salad in the other.

Dante extricated himself from the little octopus's tenacious grasp. "God, no. If anything, he's trying to corrupt me. Any time now, I expect him to pull out a cardboard box and challenge me to a game of three-card monte. The kid's going to be a real sidewalk shark when he grows up."

Tucker cocked his head, shooting his mother his best wide-eyed look. "What's a sidewalk shark, Mom?"

Dante winked at his nephew and mouthed, "Tell you later," which the child acknowledged with a nod.

Norah ignored the question as she placed the bowl on the table, then lowered the sleepy baby into the playpen next to it. "House rules. No public drunkenness and no bar bets. Got it, boys?"

All three males responded with a simultaneous "Yes, ma'am."

Norah smiled at their obedience. "That's better." The smile she gave her husband didn't quite make it to her eyes. "Oh, Bry. I had to leave the last bag of groceries in the back of the minivan. Can you and Tucker go down and get them?"

"But we're about to sit down and eat," he complained.

With the subtlety of a Park Avenue lawyer, she played her trump card. "It's just that I went to DeMarco's and picked up three dozen cookies. Your favorite."

Father and son shared a conspiratorial wink and raced toward the door. Dante knew they'd return several minutes later with only two and a half dozen cookies.

As soon as they were gone, Norah dropped into the nearest chair and crooked her finger at Dante. "You sit here. We need to talk. Now."

His stomach immediately tensed into a knot. Norah's idea of a family barbecue always included grilling him. Why did he think today would be any different? She usually rotated through three basic questions during any one-on-one conversation with him:

"Who are you dating?"

"Why aren't you dating her?"

And *"Ohmigawd, you're not dating her, are you?"*

In response to her demand, he pasted on the grin that his last girlfriend had called "charming and disarming" and sat next to his sister-in-law. "Shoot, Norah."

"Don't tempt me." She made no effort to ease into the day's chosen topic. "What in the hell is wrong with Bryant?"

It was a new question and one he was woefully unprepared for. He fumbled a bit before he answered. "I don't know what you mean."

She glared at him. "Don't give me that. You know exactly what I mean. He came home yesterday with a dozen roses. Red ones! That can mean only one thing. He feels guilty about something." She leaned closer and lowered her voice. "Is it another woman?"

"Bryant?" he blurted. "Another woman? Are you serious?" Although her expression said she wasn't joking, he couldn't stop himself. Laughter formed in the center of his chest and broke out. Between gasps, he managed to say, "That has to be the funniest thing I've heard in a while."

Instead of laughing along with him, she sniffed and swiped at her eyes with the back of her hand. "I'm serious, Dante."

He stopped, recognizing a look of honest pain in her eyes. "Norah, my brother is the original Boy Scout—faithful, loyal, clean in thought, word, and deed. He might admire the opposite sex, but trust me, he looks but doesn't touch. Ever. Even better, he's not afraid to make sure that any trolling female knows that he's strictly off-limits."

"But the roses—"

"—are red roses, not a red flag signaling that he's guilty about anything. He loves you, Norah. He talks nonstop about you and the kids to anyone within earshot. If they pay attention for more than three seconds, out comes the wallet and he starts showing them pictures of you all. Trust me, Norah. He's besotted. I'm just so damned glad he doesn't break down and start bawling like a little girl when he starts telling the stories about when Tucker was born."

She used her sleeve to remove the tears that had dared to leak down her cheeks. "I just had to check," she said in a quiet voice. "It's probably just me. I'm still a little hormonal after giving birth to the Amazon over there."

She nodded toward the little heartbreaker, sleeping peacefully in the playpen. At three months old, Dora had already begun to look as if she was destined to grow up to be either a female warrior or a star forward.

He reached over and patted Norah's hand. "I understand. And honestly? If I knew anything, I'd rat him out so fast, it'd make your head spin."

She leaned over and placed a sisterly kiss on his cheek. Then she got up, her emotional balance evidently restored. "I knew there were reasons why I like you."

The sound of a thundering herd indicated that Bryant and Tucker were returning from the garage with the cookies they'd been sent to fetch. Conspicuous crumbs on their faces suggested that the load had indeed been lightened by a half dozen or so. Bryant caught Dante's eye as if to say *Everything okay?* and Dante sent back a reassuring nod.

With the tension broken, lunch was more than enjoyable. Too

much food, too many bad jokes, and only one spill thanks to the rambunctious eight-year-old.

It was all the best elements of family—love, laughter, and lunch. After they cleaned up, Norah took the baby into the house to nap and Tucker wandered back to his game, boning up for an inevitable rematch, which Dante would graciously lose.

Left alone with Bryant, Dante immediately got down to business. He uncapped a beer and shoved it toward Bryant. When his brother waved it off, Dante shrugged and claimed it as his own, taking a deep pull on it. "Okay. So the roses. What gives?"

His brother reddened. "She said something?"

"Of course she said something. Norah's not stupid. What'd you do?" Despite his less than sympathetic tone, Dante knew his brother well and knew the answer wouldn't shock him.

"There was this woman . . ." Bryant began.

"That's always the way these things start."

"And we started talking. Something just . . . clicked between us. Maybe it was her sense of humor, her looks . . . I dunno. But for the first time in my life, I wondered what it'd be like to be with another woman."

"Bryant!" Okay, now Dante was shocked.

His brother waved his hand dismissively. "No, no, I didn't do anything or even say anything. It might have been a temptation for a half second or so, but I turned her down. Cold. No hanky. No panky."

Dante began to understand. "Ah, but the guilt of 'what might had been' ate at you long enough that you immediately decided to bring home a dozen roses for your loving wife."

"Something like that."

"Wow. This must have been some really stunning piece of work to get you all hot and bothered for even a half second. So who was she? Some pharmaceutical sales rep trying to get into the doctors' inner sanctum? A media type wanting some gossip or dirt on a patient?"

His brother's face turned a deep crimson.

"A reporter?" Dante heaved a sigh. "God, don't tell me it was Trisha Gluckheim from the *Post*."

The answer was little more than a whisper. "A patient."

Dante swore softly.

Bryant fiddled with an empty beer bottle, placing it on its side and idly spinning it. "I know, I know. But she's leaving tomorrow."

"Good riddance. Hopefully you'll never see her again."

The spinning bottle slowed, finally resting so that it pointed directly at Bryant. "Yeah. They're discharging her in the morning and I don't have to go in until the afternoon."

Dante flicked the bottle so that it spun again. "Even better."

The bottle came to a rest, again pointing at Bryant. "Yeah, but it's really too bad she hasn't regained any of her memories yet."

Every nerve in Dante's body went on full alert with his journalistic ones standing at full attention. "You don't mean the woman from the plane, do you?"

Bryant colored slightly as if only just making the connection. "Uh, yeah. That's right. She's the one you saved, isn't she?"

"And they're just setting her loose back into the wild with no help? No memories?"

Bryant reached over and snagged Dante's beer, tipping it up and draining it. "Yeah, I thought it was a bit raw."

"More than a bit."

His brother handed back the empty bottle. "It's not like there's something I can do about it.

"Maybe not you, but maybe I can do something."

Bryant stiffened, his personal embarrassment fading away and his professional security-conscious side taking over. "You aren't going to cause any trouble for me, are you?"

"For you, of course not. Not even for the hospital. But for CoastalEast? Absolutely. If those cheap bastards think they can get away with cutting her loose without any further medical treatment, then they have another think coming."

"Like what?"

"Like having their plans exposed to the public. They had no qualms about parading her around when they thought her survival made them look better in the public eye. What is the American public going to think when they learn the Angel of the Hudson is being thrown out on her ear to deal with the cold cruel world on her own without any identity?"

"Just as long as nobody makes a connection between you and me and her."

"Of course not." Dante could read the sense of concern that returned to his brother's face. He searched for an answer that might pacify Bryant's fears. A good lie for a good reason.

"Now that I think about it," he started, "if her brains are still scrambled, she might have reacted to you solely because of our family resemblance. You know . . . wanting to thank the man who saved her."

Bryant looked unimpressed with either Dante's explanation or his act of valor. Or both. "Good try. But we don't look anything alike."

A female voice interrupted from the kitchen door. "No, but you sound alike. And move alike." Norah stood in the door frame, her arms crossed and her expression just a bit shy of "grim." She left her post and took a seat at the table, commandeering the empty beer bottle and giving it a hearty spin.

"Don't try having a private conversation right beneath the baby's window."

Both men looked up, spotting the pink curtains fluttering through the open sash.

"Oh shit," Dante said under his breath, "you are so screwed."

Dante left Bryant and Norah to clear up their misunderstanding, knowing they would kiss and make up and didn't need a third wheel for that. Once he hit the sidewalk, he walked to the corner, flagged a cab, and headed back to his office.

The good thing about working for a 24/7 news organization was that the main editorial office was staffed around the clock. But the bad thing about it was that sometimes he couldn't avoid crossing paths with his nemesis, senior editor Victor Smithfield.

Although not old himself, Smithfield was nevertheless old school in his journalistic opinions. He was a legacy newspaper man brought kicking and screaming six years ago into the world of multimedia news. Wiser heads than his had realized it was the only way to save the family-owned news organization that had been hemorrhaging red ink for years.

So they turned a staid newspaper corporation into a highly visual, news-the-moment-it-happens online conglomerate. By riding in front of the virtual-news shockwave, they'd saved the Smithfield family fortune and positioned themselves as trendsetters rather than followers.

Other news organizations were just now scrambling to do what TwentyFourSeven had done years ago. When it came to online news, mytwentyfourseven.com ruled the Internet.

However, since no one person could occupy the Big Editorial Seat for twenty-four hours a day, seven days a week, each shift had its own senior editorial direction. The senior editors worked together to create a unified front with respect to the comprehensive company philosophies. But that didn't prevent each shift editor from bringing a small individualized slant to the overall picture, reflecting their own likes and dislikes.

If you wanted a freer hand for a political angle, you took the story to Charlie K, the senior editor on the first-shift weekday desk. If you had a human interest angle, Jeannine, the second-shift desk, better appreciated those.

But to get his proposed exposé of a callous airline past Victor Smithfield's radar, it would take cunning, skill, and more luck than Dante was due. Vic had a well-known dislike for any employee who accidentally or deliberately pissed off any of their current advertisers.

And of course, CoastalEast was one of TwentyFourSeven's biggest advertisers.

Dante worked hard to prepare his argument in support of publishing the story. He even went as far as to jot down notes on a crib sheet so that he could be "spontaneously" persuasive. Once he got all his material pulled together, he gathered his courage and headed upstairs.

Stopped in reception, he made nice to Lucy Minor, today's editorial gatekeeper. To get into the editorial wing, you had to first charm the dragon at the entrance of the cave.

He placed the requisite rose on her desk. You could determine how many bribes she'd taken during the day by the size of the bouquet on her credenza. Today's offerings were unusually thin.

"Lie to me, Luce. Tell me Victor's out of the office," he said, hiding his hope under a layer of humor.

Lucy pulled off the earphones of her iPod and folded her hands primly on the reception counter. "Victor's out of the office," she parroted.

He shook his head. "Don't toy with me, woman. I have a fast pitch that I need to get moving on now. So how's his mood? If I interrupt him while he's playing on his putting green, is he going to tear my head off?"

She shook her head. "Don't sweat it. You're the golden boy at the moment, thanks to the footage of the crash. He won't even think about beheading you for"—she screwed up her face as if calculating the time frame—"another two days."

Dante felt moderately more hopeful. If he was still in Victor's good graces because of his exclusive video, then maybe he had a chance. "So I'm clear to go in?"

Her serene expression didn't change. "No."

Foolish mortal, he told himself. Lucy always liked dangling a lifeline of hope in front of a guy, then ripping it out of his hand just as he reached it. His mind raced ahead, plotting how to slip past the Dragon Lady. "Why not?"

"Like I said. Victor's out of the office. He's at Avery Fisher Hall, at the charity ball for the ballet. Marguerite is taking his shift."

Glory Hallelujah and pass the ammunition. Marguerite had a hard-on for transportation issues, which probably dated back to her earliest days of being taunted by bullies on a school bus. She, better than any other editor, would be willing to let him play his own angle with his proposed article regardless of CoastalEast's substantial advertising budget.

Dante walked toward her closed door with a renewed spring in his step and fifteen minutes later emerged with her hearty approval.

Of course, if the plan worked, no scathing exposé would actually be necessary. He knew that sometimes it was just the promise of bad press that forced the wheels of justice to advance a rusty revolution or two.

An hour later, he finished the article, viewing it as a virtual line cast into the murky waters of the Hudson on behalf of its Angel.

As a fishing expedition, it was a raging success. It took less than two hours for the Powers-That-Be at CoastalEast to reconsider their plans to discharge Angela Sands.

The power of the pen . . .

As promised, Dante submitted his revised article, having removed all the pointed references to them being heartless, uncaring, and cheap bastards. Instead, the story became a revelation of how a huge conglomerate managed to retain their sense of humanity and honor in the face of adversity and economic downturn.

Although his editor Marguerite would have rather had a good bloodletting, she agreed that together, they'd done a good job of manipulating the corporation into having some sort of conscience and doing the right thing.

He just hoped that the Angel of the Hudson would someday agree.

9

The next morning, Angela's favorite nurse, Kalli, brought in the breakfast tray along with a thick stack of papers.

"What's this?" Angela eyed the forms, wondering if these were indeed the hallowed discharge papers that she'd been dreading. Or was that anticipating? She hadn't made up her mind yet.

"Breakfast. Today we have white stuff and yellow stuff."

"Not that." Angela reached out, then withdrew her hand, not even wanting to touch the pages. "Those," she said, pointing instead.

"Your discharge papers."

Dread won out. What little appetite she'd mustered up for colored stuff fled in horror. "I'm getting out of here?"

"So to speak."

Evidently, Ms. Seymour had made up her mind. Angela waited for more information, but Kalli didn't offer anything more, not even a hint of why today was the day.

Gathering up all her courage, Angela put on her best game face. "Let me guess. CoastalEast has decided to not cover my medical costs and I owe the hospital twenty grand."

Kalli shook her head. "Thank God, no. Actually, it's just the opposite. The company is still going to handle your hospital bills, but they want to transfer you to a different facility."

Suspicion grew in the absence of detail. "What sort of facility?"

The nurse chose her words carefully. "They want to send you to a place where you can work on getting your memories back."

She didn't need to say the actual words; the implication was bad enough. Put politely, they were sending her to the psych ward. Angela's mind was screaming, *Loony bin, Bedlam, the nuthouse,* One Flew Over the Cuckoo's Nest, *Nurse Ratched . . .*

"It's not what you think," Kalli said, reading Angela's expression.

Angela shrugged. "I have amnesia. I'm not sure *what* I think." She tried to smile as she studied the pile of papers, but her heart wasn't in it.

Oddly, Kalli's face displayed no emotion. It was as if she had been ordered to remain neutral. "Psychiatric facilities aren't the same as they were years ago. They're certainly not the snake pits you see depicted in the movies." She sounded like she was repeating someone else's words, reading from a prepared script.

Angela ran her forefinger along the edge of the top sheet. "What would you do if you were me?"

When Kalli hesitated before answering, Angela figured she'd already received her answer. But she learned she was wrong.

The nurse glanced at the door as if worrying she'd be overheard. "Honestly?" she said, her voice barely over a whisper. "I'd give it a try. Think of it as a halfway house, an easier transition from here to"—she pointed out the window—"there. Plus, if a friend or family member shows up, they can become your bridge back and you can get out. It's strictly voluntary."

"Oh, so I'm not being committed, per se."

"Absolutely not. The airline is just trying to minimize their costs. It'll be cheaper than keeping you here. And as sorry as I'll be to see you go, quite frankly, you don't need medical attention."

Angela contemplated her choices—she could be expelled with nothing more than a shopping bag of cheap clothes, no money, and a very uncertain future. Or she could live temporarily in a place where she could do whatever was necessary to either get her memories back or learn how to live without them.

There really was no decision to make.

"Where do I sign?"

Whereas the airline company had sprung for a private room in the hospital, their generosity only extended to a shared room at the Martin I. Shears Behavioral Health Center, known better by the unfortunate nickname of MIS-Behave.

When Angela and her paper bag of belongings arrived, she was immediately run through a battery of medical and psychiatric tests. Most of them substantiated that her problems—such as they were—had not arisen from any drug use. Yes, there were anomalies in her bloodstream, but their lab rats finally decided that the indicators didn't reflect any pharmacological abuse.

"That's not to mean that you might not have been completely clean in your days prior to the plane crash," one doctor offered. The two white-coated men seated on either side of him harrumphed in disagreement.

The three men reminded her of the three little pigs, building their houses out of materials of different strengths. The pigs in the fable had seldom agreed, either.

Mimicking their dispassionate manners, Angela addressed them, surprisingly pleased at how professional and informed she sounded. "But if you believe that, then wouldn't you be suggesting that drug addiction is more of a mental crutch than a physical dependency? If I had been addicted to any drug prior to the crash, I certainly would have shown signs of physical withdrawal once I no longer had access to the drug." She nodded toward her medical records, sitting in the middle of the table. "And as you can see, none of the medical observations substantiate that."

The doctor on the right nodded, while the one on the left leaned back in his chair, shaking his head in disagreement.

The one in the middle spoke. "Perhaps your memory loss has simply been your mind's way of protecting itself from the horrors you witnessed during the wreck. It may also be a coping mechanism that is minimizing any withdrawal symptoms, as well."

Again, the two doctors on either side displayed opposite reactions, one in support, the other disagreeing.

"She'd make an excellent subject for a case study on how memory loss affects addiction."

Angela tried not to jump when the words flowed clearly into her mind. Or when two other voices joined the first.

"I wonder if the cafeteria is going to have soup today. I want soup."

"If we don't get this over with, we're going to be late for our tee time."

Angela struggled to push back the intrusive thoughts. Now was not the time to admit she was hearing voices. She managed a polite smile. "Then explain to me why my memories start prior to the crash. Tell me why I remember waking up on the plane before it started having difficulties. If my mind was trying to shield me from the devastation that I experienced, then why do I remember it—all of it—in such vivid detail?"

"Damn, she's got a nice rack."

At the middle doctor's contemplative silence, the one on the right hand jumped in. "These are the sort of questions we need to address in your treatment in order to unlock everything. I believe you may be suffering from post-traumatic stress disorder, which may be manifesting itself in selective memory loss."

"More questions? Noo-o-o-o! Shut the hell up, lady. It's golf time."

The doctor on the left closed the folder in front of him, an unmistakably dismissive gesture. "The panel will discuss your treatment and devise a schedule of programs and sessions to best address your particular problems. Thank you, Ms. Sands."

Just before she reached the door, she heard one doctor say, "We gotta go, gentlemen. We have a two o'clock tee time and you know how pissy Harlan gets when we're late."

Once safely outside, she sagged against the frame of the closed door. Three men. Three distinct voices in her head. Could she really hear what they were thinking?

She shook away such a crazy notion. The place must be getting to her already if she believed she could actually hear people's thoughts.

A statuesque young woman approached Angela wearing an artificial smile. "Hi, Angela. I'm Sienna and I'm going to take you to your room now."

Angela cocked her head, ready for an intrusive thought, but she heard nothing. The woman's artificial smile screamed, *I know that you know that I know you're a lunatic* but that was strictly a matter of reading her expression, not her mind.

"Before we go, humor me for a moment. Think about your favorite color?"

Sienna stared at her with dead eyes. "What?"

"Your favorite color. Think about it. Don't say it, okay?"

Sienna sighed as if dealing with a hyperactive child. "Okay. I'm thinking of a color."

Angela closed her eyes, waiting for the answer. But she "heard" nothing. No words. No images. Not even any flashes of any particular hue.

She opened her eyes. "Red?"

"Excuse me, ladies." An orderly pushing a large laundry cart had stopped, unable to negotiate a path around them.

Both Angela and Sienna took a step over to allow the orderly room to pass by as the woman responded.

"No. Green."

"The color of money. That's no surprise."

The words formed in Angela's mind without any direct connection or clue as to the originator of the thoughts.

She turned to the orderly. "Did you say something? About money?"

Before the man could respond, Sienna took her by the arm. "Come on, Angela. It's time to go."

"Did you?" She turned her question to the woman. "Did you say anything about green being the color of money?"

A gleam of greed lit the woman's eyes for a moment, then flickered out. But her smile lost its artificial sheen and curled into something almost wolflike. "You're going to fit in just fine here, Angela."

That night, they bunked her in a private room, warning her it was only a temporary location. She would receive her *permanent* assignment the next day. The word contained a sense of finality that made her stomach churn. Or maybe it was the medication they insisted she take that gave her indigestion.

Once the pills kicked in, she decided that she'd been hallucinating. No sane person would believe she could read the thoughts of another . . .

Bright and too early the next morning, Sienna escorted Angela to a third wing and to a semiprivate room on the fourth floor. They were met at the doorway of Room 407 by a tall, big-boned blonde with a series of tattoos that started at her wrists and extended at least to the edges of her T-shirt sleeves and most likely beyond.

"Gretchen, this is Angela, your new roommate. I'm sure you two will get along just fine." The woman gave Angela a little nudge at her back, propelling her and her paper bag of belongings forward a couple of steps into the room.

Angela turned around to thank her, but realized Sienna had literally shoved her into the room, closed the door behind her, and fled.

Gretchen stared at her with granite-set features that reflected a distinct lack of enthusiasm to share her space. But the woman said nothing. Instead, she turned around and stalked back to her bed as if Angela might not realize which half of the space might belong to whom.

Like anyone might get confused . . .

A tattered strip of masking tape formed a line of demarcation down the center of the room. The sterile right half contained only a bare mattress on a metal bed frame and a chest of drawers pulling double duty as a bedside table. A gooseneck lamp curved toward the bed, its plastic shade missing a chunk at the edge.

Then there was Gretchen's side. If the décor reflected the woman, she was heavy into motorcycles and 1980s hair bands. Posters filled every bit of wall space of her half of the room, including the ceiling. Brightly colored rugs formed a connect-the-dots pattern on the floor. The tie-dyed bedspread in purple, green, and orange suggested that the woman was also certifiably color-blind.

In the midst of the color explosion, a semicircle of unlit white candles clustered on the top of Gretchen's chest of drawers. It appeared to be a sort of shrine crowding a silver-framed picture, a black and white photo of a man on a motorcycle.

Despite an obvious love of color, Gretchen herself wore a dingy gray T-shirt and well-worn jeans. She sat on the edge of her vivid-hued bed, legs crossed Indian-style. Holding up her hand, she began to count on her fingers.

"The rules," she said in a low gravelly voice.

One: "Don't touch my stuff. If my stuff is on your side of the room, leave it there. It's mine."

Two: "No smoking. If you even smell like smoke, I'll go apeshit on you. I can't stand the odor. Reminds me of my old man."

Three: "I don't want to talk to you. I don't care why you're here. I don't care what your problem is. If you start crying, get the hell out of my room. I don't tolerate waterworks."

She finished by skipping number four and holding up her hands.

"And number five? If I decide to spend the night elsewhere, or decide to leave, whatever, if you rat me out, I'll kill you. Understand? Cross me once and you'll wish you'd never been born. *Capice?*"

Angela stared at the woman. Her heavy-lidded eyes and blown-out pupils suggested she was already on some heavy meds. Whatever it was, Angela concluded she wasn't getting enough of it, considering her lingering aggression.

But the woman's lotus position and her basic build—stocky but strong—suggested something more troublesome. Although she might be drugged out of her gourd, she still had the innate flexibility and physical strength to back up her threats.

Someone like that only understood one thing.

"Gotcha," Angela said softly. "And here are my rules." She held up her forefinger. "You leave me alone and I'll leave you alone. Period."

Even though she'd resisted using her middle finger to make her point, Gretchen uncoiled and stood, growling as if she'd been royally insulted. A few steps later, the woman towered over Angela and shook her massive forefinger in Angela's face.

"Listen, bitch, this is my—"

Angela reached up, grabbed the woman's finger and tattooed wrist, and twisted both backward. Using the leverage of pain and surprise, she spun the woman around and down to her knees, her arm pulled behind her at an angle guaranteed to be painful now and even more so if the woman moved. In fact, the position was such that it'd take little effort on Angela's part to snap both bones in Gretchen's wrist.

The movement was instinctive and smooth. Something inside of Angela found far too much pleasure executing such a maneuver against a bully.

She leaned down and said in a low voice, "I have no desire to hurt you. I don't want to intrude on your space. All I want is to be left alone. Do we have an understanding?"

The woman spat out a few choice expletives, grunted in pain, then finally nodded. "Okay."

Angela continued. "I'm going to let you up and we're going to start all over again. Agreed?"

After a moment of hesitation, the woman said, "Agreed."

Angela released the hold and allowed the woman to rise to her feet. She stuck out her hand, knowing the gesture could easily be used against her. "Hi. I'm Angela."

The calculated stare Gretchen gave her wasn't that of a tranquilized patient. Her gaze held a distinct sense of awareness and wariness. She drew a deep breath and her lips curled in a smile that looked much more like a snarl. "I hope you don't plan to do much sleeping in here."

Angela met the woman's glare. "Don't worry about me. I sleep light." To demonstrate her lack of fear, Angela turned her back on the woman and nudged the small bag containing her meager belongings across the floor until they rested next to her bed.

Staring at the stained mattress, she sighed. "Maybe you'd tell me where to get some sheets for this thing?"

Gretchen didn't speak for a moment, then finally said, "Top drawer. Pillow's in the bottom drawer."

"Thanks."

It might not be an overture to friendship, but it was the first step toward a possible stalemate, the best-case scenario Angela could envision.

After making her bed, Angela unpacked the few items Ms. Seymour had provided. Kalli had insisted she take the hospital robe and a set of scrubs as sleeping gear. As she shook out the robe, a piece of cardboard fluttered free.

Stooping down, she retrieved it, realizing it was a business card. It took a moment, then she remembered the man who had seen her walk of shame from the press conference to the elevator. He'd been kind. Concerned. Even slightly familiar looking. But if he knew her, knew who she was, wouldn't he have said something?

She turned the card over and recognized the red logo.

Dante Kearns, reporter
dante@myTwentyFourSeven.com

A reporter. The last thing she needed.

She sighed and tossed the card in the chest of drawers and then stretched out on the clean sheets. The bed was moderately more comfortable than the one at the hospital. There was no way she was going to fall asleep, not with the glowering Biker Chick across the room, but Angela didn't feel like going out and exploring her new home.

The reporter's face loomed in her mind again. Why did he seem familiar to her? Maybe she'd seen him on television. Maybe—

"Only one change of clothes? You must not be planning on staying long."

Either Gretchen was starved for companionship, or maybe they could proceed from stalemate to possible truce. No matter which reason, Angela was glad of the distraction. Even more so, she was glad that her little "mind-reading" psychosis had evidently passed.

"It's all I own."

"I know bag ladies with more stuff than that."

Angela shrugged. The last thing she wanted to do was launch into the story of her brief life.

Gretchen continued. "This court-mandated or something?"

Angela rose up on her elbows. "Court-mandated?"

The tall woman sat sideways on her bed, leaning back against the wall. "You know. Plead to a lesser offense and get psychiatric treatment and counseling in lieu of a sentence."

"No."

Gretchen remained quiet for a while. Then she spoke again. "You actually crazy?"

"No."

"My last roomie was a real nutcase. Kept seeing people who weren't there."

And sometimes I think I hear voices in my head. You keep getting stuck with some real winners.

Heavy silence filled the void. Angela was thankful for it. On the other hand, it seemed to bother her new roommate. Gretchen picked up a magazine and slumped down, pretending to read it. Finally she tossed away the magazine and sat up.

"Sorry I came down on you hard. Doc says I have anger management issues. And abandonment issues." She narrowed her eyes in thought. "And some sort of other issues, but I can't remember what."

Seeing how Angela had been looking forward to a night's sleep without taking any drugs or being bothered by nurses or PA systems, she decided to accept Gretchen's olive branch. It was far better than sleeping with one eye open while waiting for an impending attack.

"Maybe it's memory issues?"

Gretchen glared at her, but the frosty look thawed and a glint of humor reflected in her eyes. "Sounds about right." She stretched. "So did Miss I'm-too-Perky-to-Be-Believed give you the grand tour? Show you where the phones are? The vending machines? The cafeteria?"

"No."

"The bitch. They pay Sienna to do stuff like that. They call it the 'entrance orientation' but she never does it. Just dumps and runs. C'mon. Staying here isn't so bad if you know the basics."

Drug hangover had made exhaustion crawl through Angela's veins like warm wax. It solidified at the thought of walking the facilities hallways with Gretchen the Hun. But the woman was right; it would be smart to know the lay of the land and the personalities of those living and working there.

"Sure."

Thirty minutes later, Angela had seen all the highlights of MIS-Behave from the Conservatory of Tranquility to the Nutritional Center. In layman's terms, the garden and the dining room. Gretchen had informed her that they were "guests" rather than "patients" or "inmates" and the staff members were all "facilitators" rather than mostly "orderlies" and "guards."

Along the way, Angela learned that males and females were housed on different floors of the facility and shared the recreational, meeting, and dining spaces.

Gretchen waited until they returned to the relative privacy of their room before she turned toward the more sensitive parts of the rules. "Lockdown is ten P.M. If you're not in your room, they'll go hunting for you and it's not a pretty sight when they find you. The day staff is made up mostly of bleeding heart liberals who want to talk away your problems. The night staff . . . well, they're made up the folks who couldn't get a better job than night watch at the local nut ward." She paused. "Even I steer clear of them."

"Good to know."

"Now, this next rule? It's one I break all the time." Gretchen pushed aside her dresser, revealing a neat cavity in the wall. She reached in and pulled out two candy bars, slinging one toward Angela. "No food in the rooms. So make sure to stick the wrapper in your pocket and toss it in the trash can in the garden." She stripped the paper and took a big bite.

"You'll probably be assigned a group for therapy," she said around a mouthful of chocolate, "and meet with them once a day. That's about the only time you see anyone with any medical background around here. Don't be fooled by the white coats. They give them out to everyone from the janitor on up."

"So I guess the inmates . . . er . . . guests run the asylum?"

"Pretty much." She watched Angela. "You going to stare that thing to death or eat it?"

Angela consulted the candy bar, trying to remember the taste of chocolate. Surely she'd had it before. But why didn't she remember it?

Wasn't that a sin or something to not remember chocolate?

She experimented with a small bite, the taste exploding on her tongue with the elegant ferocity of an orgasm.

At least she did remember what those felt like.

"My God, this is fantastic." She took another bite and it pleased her just as much as the first, if not more.

Gretchen stared at her. "It's only chocolate."

"Only? It's fucking fantastic!" The texture and the sensation of eating it commanded all her senses, bringing her pleasure on a level and with an intensity she'd never felt before. Even if her memories were extremely limited, the sensation was totally overwhelming.

Finally, after swallowing the last bite, she managed to regain some semblance of control. "I never had chocolate before."

Gretchen looked both dumbfounded and horrified. "What sort of God-awful cult have you been living in?"

"No cult. It's a long story." At Gretchen's expectant look, Angela added, "One I don't want to go into right now."

"Sure. Later, eh?"

"Yeah. Later."

10

"Later" occurred during the next day's breakfast. The guests lined up at the door in a manner that seemed initially unorganized. But once Gretchen arrived, a hierarchy quickly formed with Gretchen in the lead. As her roommate, Angela was evidently afforded the same courtesies.

They breezed past everyone in the crowd and entered the dining room first as if everyone had been waiting for their arrival. As first in line, they received the hottest food, the largest portions, and the choice table by the lone dining-room window. Whoever Gretchen was, she ruled by respect and, quite possibly, the threat of bodily harm if she didn't receive the respect she believed due her.

Somewhere in the back of Angela's perforated mind, she knew that she'd accidentally made a smart strategic move by befriending the biggest and evidently baddest inmate . . . er . . . guest in the population.

Angela spent the rest of the meal trying to figure out why she knew so much about the psychology of prisons and prisoners. Did it mean she'd been incarcerated in the past? If so, wouldn't the investigators have figured that out? She distinctly remembered someone coming in and fingerprinting her. Wouldn't her prints show up in IAFIS?

Her line of thought came to a screeching halt.

"What in the heck is IAFIS?"

"What?" Gretchen looked up from her third muffin. "You say something?"

"What's IAFIS?"

"Sounds like a bug to me. Don't they get all over roses or something?" She turned to a man sitting at the next table. "Yo, Bernie. What's IAFIS?"

The man didn't even look up from his meal. "Fingerprint system. Run by the feds."

Gretchen nodded resolutely, stuffing the last bit of muffin in her mouth and talking around it. "There's your answer. Bernie knows everything. He's a walking Wikipedia. Hey, Bernie, what's the name of those little bugs that get on roses?"

"Aphids." *"Stop asking me questions, bitch. I want to eat."*

Angela tried not to react to the voice in her head.

Gretchen mistook her expression for awe. "Don't look so shocked. I told you he was fucking brilliant." She eyed the wrapped muffin on Angela's tray. "You gonna eat that?" At Angela's lack of response, she snagged the item and began freeing it from the plastic. "So, who took your fingerprints?"

Angela tore her attention from Bernie. Had she heard his thoughts or just read words into his facial expressions? "Uh . . . an investigator."

"Why?"

She pushed Bernie and his complaints away. Maybe it was time to come clean. It wasn't like this hadn't been the top news story for a day and a half. "Because I don't know who I am."

Gretchen looked up from the muffin. "No shitting me?"

Angela thought for a moment before boiling her life story down to four short sentences. "I was in an airplane crash. When I woke up, I didn't remember who I was. They assume I'm the only unaccounted-for passenger. But no one has stepped forward to identify me."

Gretchen took a gulp of her coffee then whistled. "Man, that's so much better than my fingerprint story."

Relieved that she didn't have to go through the "Angel of the Hudson" recognition routine, she asked the obvious question, hoping it would turn the spotlight on Gretchen instead. "What's your story?"

"So . . . I was in this bar and this guy came in and tried to get all handsy with me. I was PMSing so I coldcocked him. And then I pretty much wrecked the place after that." Her face grew darker. "That's rule number six. Don't mess with me when I'm PMSing."

"I'll make sure to remember that. You got a calendar or something?"

"Nope. I don't have a regular cycle." She released a hoarse laugh. "I ride a Harley. Get it?"

After a string of an additional half dozen or so bad puns, they finished breakfast in time for Angela's first group meeting.

Because of the prescreening efforts by the doctors, she'd been placed in a session for people who were suffering from post-traumatic stress disorder and who also had dabbled with drug and alcohol use to help them cope.

She listened to the others recite their tales of terror, some in great detail and others offering only bare sketches of their experiences. Obtrusive thoughts interrupted her attention and she could never tell if the person thinking was the person speaking or whether she was hearing the opinion of another.

The group consisted of a session leader whom everyone seem to mistrust and five patients—all men: a cop (*"Glad he's not out on the streets"*), an emergency medical technician (*"Afraid of a little blood? Give me a break"*), and three former military types (*"Did you join and think you were going to be anything other than cannon fodder?" "I'm going to kill my CO when I get out." "Don't make me go back"*). And Angela.

When it came time for her to speak, she was at a loss for words, her mind reeling from the inadvertent bombardment of thoughts.

The session leader, a man named Nelson, nonetheless prodded, obviously assuming it was fear that stopped her rather than distraction and a lack of her own cohesive memories.

It took a while to shut out everyone else and find the right words without sounding evasive or detached. "I was in an airplane crash and I'm suffering from memory loss."

The cop leveled her with a hard stare. "You don't remember the crash?"

"No, I remember it pretty well. It's just that I don't remember me."

Nelson nodded sagely. "It's not uncommon for people involved in dangerous and tragic circumstances to distance themselves from the actual situation and remember it from a different perspective. It's a coping method to recall it like an observer rather than a participant."

She shook her head. "I was definitely a participant. I remember being there." Angela closed her eyes and her heart began to beat faster. "I remember the roaring of engines, the smell of the smoke," she said, struggling to draw in a deep breath. "Did you know that when jet fuel burns, it makes a thick dirty black smoke that smells awful?"

The memory of the smoke grew cloying as she spoke about it—almost an out-of-body experience. The only sound in her mind was metal screaming against metal. She drew in a breath, trying to tell herself that the faint smoky aroma she smelled came from the clothes of the cigarette smoker sitting next to her.

Now that she couldn't hear any unspoken responses to her tale, it was oddly cathartic to recount her experience to this particular audience. They were people who didn't want the details solely to analyze the reasons behind the crash.

"There was a man sitting next to me on the plane. The first time I remember seeing him, he was asleep." His gory image flashed in her mind and her stomach started to churn. "The last time I saw him, he didn't have a face."

Someone made a sympathetic noise.

Despite her best efforts, her voice cracked. "When we finally stopped tumbling, we were upside down. I was hanging from my seat and had to figure out how to release my belt but not fall into the fire below."

When the images of flames flickering in her mind threatened to overwhelm her, she opened her eyes. That's when she realized she had been rocking back and forth as she spoke. Looking across the circle of patients, she realized that a bearded man across the way had matched his rhythm to hers. His expression screamed he'd experienced something far too similar.

Sensing a kindred soul, she turned her attention to him. "I tried not to panic, but I think I did. I'm almost certain that I panicked." When the man looked away, unwilling to make anything but the briefest eye contact with her, she turned toward Nelson, the coolly detached session leader. "Who wouldn't panic in a situation like that?"

He said nothing, but the others spoke in a chorus of voices. "Me." "I would." "You'd be crazy not to be scared."

The bearded man finally spoke, but he still didn't look at her. "I was petrified."

"You were in an airplane that crashed?"

He nodded, his voice dropping to a whisper. "Afghanistan." Then he shut down, his brief tale told.

"Finish your story, Angela," someone else said in encouragement. "It'll help."

By the time Angela finished, mentioning about the bodies she swam around, the baby who survived, and everything else, the supportive chorus had grown silent. Everyone stared at her, their mouths gaping open.

"I know who you are . . ." someone thought.

The cop was the first one to speak aloud. "You're the Angel of the Hudson. We saw you on TV." He gave her a critical once-over. "You sure look a lot different than you did during that press conference."

A shiver coursed through her as she recalled her outburst. *A lot saner?* "I know," she whispered. "I'm better now."

"But you still don't know who you are?"

"I know who they say I am."

One of the military types uncrossed his arms and shifted forward in his seat. "SOP is to work from the manifest, identifying who was on the aircraft. If you can find all the bodies but one, then by process of elimination, the survivor must be that one last passenger, right?"

She nodded.

He continued. "But no one came forward to actually identify you? To substantiate who you are?"

"Nobody cared."

Then a second more damning thought hit her.

"God, you must have been a real bitch for no one to step forward to claim you."

She tried to chastise herself for contemplating such a depressing thought, but who's to say it wasn't true? Or maybe she was mistaking someone else's thought for her own . . .

"They probably had good reason," she said, unable to speak much louder than a whisper. "But I don't know what that reason might have been. I know my name and what hotel I'd been living in, but nobody can tell me anything about . . . me."

Nelson glanced at his watch, which Angela took as a sign that she'd taken too much of the group time. "So who do you think you are?" he asked solicitously.

"A bad mother. A lousy lover. A prostitute. A criminal. A poor excuse for a human being."

She pushed away the insulting descriptions. "I don't know." She began to cry in body-wracking sobs. The bearded man and one of the military-types showed signs of sympathy. The other faces remained untouched by her display of emotion.

Nelson glanced at his watch once more and signaled the time by standing up. "Good session, everyone. We'll pick this up tomorrow with you"—he pointed to the man sitting next to Angela—"Carl, okay?"

He was already halfway out of the room when the man seated next to Angela said in a low voice, "My name is Steve, you little shit." He turned to Angela. "Listen, don't pay Nelson any attention. He only thinks he's in charge. This is when the session really starts."

The group pulled their chairs closer until their knees touched. Angela didn't like the personal contact but she decided to tolerate it, just this once.

Whereas the official session had been facilitated to death by Nelson, the unofficial session was a freewheeling bitch session. Participants who had only responded to direct questions with a minimum of words now emptied out their pent-up feelings, their fears, and their hopes. The outpouring was as much cathartic as it was confusing.

Their thoughts still slammed into her but with less ferocity as before, but were still unidentified. Was the cop the alcoholic? Or was it the EMT? Which one had the four ex-wives? Was it meth or crack that the soldier-turned-teacher had been cooking up in the school lab when it exploded?

The facts and feelings mashed into one gigantic swirl, almost too much for Angela to comprehend. When she pushed back her chair, breaking the circle, the others didn't look shocked, upset, or even perturbed by her actions.

Steve turned back to face her. "Too much, too soon?"

She nodded, not trusting herself to speak. Doing so might let the tornado of thoughts back into her mind.

"Don't sweat it. It can be pretty overwhelming, especially after Nelson's dog-and-pony show. It's okay if you want to ease into this or not participate at all. Just know that we"—he nodded toward the others in the group—"are here and we understand how you feel."

The bearded man spoke. "All we ask is that you don't rat us out to the staff. They know what we're doing, even if they don't officially sanction us. If anybody complains, that'll give them a reason to shut us down."

"I won't say anything," she whispered, fearing that the mere effort of speaking would destroy her efforts to hold back the maelstrom.

She chanced it one more time. "And maybe . . . maybe I can come back when I feel ready?"

Every head nodded and she was suddenly filled with a feeling of strength and support that almost took her breath away. She managed to stand. "Thanks, guys. It's good to know . . . that you have each other."

The bearded man looked up, making eye contact with her for the first time. "That *we* have each other."

A week passed and the sense of security she received from the unofficial group session was the only thing that got her through the rest of the day.

By working with six different men with six different sets of thoughts, she began to be able to sort out who thought what. It wasn't as much a matter of content, but learning that each man's thoughts appeared to her differently. The cop's thoughts left a dark blue afterimage in her mind. When she looked at him, she could almost make out a blue outline around him.

But it wasn't always color. For instance, the EMT's thoughts came to her in something like soap bubbles, the words floating upward and fading until they popped and disappeared. She didn't see bubbles when she looked at him.

Nelson, the leader, only thought in jagged lines—sharp, irregular, and sometimes painful, just like him.

Group might not be helping her reclaim her memories, but it was doing wonders about teaching her more about her strange abilities. Still, as interesting and perhaps important as it was to learn about the extent of her talents, such knowledge didn't actually make life easier for her.

It didn't take mind reading to realize her inadvertent association with Gretchen made her a pariah elsewhere. Thanks to the umbrella of "protection" Gretchen extended over her, Angela hadn't been bullied by any other patient. But neither was she befriended, talked to, looked at, or otherwise included in anything outside of group. Even when she saw the men outside of their meeting time, they seldom even made eye contact with her.

But if she thought life with Gretchen was odd, life without

Gretchen was far worse. When her roommate was abruptly transferred to another facility, the resulting void in leadership caused a political struggle among the remaining patients. The tenuous peace shattered as various patients tried to assume her self-professed role of the facility's unofficial benevolent despot.

As a result, there were at least two daily fistfights in the Conservatory of Tranquility and meals in the Nutritional Center were filled with tension and, often, name-calling.

Even the after-group suffered from the general sense of unrest. Two members of the group had to be held back by the others when their arguments about military branch superiority grew unnecessarily heated. Anger and distrust tore everything apart. Their short-tempered thoughts turned jagged and red and were filled with heat, hatred, and distrust.

The worst part was the strident voices that followed her everywhere and bombarded her constantly. She'd always had a bothersome hum in the back of her head. But now with the facility in such complete disarray, the hum expanded until she heard the individual voices that comprised it, all the time.

And in a mental ward, what those voices screamed was enough to turn a sane person into something as crazy as those people who were screaming.

Angela coped by getting away by herself whenever possible. The more distance she put between her body and the other patients, the fainter the babble grew. But the wear and tear of being a mind reader in a mental facility wore on her. Thanks to a new roommate who alternated between uncontrollable crying and accusations against invisible enemies, even her room offered no sanctuary.

Instead, Angela began to walk the grounds daily, trying to build more strength and endurance. If she couldn't improve her memory, at least she could exercise her body.

Each day, she ventured farther, exploring the vast property, taking note of the surveillance cameras along the enclosure's fence line. It didn't take long for her to realize that only every third or so camera was operational. Some of the wires had been cut, the others chewed through by small animals.

Evidently, no one paid much attention to any of the security camera feeds. She supposed she should take some relief that the razor wire at the top of the wall faced outward, to repel unwanted visitors, rather than inward, to make sure the crazies didn't escape. You had to be really crazy if you wanted to break *into* the place. . . .

As Nelson had repeated several times, every "guest" had committed themselves, voluntarily. Or as Gretchen had put it, "We are all nuts but at least we know it."

Angela actually missed Gretchen.

In some perverse way, the woman had kept order and peace among the patients. Sure, she preyed on the gullible and picked on the weak, but because she did so, no one else did. There was only one great tormentor and she spread her torture evenhandedly so that no one person bore the brunt or buckled under the distress.

Even the orderlies were trying to fill the vacuum left behind by the woman's departure. Two in particular, Newcomb and Dunlap, had begun to strut around the ward during the night shift, finding pleasure in controlling people purely for the sake of control.

Angela avoided the twosome whenever possible, trying to be in her room long before the night shift came on duty. She didn't like what they thought and how often they thought it.

But one evening, she'd stayed outside too long on her walkabout. When she realized her mistake, she followed the tree line on the east lawn, hoping to reach the southern entrance of her wing unseen. That's when she stumbled across the two men.

Luckily, they were too busy smoking a couple of blunts to notice her. She stayed in the shadows, but she heard them clearly.

"So, you see that new piece of fine, fine ass on the fourth floor?" That was Newcomb, with his thick southern accent.

"Yeah, she's got a mighty fine rack." Although Dunlap was more soft-spoken, it didn't mean he was any less harmless.

Newcomb made a smacking noise. "I want me some of that."

"Me, too. So, why don't we do it? Let's get some tail. It's been too long." Dunlap lowered his voice. "We can slip the blond roommate a double dose of sleep meds and we can have as much of her roomie as we want." He snickered. "It's not like anyone's going to believe her if she bitches about it. She spends most of her time blaming invisible people for touching her. No one will buy her story that one of her invisible friends got a little friendlier than usual."

"Good thinking."

"And after we're through, maybe we'll do the roomie, too."

"That blond bitch? Nah, she's too skinny."

Despite his protests, Angela could hear his smoky thoughts. *I'll do the blonde after we finish with the tail. I like me a woman with some meat on her bones. Some muscle. Someone who can put up a fight. I like 'em to fight.*

Angela flexed her hands into fists. Energy and indignation shot through her like electricity.

You want a fight? I'll give you one.

11

It took little effort to persuade Shandra, her new roommate, to change beds. Angela simply pulled a "Gretchen" by bullying the woman into the switch. As a result, the new nurse who hadn't learned patients' names and faces yet gave Shandra the double dose of sleeping meds meant for Angela.

Fifteen minutes later, Shandra was out for the count and snoring peacefully. Angela figured she'd done a good deed there. This might be the first good night's sleep the woman had experienced since she arrived. Most of the time, she cried herself to sleep . . . eventually.

Angela rolled her roommate over, then pulled up the covers so that no one would see Shandra's telltale black hair. No one would realize an exchange had been made.

After Angela climbed into the other bed, it didn't take long for her anger to build, growing steadily until she feared she'd explode in rage. It took all her control to simply lie still.

And wait.

Sometime after midnight, the door scraped open. A slice of fluorescent light lit up the cold room and then winked away. Another noise sounded like someone dragging a chair across the floor. Somehow, Angela knew it was being wedged under the doorknob.

"Don't want any interruptions."

She smothered a laugh. They thought they were giving themselves some privacy. In reality, they were closing the cage door behind themselves.

"I'm going first," Dunlap whispered too loudly.

Newcomb sounded angry but kept his voice low. "No way, asshole. It's my turn." *"You went first last time."*

That revelation refueled Angela's anger, turning it into raging fury. It made her plans for revenge much more satisfying. These men were going to experience *justice.*

I'm going to make you wish you were never . . .

Something twisted inside of her and a more powerful sensation knocked aside her fury, replacing it with a different emotion, equally as strong.

She didn't want revenge.

She wanted . . .

Sex.

Her breath caught in her throat.

Not just sex but hot, sweaty sex on the bed, on the floor, hanging from the light fixture if necessary. She opened her eyes to see Newcomb leaning over her, obviously stunned to realize he'd chosen the wrong patient.

"Aw, fuck . . ."

He tried to pull away but she reached up and hooked an arm around his neck. "That's just what I was thinking about," she said, pulling him down toward her. "What I need is a good, hard fuck and I think you're just the man to give it to me."

She glanced over at Dunlap, who stood at the foot of bed, somewhat chagrined at being caught with his pants down.

Literally.

"And then when I'm finished with him," she purred, "you'll be next." It was a statement rather than a question.

It only took a moment for lascivious grins to replace their twin looks of bewilderment.

Her desire started out strong, but in seconds, magnified tenfold, turning into an overwhelming demand for immediate and thorough satisfaction.

She didn't just need sex.

She'd die without it.

But as much as her lustful inner woman insisted on instantaneous attention, she managed to project a more controlled exterior. "So," she said, stroking Newcomb's grizzled chin, "are you just going to sit there and stare? Or are we going to have some fun?"

The man fell on her, fumbling with her nightshirt like a schoolboy, all anxious fingers, and panting heavily. He lowered his mouth to hers, his tongue forcing its way between her lips. His hips began to grind into hers although several layers of material separated them.

She pushed him back, breaking contact.

"Slow down, cowboy," she cooed. "You act like you haven't had any in a while. You don't have to set a speed record. We have all night to do anything you want." She sat up, trailing her fingers over the pulsating bulge in his pants. "If you can last that long."

Dunlap, his partner in crime, plopped down on the end of the bed, angling himself for prime viewing.

She smiled at him. "You don't mind watching for a while, do you, sweetheart? When our boy here gets all tuckered out, it'll be your turn." She giggled. "Or is that all *fuckered* out?"

Dunlap could barely talk. "Watch. Now. Fuck later. S'okay."

"I thought you wouldn't mind. Go"—she wiggled her fingers at his groin—"amuse yourself while we get started." She turned to Newcomb. "Stand up, doctor, and let's see what sort of operating equipment the good Lord outfitted you with."

The man obeyed by shifting off of her and standing next to the bed. She pulled the string at his waistband, loosening his scrub pants. They puddled around his ankles, revealing his dingy tighty-whities that strained to cover his swollen erection.

"Ooh . . . Doctor," she said, stroking the material. "You're ready for me, aren't you?"

He stood there, his eyes shut, his hands clenched in fists at his side. "Uh-huh," he said between gritted teeth.

Angela stood, plastering herself against his side. Then she slithered to his back, molding herself against him. "Then let me allow the beast to escape." She shimmied down him, pulling his underwear down as she lowered herself. Her cheek slid down his clammy back, his butt, and then his hairy leg.

The man smelled of too much exertion and not enough hygiene. The aroma of old sweat sliced through the lust that had been driving her. Her brain suddenly severed the control exerted by raging hormones.

What in hell am I doing? Have I lost my mind?

The last thing she wanted to do was have any sex—much less consensual sex—with this pervert and his partner in porn. The whole reason she'd set up this little sting operation was to stop the twosome in their tracks. What was wrong with her?

"C'mon, baby, don't be a tease. *Do me, now!*"

There was something enticing to her basest instincts in his commanding words. A promise of extreme pleasure in his rough voice. What would it hurt to have a little fun first and to—?

Stop! she screamed at herself. *Stick with the original plan.*

But it was so hard to sever her attraction to him, to dissolve her insane desire to mate, which vied for control with her need to avenge all the women they'd raped.

"Gimme a blow job." Newcomb's voice echoed in her head, but not in her ears.

"I don't wanna watch. I want some of her now." That was Dunlap, his words as clear in her mind as if he was speaking.

The two voices in her head warred for her attention.

"I'm gonna explode if she don't do something soon."

"I could knock him out, tell him she done it, and then I could have her to myself."

"I wish she was bigger."

"I wish she was blonder."

Two voices, two sets of thoughts. She could barely keep them straight. She felt her body twisting inside as if trying to keep up with the two sets of demands.

She tried to rise to her feet but Newcomb pushed on her shoulders. "Stay there. You know what to do."

His engorged penis loomed in her face.

She reached up as if to guide it into her mouth, but she dug her nails into the tender flesh instead. Newcomb screamed like an adolescent girl.

Before he could take another breath, she shot up, slamming her knee into his groin, and clocking him under the chin with the top of her head.

A few stars exploded behind her eyes, but she managed to keep her footing and shake it off. Newcomb sank to the floor. He writhed in pain, one hand clutching his offended member, the other cradling his head. The whimpers he made didn't even sound human.

Dunlap laughed at his ailing buddy. "Bet you're wishing I'd gone first now," he said. "But now that I know what I'm facing . . ."

He stepped closer to Angela, his face distorted by lust and

meanness. His meaty fist shot out. Had Angela not ducked in time, it would have caught her in the face. A powerhouse blow like that would have surely knocked her out. She'd have been unconscious, unable to fight back.

But she'd instinctively thrown up a block, dodging the knockout blow. Her follow-through jab carried Dunlap forward, throwing him off balance. Angela took advantage of his position by hooking her left arm around the back of his neck and hitting him hard in the stomach. As he doubled up, she let go of his head and slammed her elbow into his temple and kneed him hard in his solar plexus.

Dunlap sank to the floor, doubling up in pain and vomiting.

Horrendous thoughts of retribution and revenge against her filled her mind. She wasn't sure if she was actually reading the thoughts of both men or simply interpreting their rage and pain.

As strong as her inexplicable lust had been, her anger was bigger. Her need for justice expanded until it crowded out all other thoughts.

She stalked to the door, kicking the wedged chair free. The moment before she stepped out to call for help, Newcomb pulled her back. But instead of trying to hit her, he pushed past her, stumbling into the hallway. He struggled with his pants, trying to pull them up so that he was no longer exposed.

"Code Gray," he screamed between gritted teeth. Blood dribbled down from his nose, which was starting to swell. Angela decided she'd clipped it when she'd hit it with her head.

"Code Gray Emergency," he repeated. His voice was a shaky soprano wheeze. Given how hard she'd hit him in the gonads, she wasn't surprised.

Unfortunately, the first nurse who responded was NutMeg, a woman who had earned her nickname by sharing far too many of the peculiarities of her patients. She sprinted down the hallway toward them.

Before Angela could explain what had happened, Newcomb pushed her aside and stepped in front of her. "This crazy bitch attacked me!"

Angela stepped away from him. "Only because he tried to rape me." Looking down, she realized her nightgown was still hanging open. She began to button it up again.

Newcomb held his hand to his nose. "In your dreams, skank. I wouldn't touch you if . . ."

When Angela raised her fist, he stepped back, almost cowering. The nurse stepped between them.

Newcomb wheezed, "She got Dunlap, too. I think he's really hurt."

NutMeg glared, gesturing Angela away from the door and her victim. Then the nurse peered inside where Dunlap lay on the floor, groaning in pain. Reaching in her pocket, the nurse pressed a panic button, something that all staff members carried.

Neither Dunlap nor Newcomb had thought to activate theirs; Angela had kept them too busy.

The nurse turned to Newcomb, who was bracing himself against the wall, trying to stay upright. "What were you doing in her room? And why are his pants down?"

Angela tried to answer, but the woman stopped her with an admonishing look that could have shriveled a cactus at ten paces.

Newcomb saw his opening and lied for all he was worth. "We was walking by, Dunlap and me, and we heard some strange noises. We knocked and we heard this one yell at us to go away. We was suspicious so we opened the door. We found her on top of her roommate, just a-grinding away. We separated them and that's when we realized her roommate was knocked out." He glared at Angela. "This crazy bitch drugged her so that she could attack her—you know—sexually."

"I did not!" Angela said bitterly. "I overheard him and Dunlap while they were outside taking a smoke. They were planning to drug me and rape her. But I switched places with her because I knew I could stop them."

Newcomb literally vibrated with anger. He looked ready to blow a blood vessel and stroke out. "What a pack of lies. She's loony tunes, I tell you. Soon as we pulled her off her roomie, she threw herself at me, wanting me to have sex with her." He scrubbed his hand against his leg as if cleaning his soiled palms. "Skank!"

She couldn't help herself. "Liar!"

He looked down and saw the bloody prints he'd left on his pants leg. He blanched and sagged against the wall. The tough guy clearly didn't like the sight of his own blood. "If you think I look bad, you should see what she did to Dunlap." He pointed toward the room.

Angela's temper rose up and took control. "You're a monster and so is he. You both deserved what was coming to you!" She took a step toward Newcomb, determined to shove his dirty lies down his throat.

The nurse latched onto her arm and pulled her back. "Exactly what do you mean by that? Deserved what was coming to them? Are you admitting you attacked them?"

Angela started to say "in self-defense." Then she was hit with a flood of lustful memories. Maybe self-defense was the end result, but the situation hadn't actually started that way.

The nurse read guilt into the hesitation. "Well?"

Angela felt her face flush. "I did everything I could to keep them away from Shandra." At least that part was true.

"Are you going to just stand here and listen to her whoppers? Is anyone going to help Dunlap? I think she busted his gut or something."

NutMeg pulled backup from the folks who had responded to the panic button. The two orderlies she picked from the crowd looked as if they had been offensive linemen for the Steelers in a previous life. One orderly held Angela at bay in the hallway as the other helped the nurse deal with Dunlap. By now he was playing up his injuries like an Oscar contender.

Curious patients who had been awakened by the noise now stuck their heads into the hallway, hoping to see who was causing the problems.

Once the room was cleared of combat victims and the drugged Shandra was relocated "to where she can be monitored," the nurse pushed Angela unceremoniously inside. "It's going to be hours before we get everyone back asleep again," the woman complained. "Next time you want to get laid, do it quietly." She punctuated the remark by slamming the door and locking it. "And don't do it on my shift."

Suffering from an unrelenting adrenaline rush, Angela paced the room. She tried to exercise away her energy, hoping to eventually exhaust herself, but no number of sit-ups, push-ups, or jumping jacks turned off her churning mind.

She couldn't tune out the voices.

They had invaded her head, some sounding sane, the others rambling incoherently. NutMeg had been right; it would be hours before the place settled down again.

Angela was not only a prisoner in her room but also a captive of the voices in her head, all clamoring, all demanding.

All pushing for her sole attention.

I'm never going to get any sleep. . . .

When the sun spilled from the window into her eyes, Angela woke up, startled to realize she'd fallen asleep at some point in time. She stood, stretched, and stared out the window. Her room looked out over the courtyard formed by the U-shaped building. Directly across the way, the men's wing was still dark, its windows not yet out of the shadows and its occupants blissfully asleep.

All but one man.

She could hear him clearly.

"I'm going to kill that bitch."

She recognized the voice, the thought, and the sentiment.

Newcomb.

What small sense of safety she'd found at the facility had all been destroyed last night.

By her.

What was I thinking? I thought I could beat the crap out of two men? And then what? Expect them to see the error of their ways? Why didn't I just lock the door?

The answer came clearly from her subconscious. It startled her.

Because what would have been the fun in that?

Her desire for justice and revenge had resulted in making her enemies. Even worse, these enemies were two men who had more authority than she did, meaning they could make her life miserable.

More miserable, she corrected. *And possibly much shorter.*

"I've got to get out of here."

Newcomb's threatening thoughts faded away as more voices began to fill the relative silence. She heard everything from idle thoughts about breakfast to the psychotic ramblings of someone who thought he was an alien diplomat from Centauri Prime. One person seemed to be having a conversation with himself—an argument, actually.

Then again, was she really hearing people or only thinking that she was? Had she actually heard Newcomb and Dunlap make their plans or had she only imagined what they were thinking?

Am I crazy?

She answered herself. *No. The moment those two men stepped into my room, I knew it wasn't my imagination,* she told herself. But how could she prove it? Offer to read someone's mind like a parlor trick?

What made her so different from the unknown patient arguing with himself? Wasn't that what she was doing? Arguing with herself over the voices in her head?

More voices intruded.

"All I want is one lousy drink. Why is that so bad?"

"I wonder if I can get a seat next to her again this morning."

"I like how she smells."

"I'm going to make that crazy bitch wish she'd never been born."

"I can't take this life anymore. I just want to die."

The voices grew less distinct as they increased in number. They finally blurred into a mishmash of sound. Angela covered her ears, wishing she could block out the chaos in her mind, but nothing helped.

No matter how much she told herself that these intrusive voices belonged to other people, she couldn't help but worry she was crazy. That she belonged here.

What if there are more than one me? What if those other people hearing voices actually are?

The morning staff unlocked her door at eight and Angela barely made it to breakfast before the serving line closed. She made her meal of the remaining food: crusty eggs scraped from the sides of the last pan, two pieces of cold toast, and lukewarm coffee.

Although the room was practically empty, a school of voices still swam in her head. One voice contemplated quitting. Another voice groused about a missing twenty dollars from his last pay statement.

She listened with little fascination and more dread until one thought, her own, struck her.

The voices in her head were those of men. Only men. She didn't hear a single female voice. When she looked around, that's when the revelation hit her.

That's because they're all men.

Steering clear of men was much more difficult than Angela expected. So she was glad when her usual schedule was drop-kicked by her "counselor" so that she could have a "serious discussion" with one of the psychiatrists—luckily, a female one.

Angela already had her defense prepared. The voices in her head were imaginary. She only *thought* she heard the men plotting to attack her roommate. And their claims about her trying to seduce them? She was merely trying to get them away from her roommate whom she perceived to be in danger. When she realized that wouldn't work, she'd gotten physical, but only because she felt that both she and her roommate were in jeopardy.

She added enough tears, enough air of confession, enough rapt attention to the doctor's long-winded dissertation about feminine empowerment to get out of the room with only a stern warning.

Once free, she almost ran to her group session. She needed advice and the men there were her best sounding board and the only individuals in the place she could trust. Her luck held out as she managed to miss the session leader, Nelson, by skidding around a corner and hiding until he disappeared.

When she burst through the door, she was hit by five sets of thoughts that all pretty much matched the five separate greetings she received. No hidden agendas here.

Everyone had heard about the fight, so she didn't have to answer a lot of questions as to why she'd missed the session. That allowed her to get right down to her biggest problem.

"I've got to get out of here. How do I do it?"

Ortiz, the army guy, cocked his head. "Out like in gone forever, or out like I-need-a-day-pass."

"Never to return to this God-forsaken place."

To their credit, not one of them thought or asked "Why?"

Pete the cop eyed her. "Are you a voluntary commitment?"

The words didn't register. "What do you mean?"

"Were you committed here by a court? Is this mandated for you?"

"No."

Pete cracked a small smile. "Then all you have to do is pack up and leave. They can't keep you here if you're here voluntarily."

"It's that easy?"

"Sure, but once you leave, where will you go?" It was no surprise that JD, the EMT, would cut to the chase. They all knew about her lack of memories and her dearth of financial and family support.

"I don't know," she admitted.

"Got any money?"

"A place to live?"

"Friends?"

I have nothing. Her heart sank. "The airline is covering the cost of this place. If I leave, I don't think they'll want to pay for a hotel or anything."

The brainstorming session started and continued for at least a half hour with everyone in the group tossing out ideas, but each idea was systematically shot down as infeasible or improbable by the others.

It was Pete who came up with the best solution. "You said you have nothing. What about your luggage?"

"I don't have any luggage."

"But I bet you probably checked a bag or two when you got on the plane."

She shrugged. "I suppose so but it's not like I can remember that. Plus, you saw the wreckage on the TV. There wasn't anything much left. Who's to say what was mine and what belonged to someone else?"

"I realize that." Pete grinned. "Still, it seems to me the airline would owe you some money for your lost and presumed-destroyed luggage."

A small flicker of hope flared up in the center of her chest. "How much money?"

Pete dug a cell phone out of his pants pocket. "Let's find out."

12

Dante gritted his teeth, hoping his expression looked more like a smile than the grimace of pain it was. Luckily, he knew he was out of frame and the camera was centered on the man talking about the robbery he'd eyewitnessed. Dante preferred doing his job off camera, but upper management thought they were rewarding him for the Hudson crash scoop by insisting he work on the other side of the lens.

Funny how often reward and punishment took the same form. He'd been sent on the ferryboat captain story only because Victor Smithfield had been pissed at him. Ol' Vic knew there was only one thing worse than doing an obvious fluff piece and that was doing it on camera and having to pretend that you were interested.

Dante hated being a talking head with nothing of importance to say.

But now he was back to being a big-time reporter . . . until he pissed off Victor again. Unfortunately, his lead-placement crime story had disintegrated quickly and the only thing he could do to milk it any longer was to interview the only eyewitness. Said witness turned out to be an out-of-work actor who evidently spent every free hour watching reruns of cop dramas. The young man sprinkled his answers to Dante's questions with far too much television-cop jargon and not enough factual description.

If the witness was to be believed, then a whole platoon of heavily armed, faceless "skels" had pulled off a daring and precisely timed daylight robbery. Then, they sped away in an unmarked armored van, which miraculously disappeared in otherwise gridlocked traffic.

When the "wit" paused to take a breath, Dante seized the opportunity, jumping between the actor and the camera he obviously loved.

"Thank you, sir." He listened to the blaring voice in his head, coming from his earpiece. Someone had patched his IFB into the statewide responder band, the interagency frequency that all the cops, firemen, and other first responders used in case of disasters or events that crossed city or state jurisdictions.

"We're receiving a report . . ." He digested the details quickly, distilling the information to the barest bones. "Yes, we've just heard that the New Jersey State Police have surrounded a vehicle in South Amboy and the"—he put emphasis on the word—"*car* matches the one police observed being driven by the main suspect."

So much for his eyewitness. The actor had probably recited his lines from his bit part as Patrolman Number Three in *Law & Order: OCB—Organized Crime Bureau.*

Dante heard a second voice in his head. *"Kick it back to the news desk."*

As he opened his mouth to dutifully follow orders, he heard loud noises through the earpiece. He recognized them—gunshots. Then there was an explosion of command voices. In the middle of the melee was a story.

"Do we have eyes in South Amboy?" he asked on mic, knowing his producer would respond.

The voice in his head answered above the din. *"No. We only have the audio from the responder band."*

Dante tried to make as much sense as he could out of what he heard. This was the most difficult part of being an on-air talent: listening to a half-dozen simultaneous conversations in his head and being able to talk coherently at the same time.

"Details are sketchy, but shots may have been fired. Yes, we have confirmation. Shots fired. Return fire has been authorized. We have a report of"—he paused to listen to the frantic voices— "one, maybe two officers down."

With a substantial number of years working a police beat, he could wade through everything and pick out the thread that gave the best picture of the situation as it was unfolding.

"There's been another volley of gunfire. I hear automatic weapons." The explosions died out and voices that had remained professionally calm were now more animated. "They now report that the robbery suspects have surrendered. And . . . they are taking two . . . no, make that three men in custody."

He consulted his notes. "At the scene, there was a report of four individuals involved in the crime, but there are only three men in the vehicle. It appears that a fourth suspect is . . . is still at large. Just a moment, we're getting more details."

The dispatcher repeated the APB with the description of the fourth suspect. As Dante listened, he realized that it matched the man who had been standing next to him, basking in the limelight. But now, the actor was quietly inching away.

Dante stuffed the microphone in his jacket pocket and turned to the "witness." "And he sounds exactly like you."

The man threw a punch, but Dante sidestepped it. As it whiffed by him, he grabbed the man's arm and pulled it backward, putting reverse pressure on the elbow joint. He knew from experience that the pain would be excruciating and would drop most men to their knees. The actor was no exception. But as he fell, he used his free hand to reach behind him.

Raul the cameraman yelled, "Gun!"

Dante slammed into the actor, knocking him over and landing on top of him, which trapped the man's hand underneath his body. Dante could only pray that the gun had been trapped as well.

Instead, the gun slipped out like a banana squeezed free from its peel. The weapon skidded toward Raul who instinctively kicked it to the side.

Dante and the actor struggled briefly, but Dante got in a lucky break when the young man began to flail around in an effort to get loose. As a result, he slammed his own head into the concrete steps on which he'd stood earlier to make up for his lack of height during the interview.

Poetic justice.

He loved it when the universe got even.

Dante heard a voice hissing in his ear.

"You're the luckiest bastard in the world. You know that, don't you? All of that got on the air. Send it back home, hero."

Dante fished the mic out of his pocket, surprised and pleased it was still intact. He shot the camera a brief smile. "If the cops are watching, please send a unit to our location. We have your fourth suspect in custody. This is Dante Kearns with TwentyFourSeven, only a little worse for wear. Back to you, Dave."

. . .

When Dante returned to the office, there was no hero's welcome. TwentyFourSeven didn't work on a glory-to-the-individual basis. The scale of network success rested solely on what numbers they pulled in the ratings, whether it was overnights, weeklies, or yearly as well as the Web site traffic stats.

A drop in any ratings numbers caused widespread panic on all levels from the highest vice president to the lowest and newest grip. For the general-news section, heads could roll indiscriminately, so they had an all-for-one and one-for all mentality. Glory fell to the network itself, not the individuals working there.

However, Dante's actions hadn't gone completely unnoticed. When he reached his desk, there was a cupcake sitting by his monitor, the only token of appreciation he would likely get from any of the line producers.

I'd rather have a raise. But until then . . . He peeled back the paper and took a bite.

His cell rumbled in his pocket and he wiped his mouth hoping not to ruin yet another cell phone. The caller ID came up *Unknown*.

"Kearns, TwentyFourSeven," he answered around his mouthful of cake, trying not to mumble. Whoever it was, they were going to have to compete against the glories of a red velvet cupcake with cream cheese icing. Yum.

"Umm . . . I'd like to speak to . . ." It was a woman's voice and she stumbled over his name. "D-Dante Kearns."

"You got him. What can I do you for?"

"We . . . I think we met at St. James . . . the hospital. That is, if you're the man who gave me this card."

"What card?"

"A business card. I think you slipped it in my pocket when I was waiting for an elevator. After the press conference about the airplane crash."

The dam broke and flooded him with memories. *The Angel of*

the Hudson. He'd put thoughts of her aside after his little leverage play with CoastalEast. The story of the disaster had been replaced with at least a dozen newer tragedies over the last few weeks.

Victims and their heroes were yesterday's news to an audience with an incredibly short attention span.

Unless . . .

His mind raced as he began to fashion an "After the Disaster: Where Is She Now?" pitch. The way to coerce a fickle public into caring again was to find a new element of pathos to capture their attention, however fleeting.

Had she been quietly returned to her family's loving embrace?

Or was she still playing in the shallow end of the sanity pool as evidenced by her erratic behavior at the press conference?

Hopefully, the public would either find her plight or her fortune worthy of a moment or two of their time.

"Ms. Sands, yes, I remember you. How are you doing?"

She hesitated and he could only guess the answer. *Still crazy. You?* He closed his eyes and admonished himself.

She finally spoke. "I wish I could say I've done better . . . but I still don't have my memories back. So I don't have a basis of comparison."

He couldn't help but smile. At least she seemed to have a sense of humor, if slightly macabre.

"The reason why I'm calling you . . ." More background noise erupted, drowning her out. She started again. "I'm calling you because . . ." This time, no noise interrupted her.

Finally he heard her sigh.

"I don't know why the hell I'm calling you."

"That's okay. I have to admit I've been a bit curious. You dropped out of sight pretty fast. I knew that you'd been transferred out of the hospital." He didn't add, *And into a psych facility.*

"They sent me to the Martin I. Shears Behavioral Health Center. Out of the frying pan, into the pits of hell."

"That bad?"

"God, you have no idea." The woman's laughter was rusty as if she hadn't had much amusement in her life lately. Stuck in a loony bin, that was probably the exact truth. "Then again, judging by your name, maybe you're a little more familiar with purgatory and fiery infernos than most people."

Ah, yes. The usual Dante's *Inferno* reference. It was an unavoidable part of any conversation with a new acquaintance with a decent literary education. His stock answer was to acknowledge the allusion and push on. But in this case, it spoke volumes.

"You've read Dante's *Inferno*?"

"I guess I have. How weird is that? I remember a book, but I don't remember me. Is this a screwed-up life or what?"

"You still have holes in your memory?"

"More than just holes. It's still a blank. A complete and total blank. And I'm . . . I'm having other problems, too."

"What kind of problems? Aren't the doctors in the . . . facility helping at all?"

"I'm no longer staying at MIS-Behave. I . . . I couldn't take it anymore. Too many voices. Too much noise."

His reporter instincts sent a warning chill up his back and a half-dozen story ideas sprang to life in his head, the most demanding concept being "Today's Psych Unit: Yesterday's Snake Pit?"

"What do you mean?" he asked, trying not to let a whetted appetite for news overwhelm his sense of compassion.

She released a somewhat fake laugh as if hoping to dilute the meaning of her previous words. "You know, the usual. Overcrowding. Sharing rooms with people you don't know. Institutional food. Nothing major."

"Sounds like life in a college dorm."

"We didn't have any booze in MIS-Behave. Anyway, I just want to ask"—there was a shriek of laughter in the background—"if you could . . ." Another noise drowned out her words.

If those were the voices she was hearing, then she was probably sane. He raised his voice. "Would you like to meet somewhere, maybe someplace less noisy?" he offered.

She spoke louder as well. "Sorry. This is the only phone I could find. Yes, could we talk? In person?"

"Where can I meet you?"

When she gave him the address of what she called a nearby café, he bit back his response. It was a part of Hell's Kitchen as yet untouched by the tidal wave of urban renewal.

The elite of New York had pushed into the neighborhood to take advantage of the lower real-estate prices. The original owners of the buildings had been paid fairly well, but those who lived in the buildings had been turned out without much ceremony. Those who could afford to find a new place to live, did. The rest of them, a large number of former tenants who had nowhere else to go, stayed there, joining the expanding community of homeless who camped out in abandoned buildings, flophouses, homeless shelters, and— lacking any of those—on the streets.

Dante didn't venture into that part of the city without a weapon of some sort and a cell phone with 911 already predialed.

But evidently, she didn't share his concerns.

Wow. Either a tough broad or a naïve one.

Nonetheless, he agreed to meet her that afternoon at 3 P.M., too late for lunch and too early for dinner. It would spare him from having to order and pretend to eat the Ptomaine Special.

The subway ride was uneventful, despite a clutch of tourists from Texas who had boarded the wrong line and who were twanging loudly and making entirely too much eye contact with the natives.

They trailed him from the train to the platform and up to the street, chattering away. But their conversations died out when they stepped out onto the sidewalk in a part of New York that tourists didn't routinely visit.

He heard their furtive whispers and turned around in time to see them troop en masse back into the station entrance, probably hoping to return unscathed to their expensive Manhattan tourist digs. He suspected they would listen more closely next time to the hotel concierge's directions.

Dante walked three blocks to the café, dodging the usual assortment of street people—panhandlers, hookers on the prowl, or those few dealers who decided he didn't look like an undercover cop.

The café sat in the middle of several abandoned buildings, one abandoned in midrenovation, the other still awaiting rebirth. Many real-estate speculators had folded their tents and walked away when the recession hit. As a result, a new wave of homeless were camped in the neighborhood.

Was Angela one of them?

He stood on the broken sidewalk, trying to see through the café's grimy windows and spot her. The glass was opaque with age and neglect. When he stepped inside, he still didn't see her and wondered if she'd gotten cold feet and decided to bail.

There was only a handful of patrons inside, mostly grubby men sitting alone near the tables at the window or at the counter. But one figure—smaller in stature than the others—caught his eye. He, she, or it was wearing a gray sweatshirt with the hood pulled up and was sitting alone in the last booth in the back corner.

When the figure lifted a hand in surreptitious greeting, he realized it was Angela. She reached up and pulled back the hood, revealing pale features and piercing eyes. She'd looked better at the press conference than she did now. Then again, if she actually lived in this tough neighborhood, he could understand why she might not be thriving. But at least she was demonstrating some basic street smarts, hiding her gender and sitting where no one could sneak up behind her.

He walked back to the booth, trying not to call undue attention to himself. But it wasn't easy; he didn't fit in and everyone knew it from the scruffy customers to the Korean cook in the kitchen to the waitress the cook appeared to be cussing out.

One look at Angela's gaunt features and Dante knew he'd have to order lunch for himself so that he could offer to buy for her as well. She looked like she'd missed more meals than she'd eaten. She didn't strike him as someone willing to take a charity handout, but she might be willing to share a meal.

"Have you eaten yet?" he said, sliding into the hardwood booth.

"No," she said with some hesitancy.

"I hope you don't mind if I order something. I'm starved."

The waitress lumbered over, maybe to take his order, but more likely to escape the Korean insults.

"Whatcha want?"

Dante glanced at a fellow diner several tables away who was chowing down on a decent-looking burger and some fries that ketchup might make remotely edible. "Burger and fries for me. You want the same?"

Caught unaware, she stumbled over the words. "Uh . . . s-sure."

"Coke for me and"—he nodded at Angela's empty mug—"you want a Coke or another coffee?"

She contemplated the mug. "A refill will be fine."

The waitress sniffed, scribbled something on her order pad, and headed back to the counter.

Angela wrapped her hands around the mug. "You don't have to buy me lunch."

He could have lied and said he was hungry, but his philosophy was to tell the truth whenever possible. That way you didn't have to remember what lie you told what person.

"I hate eating by myself." It was a simple answer and a true one that seemed to satisfy her need for autonomy.

Propping himself against the wall of the booth, Dante gave himself the best possible view of the restaurant and its patrons. Like Angela, he didn't want anyone coming up behind him in a joint like this. But unfortunately, it meant he couldn't help but see things that would probably make a health inspector blanch. He had an unobstructed view of the kitchen where he couldn't avoid the sight of rotting vegetables stacked in crates on the floor, overflowing garbage cans, and a rusty refrigerator making spitting noises.

Bon appétit.

"Interesting place to meet," he said, hoping it would lead her into conversation.

"It's usually quiet this time of day. I . . . I don't like crowds."

He eyed the basically unkempt and apparently homeless diners. Evidently these were the ones who hadn't turned their panhandled earnings into a cheap high.

Or they could simply be poor sods whose misfortunes never involved illegal vices . . .

Somewhat ashamed of his presumptions, he toyed with the empty saltshaker on the table. "So how's it going for you?"

She didn't answer. Instead, she stared at him, as if studying his face. "Did we meet before?" She corrected herself. "I mean before the hospital?" Her face brightened and she straightened with expectation. "Do you know me?"

"No. Afraid not."

She slumped back down, her brief flare extinguished.

"But I was the one who helped you with the baby. In the Hudson."

"Oh. That." After a moment she colored slightly. "Sorry. I didn't mean to be rude. Thank you. You saved my life."

He shook his head. "You would have made it just fine without me."

Her face softened. "The baby wouldn't have survived. At least you saved his life."

"I'm just glad I was in the right place at the right time."

A loud noise drowned out his last word. Both he and Angela watched as the cook stepped out of the kitchen doorway, brandishing a cleaver the size of a small broadax. The man yelled something in Korean and flashed the bloodied blade in the direction of one of the patrons.

Dante flinched and instinctively reached for his cell, wishing he'd brought the gun that he kept in a locked box in the bottom drawer of his desk. Instead, the only weapon he had on him was a small canister of pepper spray. But there was no way it'd stop the cook; the man would probably think it was nothing more than some mild seasoning.

Angela cocked her head, listening to the ranting man for a moment and then turned away as if uninterested in seeing the impending carnage. She didn't even jump when the cook slammed the cleaver into the counter as punctuation to his final remark. Then the cook spun on his heel and stalked back to the kitchen.

Dante tried to smile. "Times like these I wish I understood Korean."

Angela picked up the saltshaker he'd abandoned and lined it up against its partner, the pepper. "See the guy sitting next to the window?" She nodded toward a man dressed in a camouflage jacket far too heavy for the mild day. "He complained that the chili wasn't hot enough and that's why the cook was angry."

She speaks Korean? "Wow. I'm impressed that you understood that."

She slumped toward the grubby wall. "It's no gift. More like a curse."

"So how many languages do you speak?"

"As far as I know, just English."

Technicalities. "Okay, then, how many do you understand?"

Dante could only describe her expression as "stricken." The obvious pain in her eyes made something in him twinge with sympathy and he backpedaled quickly. "I'm sorry. Am I treading someplace I shouldn't?"

She leaned forward, covered her face, and began to cry. He listened hard as she attempted to speak between sobs.

"You're . . . going . . . to . . . think . . . I'm . . . crazy. . . ."

Filled with a sudden sense of helplessness, he reached out and patted her hand, hoping it conveyed an appropriate sense of sympathy. He was never sure with women. Sometimes the gesture was right and sometimes it was the worst possible thing to do.

She swallowed back a sob as if startled by his touch. But she didn't jerk her hand away. Instead, she looked up, tears tracking down her clean cheeks. "Think of something . . ."

He heard the words but had no idea what she meant. "Pardon?"

"Think of something. Anything. Your favorite color."

"Why?" Even as he spoke, he immediately thought *Red*.

"Are you thinking? Hard?" Cocking her head, she leaned closer as if he was too far away for her parlor trick to work. "You're not thinking. I can't hear you."

Oh shit. She's still crazy. He managed to keep his features from telegraphing his opinion of her mental incompetence but he feared his body language said what his face didn't. Then again, this wasn't the weekly poker game with the guys. After years of exposure, they could read the slightest nuances of the others' expressions, habits, tics, and postures, determining who was bluffing and who wasn't with uncanny accuracy.

He lost regularly. His buddies had a full deck.

But Angela Sands? She might be a card or two short.

The cynical reporter in him won out. There was a story in here, somewhere. *Time to make nice with the crazy person.*

He put on his best poker face. "So you can read minds?" *So you think you can read minds?*

She looked away, unwilling to make eye contact. "It sounds crazy, I know. But it just . . . happens. I can't stop it. That's why I stay away from people as much as I can. Like I said on the phone, too many voices."

"Oh. Interesting."

"Interesting? Hardly." She turned to face him and something akin to disgust filled her eyes. It added sharp, harsh lines to her gaunt features. "Only someone who is certifiably insane would believe they could read minds. But I can't explain it any other way. I don't feel crazy, but what other explanation could there be?"

"So what color was I thinking about?"

She leaned back until her head rested on the wall behind her. "That's just it. I don't know. I can't . . . hear you. I can hear practically every other freaking head in this room. But you? Nothing."

Dante turned around and scanned the room. There were only a handful of patrons left. One man was methodically smashing a package of saltines with the back of a spoon, turning them into a bag of fine cracker crumbs.

Dante decided to play along. "So, what's that guy thinking?" He pointed to cracker-smasher.

Angela sighed and closed her eyes. "He's remembering when his son was little and used to float crackers in his tomato soup. But his son died years ago and he can't stand the sight of whole crackers. Nowadays, soup is all he can afford to eat. And he needs the calories. So he smashes the crackers."

She pointed at the Korean cook who had grown suspiciously

quiet in the kitchen. "I don't understand Korean but I can see the images in his head. He's mad at the guy at the end of the counter. The cook's prepared a new bowl of chili with . . . with something. He keeps thinking one word. *Gochujang.* It could be something innocuous or it could be a poison. I'm not sure what *gochujang* is."

Dante sat up a bit straight. "It's a type of hot pepper paste." He could thank Steff, an old girlfriend, for that bit of trivial knowledge. Due to her incessant need to experiment in the kitchen, he had developed a cast-iron stomach out of necessity. And he learned to fear words like *gochujang, Rocoto, Fatalii* and other names for peppers hot enough to roast your eyeballs.

Evidently unconcerned about the cook's nefarious plans, the waitress stomped across the room carrying a canned soda for Dante and a coffeepot to refill Angela's empty mug. "Food'll be out in five," she said around an unlit cigarette wedged in the corner of her mouth.

"Thanks," Dante said automatically.

The woman appeared almost stunned by his small show of manners. "Uh . . . you want ketchup or mustard?"

All the better to drown the food with . . . "Both, please."

After the woman left, he turned back to Angela. "So what was she thinking? She didn't look worried about the cook's little outburst."

"I don't know. I can't get into the heads of women."

"Me, either." Dante wiped the top of the can as best he could, then popped it open. He took a deep sip of the lukewarm liquid, thankful it hadn't been served in a dirty glass. When he looked up, Angela was staring at him. "What?"

"I can't tell if you're just humoring me because you think I'm totally nuts and it might make a good story, or maybe there's a remote chance that you actually believe me."

He took another deep pull from his soda. Every bit of logic in him said he should pay the check, bid her farewell, and get back to work. But something in the back of his head, some part of his soul that hadn't been trampled to death because of his job, that bit of his conscience demanded he not ignore this woman. That he listen carefully to what she said, maybe because she was human and simply needed another human to care.

Or, maybe, just maybe, she was telling the truth.

He placed the soda on the table and pulled out his notepad and pen.

"So, make me believe."

13

Angela picked up the coffee mug and held it under her chin as if to warm herself from its steam. Closing her eyes, she drew in a deep breath.

"The man sitting at the counter, the one who complained about the chili. See him?"

Dante glanced toward the shabbily dressed man sitting on the last stool at the end of the counter. The man had already drawn Dante's attention with his arrhythmic twitches. A full plate of food sat in front of him, untouched, and the guy faced straight ahead, paying his meal no attention.

Dante couldn't see his face, but had a sneaking suspicion that the man was staring in the direction of the kitchen.

"He's . . . entertaining some very uncharitable thoughts about the cook. I don't think he's going to act on them, but he's got quite an active imagination." Angela cracked open one eye. "Kinda like Stephen King. It may be fiction, but it's still scary as hell."

Dante had already pegged the man as a thinker rather than a doer. Evidently, Angela had, too. But was that proof of anything other than the ability to read people well? "What about the guy sitting by the window?"

She stared at the man, then shivered. "He's wondering when the waitress gets off."

"Hoping for a date?"

The look she gave him dispelled that frivolous notion. But again, it didn't take a mind reader to interpret the look of undisguised and probably highly unhealthy attraction on the man's face and in his posture.

Or the way the waitress always seemed to be holding a sharp, pointed utensil whenever she walked near him. She looked like she was already extremely wary of the man.

Angela looked away. "The same thing happened at the psychiatric facility. I . . . overheard a couple of the orderlies planning to attack my roommate. I managed to distract them and—"

The waitress chose that moment to arrive with their food. Angela blushed as her story ground to a halt. As soon as the waitress departed, Angela grabbed her burger and took a big bite as if she hadn't had a decent meal in days. The momentary look of bliss on her face confirmed it.

Dante stalled for time by picking up the half-empty bottle of ketchup the waitress had deposited and pounding on the bottle's end, trying to coax out some condiment. Once he deposited a sufficient blob on his plate, he offered Angela the bottle, but she declined.

He picked up a fry, dragged it through the ketchup, and ate it. He was surprised to realize it actually tasted good. A tentative bite of the burger revealed that it, too, was actually quite tasty.

Angela noticed his sudden interest in his food. "The place looks like shit, but they really do have decent food."

"So I see." Although he'd had something that passed as lunch a couple of hours ago, his appetite woke up, tempted by the better fare.

It took her a moment to regroup, then she picked up her tale where she left off. "As to the orderlies, let's just say the staff took their word over mine."

"Sorry," he said in sympathy. "They didn't . . . get to your room-mate, did they?"

"Rape her? No. I distracted them."

Dante straightened, reading something into her words that he didn't like at all. "What about you?"

She looked puzzled. "Me?" She blushed once more. "No, they didn't 'get' to me, either. By distracting, I mean I successfully defended my honor as well as hers."

"How?"

She lifted one shoulder. "By trying to beat them into a bloody pulp. I didn't exactly succeed, but it wasn't for the lack of trying."

He paused, his burger midway to his mouth. "For real?"

"Apparently I have a variety of skills that I didn't know about."

"Interesting."

"For you, maybe. For me? It's damn scary." She attacked her food rather than continue the awkward interchange. But, halfway through her burger, she slowed down and pushed away the unfinished meal.

Dante wondered if her conscience had gotten the best of her and now she was about to recant her outrageous story. He decided to give her an opening. "Something wrong?"

She shook her head. "I've gotten used to eating a lot less than this."

He tried another leading question. "Things been tough?"

The look she gave him said a dozen things including *You're not too smart, are you?*

"Yeah. Things are tough. When it became evident I could no longer be safe in the 'luxurious' accommodations CoastalEast provided for me, I decided to leave. I was able to squeeze three grand out of them as repayment for my lost luggage, then I discharged myself from the nut ward. I've spent over half of it already on a place to stay, on food, and on clothing. So, yeah. Things are tough."

He automatically reached for his wallet. "You need money?"

"No," she said much too quickly and a bit too loudly. She leaned forward and lowered her voice. "I don't want any handouts. And you shouldn't flash a wallet in a place like this. All I want is a little information."

"What sort?"

She unzipped the hoodie a few inches and retrieved some paper from within. When she unfolded the page, it revealed a pencil drawing of a man's face. "Help me figure out who this is."

He studied the sketch, surprised by the three-dimensional and lifelike qualities of a two-dimensional rendering. "It's good," he remarked.

An expectant light flared in her eyes. "Then you know him?"

He shook his head. "No clue. I'm just saying it's . . . lifelike. If you did this, then it's yet another undiscovered talent." Dante pushed the sketch back across the table. "Is he important?"

"I keep seeing him in my dreams." She corrected herself. "In my nightmares. And I hoped you might know who he is. Or could help me find out."

There was something about Dante that earned Angela's trust. She didn't fool herself into thinking that he believed her stories. No sane man would. But maybe it was the fact that she couldn't hear him in her mind. So far, he was the only man she'd been near who didn't try to thrust his thoughts, his expectations, his ideals, or his desires on her.

So even though she lacked an open window into his mind, her instincts screamed that she didn't need to read Dante Kearns's thoughts to accept that he was a decent guy.

And she desperately needed to share the burden that threatened to crush her . . .

Angela tried not to look at the drawing when she launched into her tale. It was hard enough experiencing the dreams that caused her to wake up in the middle of every night for the past week screaming, terrified, and fearing for her life . . .

And seeing her own death, time and again. Not just seeing it but feeling it, experiencing every painful moment of her own bloody demise.

"I think he killed me," she said simply.

"Tell me about it," Dante said in a low voice.

She closed her eyes and tried to conjure up the details in daylight that she'd tried so hard to forget at night. "I'm sitting in a house. Not just a house but a home. My home. A really nice place. Expensive decorations, lush carpets, lots of polished wood. I'm standing in front of a really big desk. This man"—she felt the paper under her fingers and tapped the sketch—"is sitting at a big oak desk.

"He's laughing. Laughing *at* me, not with me. But I'm not laughing—I'm mad. Really steaming. There's a folder on the desk, one I gave him, and there are photos inside of him and women . . . no, not women. Girls. Some of them looked barely in their teens."

Dante spoke. "Photos of an . . . intimate nature?"

"Yes." She opened her eyes and reached for her coffee mug, but her hands were shaking so badly that the coffee sloshed out, burning her. However, the pain felt refreshingly good, reminding her that she was still alive, despite the foreboding nightmare.

"I'm incensed because he's been screwing these girls behind my back. One of them is pregnant and says he's the father. That means he hasn't been using protection. Not only has he been lying and cheating, but God only knows what sort of filth and disease he's exposed himself—and therefore me—to."

Angela was no longer sitting in a low-rent diner in a low-rent part of Hell's Kitchen. She was standing at the elegant desk in the equally elegant book-lined study, fists clenched at her sides to prevent her from slapping his cheek, pampered daily by a personal barber.

"So what?" my husband asks me. It's not a question but the excuse of the guilty.

"Why? Why did you do this?"

He laughs. "Because you're nothing but set dressing but you never seemed to understand that. Your role was to look good and keep your mouth shut." He leans back in the chair. "But you couldn't even do that right." He uses his forefinger to open the manila folder, exposing its pornographic contents. "Do you know how much it cost me to bribe the investigator you hired?" He picks up one photo, admiring the child in the Catholic schoolgirl outfit, bent in an impossible position to accommodate his lustful appetite. She looks all of thirteen.

"Maybe I can get a couple of eight-by-ten glossies for my collection."

I look away, unable to stomach another view of him with any other female, much less a woman-child. What happened to the man who wined and dined me? What happened to the whirlwind romance that caught me up, spun me around, and deposited me in the midst of wealth, social position. . . .

"Angela?" Dante's voice helped to sever the overwhelming visions and memories.

She shook herself, the flash of that life dissipating like water droplets on a skillet. "Sorry. I get . . . caught up in what I remember." She drew a deep breath to steady herself and tried to distill the oppressive memories down to the bare basics, to relate facts, not emotions.

"I remember confronting him and he showed no remorse at all. He didn't care because he could easily afford to bribe or bully anybody who might help me. But he couldn't bully me. So instead, he killed me."

Dante had stopped writing in his notebook.

She pressed on, trying to keep his attention before logic and doubt erased her last avenue of hope. "I know it sounds crazy, but I remember getting shot. I remember dying." She dropped her head, unable to watch him calculate just how nuts she was.

"I don't remember how he did it. Sometimes, I remember a gun. Sometimes, a knife. Other times, I remember his hands around my throat. But I died. By his hands. And then . . ." She couldn't go on. She couldn't say the words that would prove beyond any shadow of a doubt that sanity had packed its bags and departed a long time ago.

"And then?" Dante prompted softly.

When she gathered enough strength to meet his eyes, she didn't see veiled amusement or pity. His face remained passive but interested and not in the poker-face way the doctors had.

"And then I woke up in the plane. Confused and with no memories."

"Had the plane crashed by then?"

It was a simple question, but it conveyed a half-dozen encouraging messages, including his willingness to follow the story, no matter how infeasible it sounded.

"No. I woke up before the trouble started. All I knew was that I was on a passenger jet. I didn't remember how I got there, where I was going or who I was. And then we started having problems—turbulence or equipment failure or whatever. Less than a minute later, we crashed, and you know as much as I do from that point on."

He nodded. "So maybe you didn't actually die at his hands. Maybe you survived and you left him, jumping on the next plane out of town to get away from him."

She shook her head. "According to the airline, I was returning to New York after only a day or two in Los Angeles."

"Then maybe he was in Los Angeles and once you confronted him, you flew back to New York."

She swallowed hard, searching for the courage to blurt out the implausible, impossible, and unavoidable thought that had been haunting her since she left the facility.

"You're going to think I'm crazy . . ." Her voice trailed off as she ducked her head in embarrassment.

He reached over and patted her hand. "First, I grew up in the city. Second, I started with TwentyFourSeven when they were still a tabloid featuring stories of alien abductions and Elvis sightings. I'm no stranger to odd stories. I've interviewed everyone from crackheads to kings and have seen chemically dependent madness to inbred lunacy and everything in between. So I've been exposed to all sorts of degrees of crazy and trust me when I say: you're not crazy."

She leaned back in the booth, wishing she felt more buoyed by his words. If she could only read his thoughts, then she could figure out for herself if this was merely reassuring rhetoric or an honest opinion.

He picked up his pen and held it poised over his notebook. "So, where do we start?"

We?

We. She never thought such a small word could carry such a large meaning. "You want to help me?"

"There's a saying that if you save a life, then you're responsible for it. Now whether or not I actually saved your life, I still feel . . .

responsible for you. And being a journalist, I have resources that may help." He tapped the notebook with the end of the pen. "So, do we start here or in Los Angeles?"

She took a moment to think, then finally said, "Here. And I can't tell you why because I don't know, myself. All I can say is that whatever is at the heart of this, I have an unshakable feeling it lies here. I know the city much too well. The subway, the streets. Places and things that only a native would know."

She watched him transform to a reporter, letting one question lead to another, all designed to find the edges of the known facts. But she had precious little to give him.

When they circled back to the beginning, she realized she'd literally told him everything she knew about herself.

He leaned back in the booth and studied his notes.

"What I'm going to do is go back and do some digging. I'll see if I can come up with any missing persons reports starting a few days before you got on the plane headed to L.A."

Her heart sank. He didn't get it. He thought she was a missing person.

And I think I'm dead . . .

"And then I'll see where that leads me. I'll also check the records for assault and battery, any reports I can find that have any connection with an attack on a woman."

Angela stared at his notebook, filled with undecipherable scribbles, especially from upside down. Did it say anywhere in there to check the morgue?

It took all the courage she had to say it again. "I think I'm dead. I think I was murdered." She cringed, bracing for his laughter or a placating smile.

Instead, he nodded. "I'll check with a guy I know who works a desk at Manhattan North Homicide. I'll look at solved and unsolved crimes, starting there and then branch out." He glanced at his watch. "I've got to get back to the office. Daylight's burning. Can we meet here tomorrow? Around the same time?"

She nodded quickly. "Sure."

He flipped his notebook closed and graced her with a smile. "I'm curious to see what I can find. But we will get to the bottom of this. Somehow." He rose, walked over to the counter, handed the waitress some money, then leaned toward the woman and said something under his voice.

Angela's stomach seized. How dare she fool herself into believing that anyone would even consider her wild tales to be anything other than the ravings of the certifiably insane. She didn't have to read the man's mind to read his face.

Dante was just humoring her, only pretending to be interested until he could find a convenient excuse to leave.

He nodded at her and she strained to make out the pity in his eyes. She knew it had to be there.

After he left, she wrapped her arms around herself, combating a sudden chill. Voices began to seep back into her mind, the thoughts of the poor, the destitute, the hungry . . .

"Honey?"

Angela looked up, startled to see the waitress standing next to the table.

"You finished? Can I take your plates, now?"

Angela pushed the dishes toward the woman. "Go ahead."

After the woman stacked the plates, she didn't move away. Evidently, she was waiting for Angela's coffee cup. Now that her lunch was floundering, she had no desire for the last gulp of lukewarm coffee. She pushed the cup toward the woman.

"Another refill?"

Angela stared at the woman. Since when had this dive been so generous with their coffee?

"Oh, that guy you were sitting with?" The woman nodded toward the door through which Dante had escaped. Her stiff curls remained in place thanks to layers of lacquer. "He paid in advance for your breakfast and lunch tomorrow. So when you come in, just remind me. 'Kay? He said something about you two working better on a full stomach." She added a laugh. "On our food. Yeah. Right." She swept up the remaining cup and carried her load back to the kitchen.

He believes me?

"You believe her?" Raul, his usual cameraman, sat in the chair by Dante's desk. He was brandishing a switchblade, using it to peel an apple. Raul was the sort of guy who overequipped himself whenever possible. Even though the guy didn't have a driver's license, he continued to salivate over SUVs—the bigger the better.

A classic case of overcompensation.

Raul narrowly missed impaling his thumb. "She sounds like she needs to go back to the psych ward."

Dante looked away, unwilling to watch the impending bloodshed. "I don't need a running commentary. All I want to know is if you're still dating that file clerk at the Twenty-third Precinct?"

A sly smile curled Raul's lips. "Indeed I am." He gestured toward his groin, not realizing he still held the knife. "She can't get enough of her hot tamale."

Dante couldn't help but recoil. "Shit! Watch where you aim that thing. Both of those things."

Raul looked down, realized what he'd done, and had the decency to blush then flinch. "Point taken." He giggled. "Get it? Point?" He released a snort. "So whatcha need, boss man?"

"Nothing yet and don't let Victor hear you call me boss man. I have enough problems with him already. If he thinks I'm sniffing for his job, he'll make my life a holy hell. Now back to the favor

I'm asking . . . I only wanted to make sure that I have a secondary data resource in case I strike out on the primary research."

"You actually gonna do this?"

"Yep. So will you get your sorry ass out of my five-by-five-foot cubical so I can concentrate?"

Raul almost saluted with his knife hand, but aborted his gesture a split second before the blade hit his skin.

Dante shook his head. "You're a menace, Raul."

The man made a show of folding the knife and stuffing it in his pocket. "Only to myself, DK. Only to myself."

Once Raul left, Dante started his excavation into the newspaper's online and offline morgues and a handful of other databases, most of which he wasn't supposed to have access to. He tried not to abuse those hard-earned privileges in hopes that his occasional forays went unnoticed by the various police jurisdictions whose records he plundered.

Journalistic integrity in the twenty-first century.

By 11 P.M., he had a fairly complete picture of all deaths—accidental or otherwise—that had occurred anywhere in the tri-state region, from Ocean to Ulster and from Suffolk to Pike and all the counties and boroughs in between.

All in all, one hundred and thirty-two people had died during the week up to the time of the airplane crash.

Dante began reducing that total, first, by eliminating all of the victims who were male. Then he removed any females under eighteen and over eighty. That reduced the number of individuals to eight, two of whom he discounted because they died after long illnesses in the hospital. In ranking the final six, two seemed unlikely candidates but he kept them on the list, nonetheless.

And then he began to dig harder, case by case.

By 2 A.M., his eyesight was blurring and his attention was wavering. Rather than go home for a couple of hours, he retired to a saggy couch that the staff kept in a dark corner in the store-room.

Dante slept for a couple of hours until he heard the early-morning crew arriving at four. A twenty-four-hour news organiza-tion was always staffed, but there were spikes in activity, corresponding with America's need for overnight news served first thing in the morning. In just a few hours, the public would wake up, roll over, and turn on their televisions, fire up their computers, or stare bleary-eyed at their iPhones, ingesting the world news along with their daily McBreakfasts or Grand Lattes.

Dante's stomach growled at the thought of food and he realized he hadn't eaten anything since the burger, courtesy of Hell's Kitchen. After a quick trip to the vending machines and a pilfered donut from the craft table located inside the television studios, he returned to his cubicle and got back to work.

Dante excelled at tuning out those around him. It was an ability he'd acquired growing up in a large family living in a small home. The newsroom swelled with people and noise as the day got under way. But he continued his research, trying to build the best picture he could about the lives and deaths of six women.

While he worked, he kept his focus on the victims themselves, rather than worrying about the reason why he was looking so closely at them. If he examined his motives too closely, he might have to examine his head.

It was crazy to think that anything Angela Sands said had real merit. And yet, he felt compelled to help. The Boy Scout in him? Or something else? Maybe his tabloid roots really were showing. What compelled him to dig into the lives of six unlucky women who had only one thing in common—all evidently were murdered, done in by the hands of killers as yet unknown.

The police had strong suspects in three of the cases but no ar-rests had been made.

Six names. Karlene Devers, Andrea Marcoletti, Chloe Mason, Grace Marie Nolan, Roxanne Reddening, and Yasmine Thomas. Two beaten to death, one shot, one drowned, one bled out from knife wounds, and one who was pushed and/or jumped from a sixth-floor window.

Six backgrounds. Six investigations.

It was easy to get lost in the work. And for once, he had no intrusion by the higher-ups sending him off on assignment. Luck of the draw or a slow news day. Either way, he was left alone.

The next time Dante looked at his watch, it was almost 1 P.M. It wasn't like him to get quite so lost in research for so long. Like all newsmen, he was used to short deadlines, fast stories, and heading on to the next assignment. Time to really dig into a story was a luxury. But this was turning into an obsession. He finally stopped long enough to take two hours to go home, shower, change, and run by Nirav's bodega before he rendezvoused with Angela at the dinner. It'd take a little sweet-talking of Mrs. Nirav, but he was confident he could wheedle a cheap burn phone out of her so that Angela didn't have to search the streets of Hell's Kitchen for a working pay phone. He was pretty sure they didn't exist.

His errands took longer than he expected, though. Mrs. Nirav was up in arms about somebody in the neighborhood and he had to sit through a tirade in a language he didn't understand until she was calm enough to deal with him.

Even worse, the E train had delays, making Dante late getting home and even later getting to the rendezvous. He'd planned to arrive early; as it was, he was ten minutes late. When he reached the diner, it was full of customers, but no Angela. The same waitress from the day before was scurrying around the tables, overworked and, judging by the clientele, grossly undertipped.

Dante dodged her as she whizzed by him, two plates of food balanced in each hand. "Excuse me?"

"Just sit anywhere. We ain't got no maître d'." She slammed two of the plates on the table, narrowly missing one customer's hand. She pivoted, pushed past Dante, and served the next table.

"I'm not looking for food. I'm looking for a woman."

One of the customers overheard him and began to laugh. "Me, too, Doris. I'm looking for a woman. You ever get any of those in here?"

"Shut up and eat, Earl." The waitress slowed down long enough to give Dante a onceover. "You were in here yesterday. Paid for the lady's next couple of meals."

"Yes. I was supposed to meet her here."

The waitress shrugged. "You just missed her."

14

The waitress trotted back toward the serving window, where more plates of food awaited her attention.

Dante followed her. "Where did she go?"

The woman paused long enough to scowl at him. "I didn't ask."

After collecting a new load of plates, she pivoted, glaring at him until he shifted out of the way. He followed in her French-fried wake.

"Did she say anything at all?"

The waitress motioned for him to move aside as she served another table and took orders from two more. She slapped the new tickets on the counter for the cook's attention, then finally she turned and faced Dante.

"I don't appreciate being the go-between for whatever you two have going." She reached into her apron pocket and pulled out a folded piece of paper. Then she pulled the note back and held out her other hand. "Message takers don't work for free."

Dante sighed, reached into his wallet, and pulled out a five.

The woman hesitated for a moment, as if deciding whether to hold out for a larger bribe. Then she shrugged and traded the note for the money. "It's not like I'll make more than this in tips from these lousy tightwads." Slipping the bill into her bra, she turned away from him.

Dante read the note.

Too many men here. Waiting at library.

He turned to the waitress. "Where's the library?"

The waitress rolled her eyes in obvious exasperation and grunted. "Five blocks uptown."

"Thanks." Dante slipped her another five and headed outside. As he walked, he noticed that what had earlier been sporadic clouds had now fused into a solid storm front. Rain was imminent. He hurried as much to avoid getting drenched as to make up for his tardiness.

He reached the library steps moments before the downpour started. It was a small two-story building, wedged between taller buildings, as if they'd denied it sunlight and stunted its growth. At least, it shouldn't be hard to locate Angela. As expected, he easily found her, sitting in the reference area, hiding behind a book. He knew she was only pretending to read because of her posture and the look on her face. The male librarian was standing only a couple of yards from her, having a deep conversation with another man.

If Dante believed her claims, then she could hear what the men were thinking, and their subject matter was upsetting her. When she looked up and spotted him, she seemed equally surprised as relieved.

"I'm sorry that . . ." They both started out with the same words and both stopped, waiting for the other to finish. Dante gestured for her to continue, but she stood up, grabbed his arm, and pulled him away from the table and the men.

"We can't stay here," she whispered.

He allowed her to lead him out of the section and toward a set of stairs leading to the second floor. Judging by the sound of youthful voices, they were headed into the children's section.

Once they reached the floor, she released the death grip she'd placed on his arm. He could see her features relax and her breathing slow down.

"Better?" he whispered.

"Definitely. You don't want to know what those two were planning to do after closing hours." She shuddered.

They navigated around a clutch of toddlers and moms, and found a table as far away as possible from what appeared to be an upcoming storytelling event.

She kept her voice low. "So, did you find me? I mean, the person I used to be? Was I murdered?"

He reached into his messenger bag, pulling out the information he'd assembled on each victim. "I whittled down the possibilities to six women who died the week prior to the crash." As he spoke, the inner man was chiding him for playing along in something so totally absurd and illogical. And yet here he sat, ready to calmly discuss six homicides, trying to determine which of the victims might actually be the person sitting next to him.

Angela tensed as he flipped open the first file folder. She wanted desperately to close her eyes but she knew that wouldn't make her troubles disappear.

"Victim number one: Karlene Devers."

She stared at the woman, pictured through a series of headshots showing various looks from sultry siren to pouty schoolgirl to wholesome mom. The sheet gave her weight, height, and talents, which included horseback riding and a green belt in karate.

"I found her comp card online. She got her SAG card ten years ago as a bit player in *Third Watch*. Did voice-overs and commercial work more recently."

An actress. That explained the variety of poses. "How did she die?"

"Beaten to death. Her body was found in Central Park and police described it as a case of a mugging gone bad. She liked to jog in the mornings and usually did so with her iPod and her pepper spray. When they found her, the iPod was gone. She still had about half of the pepper spray left."

Shock and indignation rolled into one and spilled over Angela. "You mean someone killed her just to get some stupid electronics?"

Dante nodded. "Evidently. And according to the medical examiner, it appears as if she put up a fight rather than surrender the item." He tapped the talent portion of the comp card. "See? She trained in martial arts."

Angela shook her head. "I can't imagine doing that." She thought back about her brief tussle with Gretchen and the more prolonged fight with the two orderlies. If anything, her success in defending herself indicated that she'd earned something far beyond a green belt. Certainly, it wasn't the idea of fighting back that she couldn't fathom.

But fighting back and *losing* . . .

"That's not me."

"Are you certain?"

She nudged the file away. "Who's next?"

Dante looked a bit miffed. "You don't want to know more about her?"

"No." She struggled to find a suitable explanation. But how could she explain her willingness to listen to her intuition in a situation like this? That she knew the woman didn't . . . feel right? "I just know . . . that I'm not her."

He closed the file and opened a second folder. "Candidate number two is . . . er . . . was Andrea Marcoletti. According to her friends, she'd been despondent over a recent breakup with her fiancé and it's believed she jumped to her death from her apartment's roof."

Angela read the other possibility in his voice. "Or was pushed?"

He nodded. "Possibly. Three reasons why: First, there were no witnesses. Second, neighbors said the roof was off-limits to the tenants and the door always kept locked. And third, she lived on the top floor of the apartment complex. She didn't need to jump from the roof to kill herself. It would've been easier and just as effective to jump from her own balcony."

Angela studied the grainy black-and-white picture of the dark-haired woman. Would she . . . could she even recognize herself if presented with the opportunity? Or was she just fooling herself?

Dante continued. "They're looking hard at the fiancé. His alibi isn't holding up well and he was good friends with the super who had roof access." He cocked his head. "Any vibes?"

She stared at the picture. Not only was the face unfamiliar, the concept of killing one's self seemed equally as strange. "If that's me, I was pushed. I wouldn't have jumped." When she turned away from the picture, Dante was staring at her.

"I agree," he said softly. "You're a survivor." After a moment, he broke eye contact, busying himself with collecting the papers and stuffing them back into the folder. "So, let's put this in the 'maybe' pile. On to the next. For your consideration, number three. Chloe Mason." He opened the next folder, revealing a candid snapshot of a woman with her head thrown back in laughter.

The temperature of the air around Angela dropped several degrees. She struggled to drag in a breath, but it froze in her throat.

Dante said something to her, but she didn't understand his words. Her vision narrowed until she could only see the woman's face. It was only when he reached over and touched her that her senses rebooted.

"Are you okay?"

Angela found her voice. "Wh-who is she?" she stuttered.

"Her name was Chloe Mason. She was—"

"Shot." She splayed her hand across the center of her chest, feeling a blossom of phantom pain erupt under her palm. "Right here."

Her mind whirled with a dozen different thoughts, images flashing behind her eyes. She forced herself to remove her hand from her chest and to touch the photo. She was almost surprised that it didn't burn her fingers, but she jerked her hand back nonetheless.

"So you're saying . . . that's you?" Dante asked, lowering his voice.

She sat back in the chair, trying to put as much distance as possible between the folder and herself. When she turned to Dante, it was clear that his incredulity was warring with his sense of compassion.

"Tell me about . . . Chloe," she said.

He cleared his throat and began. "She lived in Scarsdale, but her body was found on the Lower East Side." He pulled out a printout of a Web page. "Evidently, she was on the board at a museum in the area. According to the police, she'd received a text message from one of the docents, asking to meet her there. There was a problem with one of the exhibits."

Angela shivered.

"Her body was found in an alley that ran alongside the museum. They think she was attacked moments after her cab pulled away. Unfortunately, the cabdriver saw nothing. There were no witnesses and no cameras in the area."

"Who found her?"

"Sanitation workers." He rustled through some papers. "A Ms. Thomasina Hale identified the body. She also said she'd gotten a text from Mrs. Mason instead of the other way around."

"*Mrs.* Mason? She's married?"

He nodded, again riffling through the report. He selected a page and pulled it out. "To this man, Lawrence C. Mason, better known as—"

The name burst out without any warning. "Lars. Everyone calls him Lars." Images flashed behind her eyes, partially formed memories that danced just beyond her reach. She leaned forward, pressing her hands against her temples hoping that by holding her head, she could calm the memory storm.

"So . . . you think you might be Chloe Mason?"

She fought against the storm to answer. "Yes. No . . . I don't know." A single thought fought its way through the mental mess. *When did she die?* She repeated the question aloud.

Dante ran his forefinger down an official-looking document. "According to the police, she was still alive when she was found but died in route to the hospital. Time of death was . . . here: 10:45 A.M." He stiffened in revelation. "Your plane went down at 10:48."

The blizzard of images began to subside, allowing her to process what Dante was saying. "That'd be about the same time when I woke up in my seat, not knowing who I was or where I was."

It was an impossible explanation. Unreasonable. Implausible.

But she said it nonetheless. "Maybe when Chloe Mason died, her . . . spirit, her essence . . . whatever you want to call it moved into"—she gestured toward herself—"this body. Maybe she's possessing me."

Dante sat back in his chair and crossed his arms. She might not be able to read his thoughts, but she could read his face. The message there seemed mixed. His brow furrowed as he switched his gaze to the remaining folders. Then he uncrossed his arms and raised one finger.

"Let me try something. Turn around for a minute."

She complied but wondered if he'd still be there when she turned back around. She heard papers rustling and the scratch of a pen.

"Okay, you can turn back."

He'd stashed the file folders and placed three single sheets of paper facedown on the library table. "Three pictures. Three men. One of them is Lars Mason. Tell me which one."

Angela turned over the first page that featured a candid shot of a man standing next to a boat.

No shivers.

The second page was a blowup of a driver's license with the name and address marked through. She felt nothing when she saw the picture.

When she turned over the third page and looked into the flat two-dimensional eyes of the man pictured there, her fear was three-dimensional. Her stomach seized and she recoiled, pulling back her hand, which felt as if it'd been singed.

It took a few seconds before she could speak again. "That's him. That's Lars Mason."

Dante wore his doubt like a great overcoat—his expression was far too heavy for the current conditions. "Are you sure?" he asked.

She dared to touch the page again, but only to cover up the smirking face. "Absolutely." She took stock of Dante's overly dramatic expression. "I know what you're trying to do. And it won't work. This is Lars Mason. I'm sure of it."

His mask of doubt melted away, revealing a more reasonable mixture of awe and confusion. Resting his elbows on the table, he templed his fingers. "Wow," he said in a low voice. "I really didn't expect you to know."

When his gaze met hers, she decided his scrutiny was one of

curiosity rather than rudeness. But it was his next question that stopped her cold. "So, if you're Chloe Mason, where's Angela Sands?"

A chill went up her spine.

"I don't know."

It took a lot of persuasion to get Angela to agree to come to the TwentyFourSeven headquarters. Dante wanted to dig deeper into the murder of Chloe Mason and even though Angela's memories were spotty, he needed her there to guide him.

For instance, she remembered getting shot, but didn't remember the back alley. She recalled the face of Lars Mason with abject fear, but couldn't place him as the shooter. Dante knew that if he took her to the cops with her story of ghostly possession or whatever, they'd laugh him out of the station and offer to drive her back to the psych ward.

After they left the library, he walked her back to her "hotel." It turned out to be a flophouse. After some prodding, she confessed her "room" had actually been a closet in an earlier life.

She called it cozy.

He called it cramped, dangerous, unsanitary, and a few other choice words.

So thanks to his insistence, she was now staying in a hotel that one of his buddies managed. The top floor of the building was being updated but the owners had hit a patch of rough road, financially speaking, and the renovation had ground to a halt, half done. Even though two of the twelve rooms on the top floor had been completed, no hotel guest wanted to wade through a maze of unfinished hallways and stacks of drywall and wood to reach them.

This meant Angela had a safe, no-frills room in a decent hotel.

Even better, there'd be no foot traffic on her floor, male or female.

The plan was for Angela to rest for a couple hours, then meet him at the TwentyFourSeven building at 11 P.M. Once the day and evening shifts left, the number of the people in the building would have dropped from a thousand to less than a hundred.

In the meanwhile, Dante rushed through a couple of stories that had popped up in his assignment queue. His boss had a big problem paying a guy who didn't actually turn in any work. *Will write for food . . .*

At precisely eleven, his cell rang.

"I'm here," Angela said simply. "Hurry."

"I'll be right down."

When he arrived, he was dismayed to see a flock of people in the building's foyer. "What's going on?" he asked the guard as he waited to get out of the security area.

"JC Strutts was on Mike's show." The man glared at the throng with a great deal of distaste. "Behold. His adoring public."

Both fans and paparazzi clustered in the foyer in anticipation of the infamous bad-boy Giants quarterback's departure from the building.

That's when Dante spotted an ashen-faced Angela, standing in a far corner, her back against a wall of windows as if trying to put as much distance as possible between her and the crowd. He bullied his way through the multitude, made up mostly of male autograph seekers and the quarterback's infamous *Strutts Slutts,* his self-named squad of adoring female fans.

Finally, Dante reached her. "You okay?"

"Get me out of here please," she whispered.

Before he could do anything, the crowd surged toward them, having spotted the football star through the window behind Angela.

The fans swarmed them, pushing and shoving. Dante braced himself, trying to hold them off. But to his surprise, Angela's fear faded away and she suddenly became one with the fanatics.

She turned around within the protection of his arms and pounded on the glass to get Strutts's attention. Then Dante watched in amazement at her reflection in the glass as changes rippled through her face and body. Her face narrowed and a deep tan replaced her previously pale skin. Her eyes changed from a nondescript brown to a brilliant green. Her hair lengthened slowly and darkened from blond to dirty blond to light brown. . . . Her cheekbones shifted higher and her posture changed, making her appear at least a couple of inches taller.

Or maybe she *was* taller . . .

Although stunned, he held his position, hoping to shield her transformation from those around them. Luckily, nobody seemed to notice her except the usually stoic football star who waved back at Angela, displaying an uncharacteristic enthusiasm.

That's when it hit Dante. This "new" Angela now looked like a typical *Strutts Slutt*: thin, tall, tan . . .

Vapid.

"JC!" She pounded on the glass like the other women who'd been waiting around, hoping to get his attention. All she lacked was his jersey to complete the look.

Strutts blew her a kiss and then mouthed something of a salacious nature with an accompanying gesture. Cameras flashed, luckily at the jock and not toward her.

She reached for the edge of her shirt. *Slutts* were notorious for flashing the Louisiana-born quarterback in the grand tradition of a Mardi Gras parade-goer.

Dante grabbed her arm. "What are you doing?"

"Trying to get my man's attention," she snapped, wrenching out of his grasp. "Hey, JC, over here!"

"Angela, get ahold of yourself!"

She turned around, green fire dancing in her eyes, and she jabbed him in the chest with her forefinger.

"Who in the hell do you think you are?"

"Your friend," he said, pushing away her hand. "Your only friend at the moment."

Her fiery gaze wavered for a moment, then subsided when a look of confusion replaced her anger. "What's going on?"

Her green eyes began to turn murky brown again. If her eyes were changing, did that mean the rest of her was going back to "normal"? If so, he had to get her the hell away from the collection of journalistic predators, who'd camped out to ambush Strutts.

If any of the press noticed her metamorphosis, she'd be the queen of the tabloids for the rest of her life.

15

"C'mon." He grabbed her arm again and this time she didn't jerk away. He pushed his way through the crowd, heading for the security desk. Once there, the guard slapped a visitor badge on the desk. He waved them both toward the elevator lobby, foregoing the usual sign-in process.

Dante nodded his thanks and hustled Angela into the elevator as soon as possible. As luck would have it, nobody seemed to have noticed their departure, but he didn't relax until the doors slid closed and the car began to rise. He punched the twelfth-floor button three times for good measure.

Angela sagged against the wall, then turned her face into the corner.

"What the hell happened out there? You . . . changed. Not just physically, but your personality, too." Even as the words spilled out of him, he marveled that he was able to say something so completely absurd without doubting his own sanity.

Her shoulders shook and he wasn't sure if it was emotion or another weird physical reaction. He reached out and touched her shoulder. "Angela?"

The moment he touched her, she released a heavy breath and turned around. "Th-thanks," she stuttered. Her face was almost back to normal. At least she looked like she did before.

"What happened back there?"

She rubbed her hands down her face, as if assuring herself this was indeed her face, now. "Sometimes, when I hear what certain men think, something else . . ." She gestured in circles, struggling for the words. "Something else tags along. Their emotions, their desires. I'm not sure. But whatever it is, something inside me responds to it. It's like I can hear what they want . . . what they want me to be and I become that." She shivered. "It's not what you'd call the reaction of a normal modern-day woman. . . ."

Despite her earlier demonstrations of her mind-reading skills, he had walked into the building lobby still doubting her abilities. But what he'd just witnessed pushed his threshold of belief about forty feet above flood stage.

But it was impossible, wasn't it?

"Take how you feel," Angela whispered, "and multiply it by ten. That's how freaked out I am right now."

As the elevator slowed to a stop, he watched her tense up. She held the railing with one white-knuckled fist and his arm with the other.

When two women stepped into the car, he could feel the tension lessen in Angela's grasp. Luckily, the twosome ignored them and only stayed in the elevator for three floors before departing.

They continued to ride in silence. When the car stopped on the twelfth floor, Dante stepped out first to make sure the hallway was empty. Then he signaled for Angela to exit.

As soon as they stepped into the hallway, the motion sensors activated the overhead lights. She followed him wordlessly to his cubicle and accepted the chair he cribbed from the empty cubicle next to his.

She looked disengaged at best, blank at worst.

"So, let's take stock of the situation. You don't remember much before the airplane crash, but you do recognize the face and name of Lars Mason. You believe you're his deceased wife, murdered by him. Your soul or essence or whatever appears to have jumped ship and ended up in the body of Angela Sands, who has no paper trail, no identity previous to making her airline and hotel reservations. Somewhere along the way, you seem to have picked up the ability to change your face and body to conform to the desires or wishes of any man within a certain proximity of you."

"I'm a freak," she said with an air of defeat.

"You're a miracle," he corrected. "A woman with miraculous supernatural powers."

"Like I said, a freak."

She was going to be useless to him if she succumbed to depression. Time to stoke her inner fire. "You want to figure out who killed Chloe Mason and why? Or do you want to continue your little pity party?"

"I'm not asking for any pity. Just clarity." She stiffened with obvious rage, her face growing red. "Do you know how humiliating it is to realize I couldn't stop myself downstairs? I had no control at all over myself. How in the hell can I keep myself from doing it again? From automatically changing to fulfill the whims and desires of any man who just happens to cross my path?"

"Practice, I guess."

"Easy for you to say," she spat back.

He nodded to the picture of the leggy Miss March from the "Girls of the SEC" calendar that Bryant had given him. The picture had hung in permanent display in Dante's office, long after the year had ended. "Look, I have a well-known weakness for redheads with long legs. I don't see you changing to fulfill my desires."

She glared at Miss March, then at him, but didn't respond.

"So ask yourself: Why aren't you changing? To please me. To become my ideal woman."

Her gaze narrowed. "I don't know why."

"Exactly my point. Somehow you can resist me and my thoughts. So why don't we figure out how you're doing that? Once we know, maybe you'll be able to contain your abilities and use them when you want, not when someone's thoughts overpower you."

Angela sat in the chair, evidently mulling over his words.

"Okay, but that doesn't mean I want to forget all about Lars Mason and how he killed Chloe—me." Anger colored her face. "He should fry in hell for what he did to me."

"The problem is proving it. It's not like you can walk up to the cops and explain who you think you are and how you know what he did."

Her brief flare of anger faded as did the flush of color in her cheeks. "True."

"It's not like you actually remember the incident or any of the exact details."

"Not yet."

"Kearns? That you?" It was an unexpected interruption from the hallway that echoed through the quiet office.

Dante's stomach twisted. What the hell was Victor Smithfield doing here at this time of night? He gestured for Angela to stay quiet and pointed toward an empty cubicle. She caught the hint and ducked into the shadows moments before Smithfield turned the corner and marched down the corridor to Dante's workspace. Dante had piled books in her vacant chair, which would forestall questions about an unexpected second seat and also make it un-available for a boss who might decide to sit and talk.

Smithfield towered in the entryway. "Burning the midnight oil, eh, Korns? I didn't expect to find anyone here."

Dante resisted the urge to correct the man. They'd known each other for ten years, and Smithfield delighted in screwing up his name. Instead of reacting to the taunt, Dante pasted on an innocu-ous expression. "I needed to catch up on a few things. You know it's always quieter after hours. Easier to concentrate." He remained in his seat for two reasons. One, it demonstrated his dedication to his awaiting work. Two, Victor enjoyed using his height to increase his position of superiority. If Dante stood, they'd end up in a pissing match of posture with Victor trying to outdo him and maintain his sense of authority. Dante didn't have the time or the patience for that kind of silliness now.

Victor loomed over him. "Indeed. You've never been a real nine-to-five guy, have you?" As usual, his expression suggested that Dante's oddball schedule was a supreme disappointment.

Dante shrugged. "You know my motto. I go when and where the news is. And somehow, all the more interesting news seems to hap-pen before five A.M. and after nine P.M."

"What are you working on right now?" Victor glanced at the pile of books in the chair.

Don't sit down. Don't sit down. Dante allowed his imagination full rein, something he was encouraged to do in the paper's tabloid days. "I'm looking at a couple of suspicious deaths that occurred around the same time as the Hudson River crash."

"Why?" The man leaned forward like a bloodhound catching a scent. "You think they're related?"

Shit. I made it too interesting. The last thing he needed was to pique the man's interest. Considering Angela's little problem with proximity to men, he needed to get Victor out of the office, pronto.

He thought fast. "Nah, not related. Just overlooked. You know how the crash dominated everybody's attention. It literally filled all three rings of the media circus. I have a source who says that because of the amount of manpower diverted to the crash, one or maybe two possible homicides have not been properly investigated."

Victor rubbed his hands in near glee. "Excellent. You know I love it anytime we can point out the failings of city government. Makes for great headlines."

Dante kept his opinion of that out of his face. The man didn't know news. He was tolerated in the office simply because he was the last generation of the old guard, the Smithfields who had owned the original newspaper. But that wasn't enough for Victor. He had rewritten history, glorifying his family's roots, acting as if they had founded an honored journalistic dynasty rather than the biggest scandal rag of its day.

Even worse, he was the wrong person to be groomed for the job. As the reigning representative of Smithfields, The Next Generation, Victor couldn't operate a television remote, much less a round-the-clock twenty-first-century multimedia news organization.

The man glanced at his watch, his usual gesture to indicate he'd done his duty for the day by speaking to an underling and that he'd run out of small talk. "Well, look at the time. Keep up the good work. You're one of our shining stars, Karns. We're damn lucky to have you."

Dante maintained an innocuous expression, even while cursing the man under his breath. Smithfield was an inept prick, pure and simple, tolerated only because of the undeserved position he would someday hold in the company.

"Thank you, sir."

The man began to whistle as he walked away, yet more proof that he knew nothing about the business.

Everybody knew whistling in a newsroom was bad luck. . . .

Then the whistling stopped.

"Pardon me, sir, but could you possibly help me?" It was a female's voice, dripping with molasses and magnolias.

Angela!?

As she huddled in the shadows, she held her hands over her ears, hoping that by blocking the man's voice, she could stop his thoughts from entering her head.

But no such luck.

His mind whirled with a rapid firing of images and concepts, the strongest of which appeared to be contempt for Dante, mixed with something else.

Jealousy?

Excitement?

He was planning something. Something to do with Dante. Something that would put Dante in a bad light. That possibility excited him. Pleased him. She dug deeper.

He didn't expect Dante to be at his desk this time of night.

It was putting a kink in his plans.

There was something on Dante's desk that he wanted. That he needed. The image he projected was that of a plant. She tried to recall: did Dante have any plants on his desk? He had a flat-screen monitor, a keyboard, a pile of books, a stained coffee cup, a couple of pictures of a child.

His child?

She pushed aside her personal curiosity. But was there a plant? She didn't remember seeing one. The only plant she'd seen was in *this* cubicle, a half-dead potted one she'd moved in order to hide in the narrow gap between the file cabinet and the wall.

The man's thoughts grew stronger, harder to ignore and resist. She clenched her fists, her fingernails digging into her palms. Anything to stay in control. The pain helped her maintain a thin sliver of sense of self.

But it didn't stop his mind from supplying her with a rush of colorful images. Suddenly, they changed away from all thoughts of a plant. A plane. A parade. Scantily clad women. Booze. Beaches.

Freedom. Soon. *Freedom.* Soon.

His mind chanted the words like a mantra. Then something snapped in her head and suddenly, she heard his thoughts, just as clearly as she heard his spoken voice.

"All I have to do is bide my time. Then once I plant the papers, I will be able to make this asshole look guilty of everything. They'll haul him away. And then I can stroll away. With everything."

She saw images of Dante in a cartoon jail, dressed in black and white. A guillotine. Off with his head. Then back to the images of a carefree life of luxury on some swanky beach, being catered to.

"Well, look at the time . . ."

The images suddenly lost their color and faded away along with his voice in her head. He was departing, his thoughts growing weaker, unreadable.

No, come back, she demanded. What are you planning? How does it involve Dante? What's in those papers?

She had to stop this man. She had to get close enough to him to learn his plans. She had to protect Dante because that was her mission. Her responsibility.

He'd saved her life. It was time to repay him.

She inched soundlessly out of the cubicle and slipped around the corner. Running on tiptoes, she moved quickly and quietly toward the light spilling in from the hallway. She paused only long enough to snatch up a vase of wilted flowers from someone's desk.

Dashing back toward the entrance Dante had used, she paused to calm herself but instead, felt herself changing.

By the time she reentered and took a few steps, she found herself in the path of a tall, well-dressed man.

He took one look at her and grinned.

She knew her smile was engineered perfectly to attract him. She knew this because the desire to entice him suddenly filled her mind. She fought hard to hang on to herself. "Pardon me, sir, but could you possibly help me?" The strength of her accent surprised even her. Evidently, he preferred Southern women.

"I'd be delighted, ma'am," he said, exaggerating the "ma'am" with a stiff bow. "How may I be of service?"

He was somewhat cute. And he did have manners.

No, remember what you're doing! she screamed at herself.

"A friend of mine asked me to deliver these flowers to a Mr. Dante Kearns. Could you possibly direct me to his desk?"

The man cocked his head. "It's a little late for a florist delivery, isn't it?" He had a 1,000-watt grin that made her a little weak in the knees.

She felt herself blush. "I could lie and say that I forgot to deliver them this morning." She pretended to study the flowers, but in reality, she was pinching herself as hard as she could. "But as you can see, these are long past their prime." She leaned forward. "Can you keep a secret, Mister . . . er . . . ?"

"Smithfield. Victor Smithfield." He sketched an *X* across his expensive suit jacket. "Cross my heart."

"She wanted to send him a pot of poison ivy but I convinced her that dead flowers would get the same message across. She's not been . . . shall we say . . . very happy with their relationship. I was to deliver this and give him a message: she never wants to see him again."

The man seemed overly delighted with the concept of Dante

getting dumped. "He's sitting at his desk, four offices down," he whispered with a sense of conspiracy and glee.

"Oh. He's still here?" She hoped she was pouting rather than grimacing. She was pinching her own arm so hard she knew she'd have a bruise to show for her efforts. "I was so hoping to just leave the flowers and a written message. I suppose I'll have to face him now."

"Would you like me to accompany you? For safety's sake?"

She pretended to contemplate the offer but his mind was spewing a dozen salacious thoughts and none of them had to do with her safety. "Perhaps you could wait for me here? I think I'd feel more comfortable if I knew someone was waiting to escort me out after I'm finished."

"I'd be glad to be your bodyguard." His mind translated the word into *master*. Then he hit her with a stream of images of women in bondage that made her almost drop the flowers.

Her body and her brain warred for control. Her body desperately wanted to drape herself across him and demand that he dominate her right then and there. Her brain screamed to be released from his overdeveloped and overpowering desires.

She only hoped he didn't spot the blood dripping down her arm where she'd dug her nails into herself. Fighting the influence of his cloying thoughts, she pasted on an encouraging smile. "Then I'll be right back, Mr. Smithfield."

"It's Victor," he called after her.

She walked toward Dante's cubicle and stepped inside. It took a long, uncomfortable moment for him to recognize her. "Angela?" he said in a hesitant whisper.

Am I?

She nodded, then spoke loud enough for Victor to hear her. "I have a message from"—she paused, searching for a suitable name— "Gretchen. She sent you these to tell you that it's over."

He stared dumbfounded at her.

Angela glanced toward the hallway. *He can hear us,* she mouthed. "She never wants to see or hear from you again."

"What's going on?" he whispered.

"That's your boss, right?"

He nodded.

"He's planning something. Bad. And it involves you."

16

A strange woman. In Angela's clothing.

What the fuck?

It took a moment for Dante to process what he saw. Then one dope slap later, he realized this strange woman *was* Angela. She no longer possessed her blond, girl-next-door looks, but had transformed into an exotic, leggy beauty with jet-black hair. Her perfect nose looked like it'd been sculpted by a very expensive surgeon. His eyes roamed lower. The surgeon, it seemed, also did breast implants.

She'd transformed into a shining example of Victor's usual taste in women, as evidenced by the beauties he was always pictured with at high-profile events.

Angela shoved a bunch of dead flowers at him. "He's planning to frame you for something," she whispered.

"For what?"

"I'm not sure yet. He came here to hide some incriminating papers in your files. Something the police will use as evidence when they arrest you."

He tried to process this sudden flood of information but it didn't make sense. If Victor wanted to mess up his life, all the man had to do was say, "You're fired." It was preposterous to think Victor needed to make elaborate plans to frame Dante for some mysterious crime.

"He's going to make the authorities think you've done something wrong and then they'll find papers proving that you did it."

"Did what?"

Frustration filled her unfamiliar but beautiful new face. "I don't know. Not yet. But I think I can get it out of him if I stay with him a bit longer. He's going to ask me out for coffee as soon as I step out there."

"How do you know that?"

She rolled her dark eyes. "Hello? Mind reader here, remember? We don't have long." She raised her voice. "I don't care what your excuse is. You've broken Gretchen's heart and she doesn't want anything to do with you. Ever again. Understand?"

"Uh . . . sure. Tell her I'm sorry." He lowered his voice again. "Don't go out with him. He's a real asshole."

"Trust me. I know that already. I won't leave the building and I'll only stay with him long enough to figure out what he's planning."

But how do I keep you safe? An idea hit Dante hard and fast. He tossed the dead flowers into the trash can and held out his hand. "Give me your cell."

She reached in her pocket and produced the phone. He dialed his own number and his ringtone echoed through the quiet office.

"I'm sorry," he said in a raised voice. "I've been waiting for this call. Tell Gretchen it was fun while it lasted." He leaned closer to her, handing back the phone. "Keep the line open. I'll be able to hear everything. And if he tries anything, I'll be just around the corner." He paused.

"And I don't care if he's my boss. He'll be toast."

She slipped the cell down the neck of her shirt, evidently tucking it into her bra. "Good idea."

He reached out to touch her arm, but she jerked away, taking a step backward. "No, don't touch me."

Her reaction confused him. "What's wrong?"

"You might make me change back." She glanced over her shoulder toward the hallway. "Wish me luck."

He gave her a thumbs-up and a lukewarm smile, wishing he could dredge up a more encouraging response. But he'd already experienced his six impossible things for the day. He was reaching the point where his ability to process any more strangeness was badly overtaxed.

Victor wants to get me arrested. . . .

Dante grabbed his Bluetooth, switched it on, and stuck it in his ear. He listened as he shrugged on his coat. After a second and third thought, he grabbed the gun and ammo from his bottom drawer.

If this got ugly, he wasn't sure he could stop it without killing the guy.

He listened to the transmission as he peered cautiously into the hallway. The twosome stood near the elevator, waiting for the car to arrive. Victor held Angela's elbow.

"How did Kearns like the flowers?"

Dante couldn't hear Victor directly from his position, but the cell did a decent job of picking up the words. Angela's voice came through loud and clear, probably due to the cell's position.

"Not very much. I don't think he expected Gretchen to break up with him, especially not like this."

"You must be an extraordinarily good friend to handle this for her."

Smarmy bastard.

"She hates confrontation. But I can't say I liked doing it. Things like this leave me feeling queasy."

"Are you all right? Is there anything I can do to help?"

"Is there a bathroom around here? If I could splash some water on my face, I'd feel better."

"Sure. Right down here." He led her around the corner, away from the elevator bank.

After a few seconds, Angela said, "Thanks. I won't be but a minute."

Dante heard the squeaky protest of a set of hinges that needed oil, then a couple of other unidentified noises. Suddenly, he could hear Angela clearly.

"It's me. I'm alone for the moment."

"What are you doing?"

"Stalling. I only have a minute. He's going to make an excuse to get me upstairs to his office."

"And?"

"And what do you think? He's going to try to seduce me."

"Then for God's sake, don't go."

"Don't be stupid. I can take care of myself. And the only way we can stop him from causing you problems is to find out what he's planning to do and why."

"And then what? He may be an asshole but he's a well-connected asshole. If it boils down to 'he said, she said,' then I'm sorry, but the world is going to believe him over you and me. Money speaks and he's—"

"Shut up. I don't have time. Quick—get upstairs to his office and hide. I know he left the doors unlocked when he came down to your desk. I gotta go."

"But, Angela . . ."

He heard the hinges squeal again, then Angela's fainter voice. "I'm so sorry that took so long. I couldn't get any of the faucets to turn on. Could you guard the door and let me use the men's room?"

"Certainly. Here."

Dante hit the fire exit at a dead run, pausing only long enough to keep the door from slamming shut. He winced at the sound of his footfalls ringing on the metal stairs. The staircase was well shielded; it was a fire exit route. Perhaps his boss couldn't hear them. Luckily, the executive offices were only three flights up. Victor was likely completely focused on Angela. Maybe he could pull this off. Once out of the stairwell, Dante ran toward Victor's office, discovering the outer and inner doors were indeed unlocked.

Angela was right again.

But when he stepped into Victor's office, he realized a big and possibly fatal flaw in this plan.

There was no place to hide.

Victor had redecorated since the last time Dante had been there. Instead of thick curtains muffling the windows and a polished desk large enough to land a carrier jet, the new style was minimalism at its finest. Nobody could hide under a glass desk or behind motorized blinds sandwiched between the window panes.

Various noises in his ear suggested that Angela and Victor were entering the elevator. The next few noises were hard to interpret until he heard her groan.

The hair on the back of his neck rose. What in hell was the bastard doing to her? He spun on his heel and reached for the doorknob but stopped when he heard her breathless words.

"Oh, God, that feels so good . . ."

"Why don't we go to my office and I can demonstrate exactly how good I can be?"

"Take me there." She giggled. "Then take me."

"Sure, baby. Going up!"

Something smothered her giggle—the sound of rustling fabric. Then there was a *ding*.

"Time to teach you exactly what TwentyFourSeven really means."

Panic hit Dante as solidly as a fist in the solar plexus. *Think fast!* he demanded of himself. *Where can I hide?*

Victor found the phone in her bra when he pawed at her boobs. But luckily, he didn't notice it was connected. Instead, he guffawed and pulled at her neckline. "Any other goodies you have hiding in there?"

Angela rubbed against his hip. "You men are so lucky. You always have pockets in convenient places." She demonstrated it by reaching into his pocket and palming his cell phone. "We women just have to make do with what nature and the fashion industry gives us."

Evidently, in a previous life, she'd been a helluva pickpocket. She slipped the cell into her own back pocket.

"There's making do. And then there's"—he reached down and nipped at her breast through the material—"making do." He made a smacking noise. "I don't know whether I should applaud or criticize the man who invented the bra." He reached up under her shirt and fumbled with the clasp in front. "So confining. So restrictive . . ." He released the clasp. "There. Isn't that better?" He looked down as if admiring his handiwork. "My God, you're even bigger than I realized. Magnificent!"

"That's because I want to please you. I can be whoever you want me to be." The words tumbled out of her and Angela snapped her mouth shut. *What am I doing? Get control of yourself.* Despite her reprimand, she felt herself expanding to meet his ideal.

He cupped one breast, then squeezed it lightly. "Oh, baby, I had no idea you were hiding such treasure in there." He pulled her closer until she was pressed fully against him, feeling his arousal push against her leg.

"Look what you're doing to me," he growled in her ear. He punctuated his words with demanding kisses. "It's. All. Your. Fault."

"Then we should do something about it, don't you think?" She licked his ear while reaching down and fondling his throbbing bulge. "But wherever shall we go? And whatever shall we do? Over and over again?" Oh, God, with her syrup-thick accent, she sounded like Scarlett O'Hara on steroids.

"Baby, you're reading my mind. My office is just down the hallway. I've got everything we need. A couch, a killer view of the city, fine wine, and all the privacy we need."

She kissed him, hard and deep, with a ferocity that scared her. In return, he slammed her into the wall, pinning her there. He fumbled with her pants, trying to release the waistband button.

Her first instinct was to hit him, but soon that instinct faded as the strength of his needs invaded her mind, threatening to take control.

"Not here," she complained, pushing him and his enticing lust away. She tried to clear her mind of his desire. But he pressed harder with his body and his thoughts, overwhelming her physically as well as mentally.

"Where's your office?" she gasped between their frenzied pawing.

Does it matter? Her inner slut didn't care. He could screw her right there in the hallway and she'd be happy.

But Angela dug in, attempting to hold on to the last shreds of her self-control.

NICOLE "COCO" MARROW AND LAURA HAYDEN

However, fighting the change, resisting his desire hurt so very much . . .

Then give in, she told herself.

It was an easy answer, a tantalizing one. Just let go and become his perfect sex partner and go along for the ride.

Give in.

No more cares. No more concerns.

No more . . .

"I wonder if there are horny bitches like her in Rio?"

Up to now, she'd had to strain to hear his thoughts, like listening to an AM station that was more static than music. But now his thoughts echoed through her mind with crystal-clear high definition.

"Hell, I could just bring her with me. For a while . . . at least . . . until I got tired of her. Until I fucked her out. We could fuck all the way there—Mile High Club and all. I wonder what sort of stamina she has?"

Something changed.

Some switch had flipped inside of her, but what? How? She felt disconnected from her body—the same body that at the moment was responding with enthusiasm to his seduction efforts.

Her mind was clear. Focused. She knew exactly what she needed to do.

"Slow down, cowboy." She pushed his hands away and backed up a step. "Let me freshen up before we get all hot and bothered."

He reached forward, his hands clawing at her clothes. "C'mon, babe, the engine's running."

She pretended to pout. "You're not telling me that you're going to run out of gas soon, are you?"

"Me?" He puffed up his chest and gave it a "Me-Tarzan" thump. "I can go all night. All day and all night."

She gave him an admiring once-over. "I bet you can. Now show me to a working bathroom."

He detangled himself from her with a dramatic air of reluctance. "Here. This is my private washroom. Don't be long. I'll be in my office, pouring us a couple of drinks."

She kissed him, plunging her tongue into his mouth and lingering for a brief moment, as a promise of delights to come. "I'll be out in a minute."

Stepping through the door he'd indicated, Angela waited until it closed completely before she pulled out her phone. She already realized Victor had disconnected the call when he pulled it out of her bra.

But they had a bigger problem. There was no place for Dante to hide in the office. So where was he? She hit redial and waited. Dante picked up on the first ring, but said nothing.

"Dante?" she whispered.

No answer.

"Are you there?"

No response.

Panic began to well up in her throat. She never liked going into an operation like this without a backup. The thought chilled her.

Wait . . . what operation?

Victor interrupted her from outside the door. "I'm getting impatient."

She almost dropped the phone when she heard his voice echo through it.

"Dante . . . are you in Victor's office?"

She barely heard his whispered response. "Yes."

"Oh, God. What do we do? What if he finds you?"

"Distract him." He disconnected the call.

Distract him? She looked around for inspiration. All she saw was an unfamiliar face in the mirror. She watched as the terror faded from the woman's eyes—her eyes.

She knew the best way to distract a man. . . .

When she opened the door again, she wore only the spare white shirt that she'd found hanging up on the back of the door. She'd left everything else behind, including both phones.

"What shall we play, Victor?" She walked toward the inner office, trailing a tie she'd also found behind her like a leash. "You strike me as a man who likes more than the usual slap and tickle."

"I'm . . . oh, hell . . ."

She'd interrupted him as he was pouring two snifters of brandy from a crystal decanter. When he looked up, he almost dropped the decanter.

He made a show of saluting her with one glass and then taking a healthy swig of the contents, coughing and sputtering when he realized his mistake.

"I believe you're supposed to sip brandy," she offered.

He waited to catch his breath. "I was mesmerized by your beauty."

"Sweet-talker."

"I always liked that shirt." His grin grew more lascivious. "But I like it much better on you."

"I hoped you wouldn't mind."

This time, he took a careful sip of his drink. "Turn around. Let me see the complete package."

As she slowly turned, she scanned the room, trying to figure out where Dante could be hiding. There were no drapes and the glass desk hid nothing. That left only . . .

She spotted something behind the couch.

Or someone?

Victor crossed the room in a couple long strides. "God, you've got yourself one fine-looking ass. Just the right size to spank." He demonstrated it by giving her a hard slap.

It took every bit of control she had not to slug him back. Instead, she smiled as if contemplating the fun to come. "Hmmm. We could play naughty schoolgirl. It's always good for a few laughs."

The hungry appraisal he gave her made her feel like a leg of beef hanging in the butcher-shop window.

"Darling, with that body, I'm looking for more than a few laughs. I'm looking to laugh for a very long time." He gulped down his drink, placed the empty glass on his desk, then grabbed her waist, pulling her closer. He stuck his hand between her legs, his awkward fingers fumbling like a schoolboy's in search of something he'd only heard of, but never seen. "My God, you're perfect," he moaned against her neck. "Absolutely perfect. A dream come true."

She allowed him to continue pawing her and trailing sticky kisses down her cleavage. He paused to suck on her breasts, then began to work his way down to her pubic hair.

The odd thing was that although her body was responding to his touch, causing her to experience visceral reactions to his efforts, her mind remained remarkably clear. Detached.

That's why she wasn't so distracted by Victor's ministrations that she missed Dante's approach. He'd abandoned his hiding place and was striding toward them, full of righteous fury.

17

She didn't have to read his mind to know he wanted to save her from Victor, probably by beating the holy hell out of the man.

Nice sentiment, but that would so ruin everything . . .

Angela waved him off, still trying to keep Victor completely occupied with his effort to seduce her. Dante stopped and stared soundlessly at her, confusion momentarily derailing his anger.

She nodded at the phone he was still holding in his hand and then formed a circle with her fingers and held it to her eye. She couldn't risk using both hands to make the universal charade sign for "movie."

Record this, she mouthed.

He gaped at her, moving only when she made a threatening face and Victor attempted to rise from his knees. She shoved the man's face back into her groin where he moaned in satisfaction.

Once Dante overcame his momentary shock, he nodded and then tucked his phone between two upright books in the bookcase so that it was aimed in the general direction of the couch.

Somehow, she didn't believe Victor was such a traditionalist as to limit himself to just the couch, but she'd make do.

Dante held up five fingers.

It either meant *Five minutes and I'm coming back* or *You only have five minutes' recording time.* She wasn't sure, but in any case, she'd get what she wanted by three.

Dante backed soundlessly out of the door into the bathroom where she hoped he would wait patiently. Even though she couldn't read his mind, Dante's face betrayed his every thought. Right now, it was clear most of his thoughts centered on killing or maiming Victor. Bringing the man to justice didn't seem to be Dante's preferred course of action.

But justice was exactly what Angela planned to provide.

Time for the show, she told herself.

She turned her attention to Victor, her mind racing through a dozen different scenarios, evaluating each one and selecting the one that best meshed with the tangled web of thoughts filling his head. "You said I was your dream come true. Tell me about your dreams, Victor."

"To make mad, passionate love to you."

"And after that?"

He buried his face in her groin. "To leave this place and never look back."

"This office? But it's so nice!"

He lifted his head long enough to glance around the richly appointed room. "This dump? It's a jail cell in disguise."

"You don't like your job?"

"I don't want to talk about my job. I want you."

He rose to his feet and, using both hands, ripped the white shirt from her shoulders, the buttons popping off in the effort.

She slapped his hand. "Bad boy! See what you did? You've torn my shirt."

When she clawed through his tangled thoughts, she learned his strongest desire wasn't hidden particularly deep in the recesses of his brain. Instead, it danced on the edges of his imagination as a fully formed wish.

His idea of the perfect foreplay . . .

She wagged her finger at him. "Now I'm afraid I'm going to have to punish you." While she talked, she fashioned a slipknot in his tie.

His eyes lit up along with his libido. "I'm sorry, ma'am." Expectation made him salivate, his heart race, his palms dampen.

"Lie down on that couch. Now." It was a leather and metal monstrosity, perfectly designed for her current needs. Then again, she already knew she wasn't the first woman who had used it in such a manner. In fact, it was hard to separate the fact from the fiction within Victor's mangled mental images. But whether they were wishful thinking or actual memories, they all had a central theme: his delight in being dominated by a strong woman, a woman who'd tell him exactly what to do.

"Yes, ma'am," he said with undisguised eagerness. He lowered himself onto the couch, then reclined, stretching his arms out in anticipation of her domination.

Angela loosened his belt, sliding it free from his pants. She positioned his hands through one of the side supports of the couch. Looping the belt around his wrists, she cinched it so tightly the leather bit into his skin.

"I've been a very bad boy," he said, groaning in pleasure, as she used his tie to secure his ankles to the opposite end of the couch.

"Yes, you have. And bad boys deserved to be punished."

Stripping off her torn shirt, she ripped it, forming a makeshift blindfold that she wrapped around his eyes.

"No!" he protested. "I want to see you!"

She slapped him hard across the face.

"You have to earn the right to see me, understand? Answer all my questions correctly and promptly and I'll make sure you enjoy what you see. Lie to me and you get nothing—no pain, no fun. Understand?"

"I'm not sure I want to—"

She reached down with both hands and gripped his throat, surprising herself with her show of strength. She wasn't cutting off his oxygen supply, but she had his undivided attention. Bending down, she whispered in his ear, "I can show you pleasures you've never even dreamed of before. You want that, don't you?"

She loosened her hold a bit and he managed a nod.

"Good." She released his throat and reached over, pulling Dante's cell from the bookcase. It was critical to capture his confession, so she watched Victor through the display screen to make sure it was recording.

"First question. What is your name?"

He coughed a few times before answering. "V-Victor Smithfield."

"Very good, Victor," she purred. "Next, do you like me?"

"Oh, yes," he answered. His breath caught on the words.

She reached into his mind. "Do you love me?"

He paused, his brow furrowing for a moment.

You love me. You adore me. You can't imagine life without me.

"I . . . I love you. In fact, I adore you." His ardor began to build along with his erection. "I can't begin to imagine life without you."

It worked. God help her, it actually worked.

You need me. Wherever you go, you want to take me with you.

This time, Victor paraphrased rather than parroting her words verbatim. "I don't want you to ever leave my side." That was good. It was a signal that he was not only accepting her thoughts but expanding on them.

"Tell me, Victor. Where do you suggest we go to be together?"

He grinned. "I know just the place. Everybody thinks I'm headed to China. That's where my plane will mysteriously disappear over the ocean, never to be found again."

"But in reality, you're going to . . . ?"

"Rio de Janeiro. The decoy plane bound for China took off about two hours ago. So I have to leave tonight. In fact, just as soon as we get through having our fun here, we can head straight to the airport and take off for Brazil."

Where you can't be extradited for your crimes . . .

"What? Leave? Just like that? It's so sudden. I'd need to pack some things—clothes, stuff like that."

"Forget it. I'll buy you anything you want or need. I can afford it," he boasted.

She toyed with his pants, loosening them and pulling them down to his knees. She had to increase the stakes so that he believed a bigger reward was forthcoming. "You must be a very rich man, Victor. Wherever did all that lovely money come from?" She stroked the bulge that strained against the material of his briefs.

He sucked in oxygen to speak. "The family business."

"You inherited it?"

"No, I couldn't wait for the old man to kick. I took it."

"Why?"

"My idiot father keeps sinking more and more of the family money into this stupid company. It's bleeding out faster than he can put it in. So I'm taking it now. All of it, before he can piss it all away."

"And no one suspects?"

His boasting grated on her nerves. "Of course not. I'm the

golden boy. I can do no wrong. I've been siphoning off the money and channeling it into an offshore account for the past two years. I've set everything up so it looks like Kearns was embezzling it. That's why I've kept him on staff despite the fact that I hate his guts. I was headed to his office tonight to hide the papers incriminating him in his files. And then I found the asshole was still at work." A grimace creased his face. "But that's how I met you so I don't mind the interruption of my plans." He smiled at that thought.

His smile went from sappy to cruel in a nanosecond. "This will be even better. About nine hours from now, the news of my unfortunate death will surface and an anonymous tipster will contact the feds about some financial irregularities at TwentyFourSeven. The trail will lead right to Kearns. If he tries to point the finger at me, he'll be branded a liar because there are a dozen witnesses who saw me get on the plane for China. Even better, he won't be able to find the one witness who can corroborate that he did see me: you."

"So you're only taking me with you so I won't testify against you?"

"Of course not. I'm taking you because I'm madly in love with you. All we have to do is wait until he leaves and then I can hide the paperwork."

"What paperwork?"

"Inside my jacket pocket. I had some pretty damning proof manufactured that will send the auditors on a wild goose chase. They'll find Dante and string him up at the end of it."

Angela found Victor's jacket puddled on the floor where he'd discarded it. Inside the inner pocket, she spotted a folded sheet of paper.

"It's just a bunch of numbers."

"No, it's a bunch of offshore accounts created in his name. I transferred the funds from TwentyFourSeven a week ago, using his computer. Then when I get in the air, I'll transfer the money from the offshore accounts into my anonymous Brazilian accounts."

"You don't think they'll ever realize that it was you all this time?"

"Perhaps. But by then, you and I will be living a life of luxury in Rio. No worries. No cares. No extradition."

She turned to see Dante standing next to her, her discarded clothes clutched in his white-knuckled fist. He shoved them toward her and held out his other hand for his phone.

She understood. She made the trade.

Dante angled the camera at the man tied to the couch.

"Just one more question," Angela said while pulling on her clothes. "Why Kearns? Why him?"

"Because my father keeps shoving the fucker and all his fucking achievements in my face all the fucking time. 'Why can't you be more like this guy?'" Victor struggled against his bindings. "I hate the bastard and he hates me. So why not make his life as miserable as he's made mine?"

Angela tugged on her shirt and turned to Dante. "That's all I need to hear. You?"

Dante nodded. "It should be enough to hang him. Between this and his fingerprints on the papers he was going to stick in my files."

Angela reached down and whipped off Victor's blindfold.

Dante's voice changed to a deep resonating news reporter's voice. "You've just heard the freely given confessions of Victor Smithfield, senior assignment editor of TwentyFourSeven news, confessing to a major embezzlement of the company owned by his family and his attempts to frame this reporter for the theft."

"What the hell?" Victor turned his head, either trying to shade his eyes from the sudden brightness or to shield his face from the camera. "You bastard!" He began to struggle furiously against his bonds. "I'll kill you!"

"Oh, dear. Those are death threats, aren't they?" Angela pointed out.

"Indeed they are."

Victor flailed wildly. Thanks to his efforts, he managed to knock loose one of the uprights on the couch's side. A moment later, he worked his bound wrists free from the couch, and began to gnaw at the belt wrapped around them, trying to release the buckle.

Dante reached forward and grabbed Angela, pulling her behind him. The man was a knight, alight with chivalry and a desire to protect her. He shoved the camera phone into her hands and pushed her toward the bathroom. "Lock yourself in there and send the video to Chaz Brooks. He's in the address book under 'NYPD.'"

"Don't you dare, bitch. I'll make your life a holy hell." Victor lunged at her, his fingers just grazing her arm before he realized his feet were still attached to the couch.

Somehow, when he fell to the floor, it exerted enough torque on the couch to break the uprights imprisoning his feet. A moment later, he scrambled toward Dante, his head down like a football tackle. He caught Dante in the stomach, driving him backward and off balance.

Although Angela screamed a warning, it'd been too late. The two men exploded into a fury of arms and legs. They both threw punches and epithets. Victor had four inches of height on Dante. He'd also had some martial-arts training, enough to make him a hazard to everyone in the office, including himself. Dante offset the difference in their height and weight with some effective fighting skills he'd learned on the streets.

Angela couldn't bring herself to hide in the bathroom like a coward while sending the video file. Instead, she started the upload process, then hid the phone behind the curtains on the windowsill in the bathroom.

When she emerged, Victor was standing over Dante. He had Dante pinned to the floor.

Angela looked around for a weapon. The first thing she saw was the broken upright from the couch. Grabbing it, she swung it at Victor's head.

And connected.

Victor fell over and sprawled on the floor, a small dribble of blood from his temple marring the expensive carpet.

She looked down at Dante. "You okay?"

He groaned as he pushed up into a sitting position. "Yeah. I've faced worse on the playground. For a man of his size, he fights like a girl."

Angela stared at him. "You didn't just say that."

He rubbed his jaw and winced. "Sorry. I didn't mean it the way it sounded."

"I hope not. After all—"

She caught movement out of the corner of her eye. Victor had sprung to his feet and was lunging at her.

She acted out of instinct, snapping out a high kick that caught him in his injured temple.

Blood sprayed across the room as she connected with his head. He collapsed like a wet sack of potatoes, falling into an ungainly heap.

She waited for him to rise again, but he remained limp on the floor. Satisfied that he was out for the moment, perhaps even several moments, she turned back to Dante and smiled.

"You were saying something about fighting like a girl?"

18

By eight o'clock, the story had broken on TwentyFourSeven and the other news networks were scrambling to catch up. Auditors swarmed the building and Dante had been interrogated by three different teams: the police, the FBI, and the FCC. He told each group the same story. He'd been called by a mysterious woman and warned of Victor's plans. When he got to Victor's office, the woman already had Victor tied to the couch under the guise of sexual play. The video showed that his confession was not coerced, but freely given.

And no, Dante had no idea who the nude dark-haired woman in the video was, where she came from or where she went when she left. The security cameras only showed one woman with a visitor's pass, the blond Angela Sands who had been cooling her heels in Dante's office all night, waiting for him to return from his boss's office. She'd been questioned and remained a person of "distant interest."

When the Smithfield family weighed in, it wasn't in support of their black-sheep son, but to condemn him. Victor broke shortly afterward, confessing everything: his embezzling success, his attempts to divert suspicion by putting a timed bomb on the plane headed for China, the fake trail of clues designed to put the blame on Dante, and a host of other, smaller crimes. Luckily, the plane had been diverted in time to land and the bomb detected and defused.

He even admitted that he had no real idea who the dark-haired woman was or why he'd professed such uncharacteristic adoration for her. He said that he must have been drugged so the police drew blood samples for screening.

However, with his second confession duly recorded for the prosecution, the first confession, exacted by the mysterious woman, became less important in terms of evidence, but became viral in terms of news reporting.

By noon, a sanitized version of the "bondage confessions" had hit every major news outlet and was the top download at YouTube.

Victor Smithfield's lovestruck confessions had made him the laughingstock of the nation and the world beyond. Plus, the mystery of the identity of the "Dark, Double-D Dominatrix" became a global phenomenon with hundreds of women identifying themselves as the infamous "4D." Since the camera never quite captured her face, the only way to identify who might be 4D was by the nude body.

It was every porn-loving fanboy's best wet dream.

However, it wasn't the sort of viral promotion that Twenty-FourSeven wanted to be associated with their news organization's profile.

So Dante wasn't surprised when he received a summons to appear in Alistair Smithfield's office at 5 P.M. that evening. As CEO and self-identified Grand Pooh-bah of TwentyFourSeven, Smithfield prided himself on not living in an ivory tower but, instead, being accessible to his employees. It was a nice fantasy for him, but everybody else still knew him as the Old Man who still referred to "That Internet Stuff" and who spent his time recounting stories of the great journalists of the past.

The real power behind TwentyFourSeven was Marcus Smithfield, Alistair's oldest son and Victor's younger brother.

But a summons to the Old Man's office meant official business, sanctioned by the younger Smithfield. In Dante's case, it could mean anything from a quiet firing to a big promotion.

When he arrived, the usually stern-faced Rose Shepherd, the Old Man's secretary, graced him with a rare smile. That gesture turned out to be a harbinger of things to come. Once inside, he was treated to extremely expensive brandy, an aromatic Cuban cigar, and was invited to sit not on the uncomfortable chair facing the massive mahogany desk but across a gleaming coffee table in one of the two red leather chairs facing the window high over Central Park.

It took a few moments for Alistair Smithfield to get everything situated correctly. Although Dante didn't smoke, he followed suit as the Old Man snipped the end of the cigar, admired it, and lit it. Soon, great clouds of smoke hovered over their heads.

"It feels odd, thanking you for exposing my own flesh and blood for the murderous asshole he is, but nonetheless, thank you. From the bottom of my heart."

The only response Dante could manage was "It seemed the . . . right thing to do at the time."

"I appreciate the sense of ingenuity you demonstrated. And I won't ask you how you coerced that young lady into playing along with my son in the rather unique manner she did. I won't even ask who she is." He paused as if waiting for Dante to volunteer the information.

Dante knew the proper answer. "Well, sir, as you know, a newsman doesn't reveal his sources."

The Old Man beamed. "Excellent. I always knew that deep inside of you was a traditional journalist, despite your checkered tabloid past when this was still the *New York Daily Compass*. It's one of the reasons why I insisted on keeping you on staff—you're young enough to embrace all this twenty-first-century technical stuff, but you still have some old-school values."

Shit. I'm only thirty-four. You make me sound like I'm a spry sixty. But Dante kept his thoughts to himself, and merely said, "Thank you, sir."

"Just convey to the young lady my thanks and my hopes that she will choose to remain unidentified, for her sake as well as ours."

"I'll tell her, sir."

"Now, the reason why I called you up here is this. Victor was never suited for the assignments job. I suspect he was a truly lousy boss with abysmal leadership skills. I fear that because he took liberties as the owner's son, your department had to suffer in silence."

Dante didn't know whether to agree openly or remain stoically closemouthed.

Smithfield chuckled. "I see you're very accustomed to the 'keeping silent' part. I appreciate that you don't want to bad-mouth my own son to me even after I've admitted what a complete and total disappointment he's been to me, the family, and the legacy of our business. I very much appreciate your sense of loyalty. In fact, that's one of the reasons why I want to give you a new position."

A promotion?

The Old Man read his face. "It's not only a promotion for you, with a better salary and management authority, but it's also my chance to restructure the division. Instead of the hard news, I want your people to go back to their tabloid roots, dig up those decidedly oddball and offbeat stories that were the hallmark of our old days as the *Compass*."

Visions of Bigfoot sightings and UFO abductions filled Dante's imagination. Old-school tabloid shit. His gut began to churn.

"Not all that imaginary crap some of your compatriots made up in order to create sensational headlines, but real stories about the real oddities of the world. The story behind the stories. Human-interest stuff. The heart of a news organization. Got a kid who can't bear sunlight on his skin? Go beyond the obvious vampire-child story and tell the world about the parents' attempts to provide their special-needs kids with a normal lifestyle. Or that story about the image of the Virgin Mary in the tortilla? Go talk to the folks in the town and learn more about the role of religion and faith in their community."

Dante's mind spun with possibilities. This could be the gig of a lifetime. "So we use the tabloid concept as a hook, but dig deeper beyond the implied scandal or sensation and get the real story."

"Exactly. Right now, TwentyFourSeven isn't much different from every other news channel out there. News, politics, sports, and celebrity entertainment. Newspapers are dying left and right because of declining readership and the fact that cable networks like us can get the news on air minutes after it's happened rather than wait for the next morning edition. But the death of newsprint is leaving an intellectual hole that I want us to fill. I want to shift our paradigm back so that we mirror the newspapers of old: news with more balanced divisions beyond just that of news headlines but with areas covering nonpartisan politics, government, society, entertainment beyond the escapades of today's Hollywood darling, sports, human interest, economy, history, environment . . . you see where I'm going?"

"I think so, sir."

"What it means for you is that I want you to concentrate on human-interest stories. Your work is going to be the heart of the difference from the other cable news networks. Because of that, I'm going to give you carte blanche for one year. No cap on your division's budget as long as you produce usable material for us for two major stories a week. You can pick your team and set your own schedule."

Dante stared at the man, trying not to gape but failing miserably.

The Old Man laughed. "I never thought I'd see the day when I caught you speechless."

"I-I don't know what to say, sir."

"Say thank you. And remember that I'll be reviewing your expense reports myself, so the carte blanche only goes so far."

"Th-thank you, sir."

The Old Man rose from his seat and stuck out his hand. "I'm glad to have a man of your caliber in our organization. Show me what you've got and we'll be riding the train for a long time to come. Don't make me regret my decision a year from now when I review your division."

"I won't, sir. Thank you, sir."

When Dante stumbled out of the inner sanctum into the outer office, Rose held out an ashtray. He stared dumbfounded at it until he remembered he still had the cigar clenched between his teeth.

"It's a nonsmoking building outside his office," she reminded Dante.

"Thanks." He dutifully ground out the cigar.

"Here." Rose handed him a black keycard. "Your access code is 3971."

He examined the object, noting that it had no writing on it at all. "Access to what?"

"Your new office. You're in suites 2507 and 2607, the two-story corner office. Your staff will be relocated to the twenty-fifth floor. Just give me their names and I'll clear them for transfer and access. I can make a recommendation for your administrative staff, if you like, or you can hire a personal secretary yourself from the outside. You don't have to go through Human Resources." The woman studied his face and then grinned. "You're in shock, right?"

He nodded.

"Go home and take tomorrow off. Let all this sink in. Then come back on Wednesday and we'll work out all the details."

"Th-thanks." Dante started out of the office, but stopped before reaching the door. "Why is he doing this? Can you explain it?"

Rose stood, resting against her desk, and took a moment to contemplate his questions. "He gave Victor the same sort of direction a year ago. And you can see what sort of mess Vic made out of the opportunity. He took advantage of his father, stole money, and produced practically nothing. Your team kept the division afloat without any real leadership or guidance. So by giving you the same opportunity, Mr. Smithfield wants to prove that his idea is sound. It was just his faith in his son that was badly placed."

"I thought blood was thicker than water."

She shook her head. "You have to remember—Alistair is an old-school newsman at heart. Blood may be thicker than water, but it's not as thick as ink."

As soon as Dante exited the TwentyFourSeven headquarters, he called Angela. He'd sent her back to her hotel as soon as the investigators decided she wasn't a person of interest. Luckily, she'd been interviewed by a female investigator and had remained "herself."

Angela answered on the first ring. "Thank God. I was starting to worry."

"Sorry about that. Everything's fine. Better than fine. You hungry?"

"Starved."

"You wanna go out or eat in?" As soon as he said the words, he realized it was a foolish question. "Strike that. What would you like me to pick up? Between here and there, there's Chinese, Mexican, a Thai place, Moroccan, a couple of sandwich shops, a good pizza place and—"

"Pizza. Anything with meat."

"You got it. I'll be there in a half hour or so."

True to his word, Dante showed up at Angela's door twenty-nine minutes later. When she answered his knock, she found him juggling a bottle of champagne, a bottle of wine, a pizza box, and a full grocery bag.

Another half hour later, she sat on the bed, dotting at the crumbs from the empty pizza box. He'd told her all the things that had happened after she'd left including the good news of his promotion, which had required the champagne for a toast.

Now, Dante sat in the room's only chair, his shoeless feet resting on the edge of the mattress. "I haven't forgotten about Chloe Mason and the research we were doing on her death. I'm sorry it got shuffled under my problems and the resulting excitement."

"That's okay. As hard as it may be to believe, I forgot about her, too. I was too busy becoming someone else to think about her. Or me. Or . . . whoever we are." She felt a twinge behind one eye. "It makes my head hurt, just thinking about her. Me. Us."

"I can imagine so."

They both fell quiet for a moment, busying themselves with faked interest in their empty glasses. Then Dante broke the awkward silence. "I'm curious. How much control do you have when it comes to changing your looks?"

"None, as far as I can tell." She drained her glass and held it out like Oliver Twist asking for seconds. But in her case, it was thirds. Or fourths. She couldn't remember.

Dante turned the bottle upside down to indicate it was empty. A few drops slid onto the floor and he made a face as he rubbed the carpet with his napkin. "When I was in the bathroom, listening to you, I was concerned that the real you had gotten lost somewhere in the . . . what do we call it? Masquerade? Impersonation?"

She mulled over his description. "Neither. It's not like I can just slap on or pull off a new face any time I want, and I'm definitely not pretending to be someone else. Whatever the hell it is that I'm doing, it's real and damn annoying, too, because I don't seem to have much control at all. I can't make it happen when I want and I can't stop it when it does."

"But you did, with Victor. You were completely changed physically, but it looked and sounded like you held on to the inner you. You realized that a taped confession would be the right way to catch him red-handed and you set him up perfectly. If you'd surrendered to his . . . what . . . desire? . . . you wouldn't have asked the right questions or gotten the most damning answers out of him. Maybe it's like any other extraordinary talent; you have to practice to get really good at it."

"Talent," she repeated. "I like that word. It makes me sound less like a freak and more . . ." Her voice trailed off when her vocabulary failed.

"Normal?"

She shook her head. "There's nothing remotely normal about who and what I am."

"True."

His honest answer startled her into silence and she took the opportunity to study his face more closely than she'd dared before. In all honesty, he wasn't a classically handsome man, but he was good-looking in a nondescript sort of way. That is, until he smiled.

When he grinned, the sparkle in his eyes lit up his entire face, turning him from average to extraordinary.

But his looks weren't nearly as important as the man he was inside. After all, this was the man who'd abandoned his duties as a reporter to jump into the Hudson to save her and the baby. At the hospital, he'd possessed the only sane voice in the sea of intrusive voices that swamped her during the press conference. She hung on to that small act of kindness as if it was a life preserver in a sea of sharks. And then he did even more—he fed her, clothed her, housed her . . .

It'd been no accident that she'd turned to him and put her trust in him. It was more than even instinct. There was simply something about the man . . .

She froze.

Am I doing it again? She dug her nails into her palms, hoping that pain would help clear her focus.

He cocked his head. "What's wrong?"

When amorous thoughts invaded her mind, it usually meant only one thing. "Am I . . . am I changing?"

"You mean, right now?"

She gave him a slight nod, worried that any movement might hasten the transformation.

He sat up straighter in his chair and studied her with a sense of concern that both worried her and attracted her. "Not that I can see. Do you feel as if you're starting to change?"

"I can't tell. Look closer." Angela turned her head gingerly from the left to right and back again. "Anything?"

A furrow formed between his eyebrows as he squinted at her. Finally, he pulled back, his scrutiny and his face relaxing. "Honest, I don't see any changes." He pointed to the mirror that hung behind the dresser. "Look for yourself."

Angela shifted, moving closer to the mirror, and studied a face that seemed both familiar and foreign to her. Her reflection looked the same, didn't it? Same blue eyes as before. Same shade of blond hair. She glanced down. Same basic shape. Everything was hers, so to speak, the "hers" that she'd gotten used to since waking up on the plane.

She was still Angela Sands, whoever she might be.

She squeezed her eyes shut. Did that mean that her attraction to him was real? Or was this Angela persona nothing more than the indelible imprint of the innermost desires of the first man she'd met?

Him . . .

He spoke from behind her. "I do see some change now. You're getting a little pale."

"Close your eyes," she commanded.

"Why?"

"Humor me."

She watched him shrug in the mirror and then comply. She turned around to face him and tried to open herself to his thoughts. Even though she heard and felt nothing, she persisted. "I want you to think about the perfect woman for you. Your heart's desire. What does she look like? Tall or short? What color hair and eyes? Think about her and then describe her to me."

"I thought we established that—"

"Dante, please." She hated how her voice shook. Or was it even her voice?

He released a heavy sigh, but still kept his eyes closed.

"Maybe someone from your past," she prompted.

Something flickered in his face.

She could sense that she'd hit a nerve. "There's someone."

He hesitated as if weighing whether he would reveal his thoughts or not. He finally spoke. "She was a professor of mine in college."

"Tell me about her."

"There's not much to say. Dr. Taylor was famous for picking a male graduate student each year to be her TA, her teaching assistant. But it didn't take long to realize that the TA's duties extended beyond the classroom. Had she been a male professor, selecting a female student as a yearlong lover, the university would have been up in arms. But no one seemed to notice or even really mind an older woman choosing a younger man as a temporary lover."

A smile pulled at his lips.

"And you didn't mind either." It was a statement rather than a question. Was she reading his mind or simply his expression?

"It should have bothered me, but in reality, it was fantastic. Even though I'd dated and been with college girls, I was still pretty inexperienced when it came to women. She took care of that fast. My God, that woman was insatiable. But it wasn't all sex. She also taught me how to dress, how to act, how to talk to people . . . talents I needed to learn in order to become a better journalist. At the end, she gave me a fantastic reference and used her authority to set me up at a series of jobs that eventually landed me here."

"How long did you two last?"

"Nine beautiful months."

"That's not very long. Why did you break up?"

His smile flickered, then faded. "Because the academic year was over. Time for me to graduate and step out into the real world. And time for her to select her next lover for the following year."

She ignored the twinge of jealousy that knocked at her conscience. "And this Dr. Taylor, she's your ideal woman?"

"I guess so. At least she's the one person I'd do anything to be with again."

"Why can't you be with her?"

His head dropped along with a perceptible drop in his spirits. "She died three months later. Ovarian cancer. She never even had a chance to pick the next lucky bastard. So I was her last lover." He paused then cleared his throat as if trying to clear away the emotion that accompanied his words. "I'd give anything to see her again. Anything."

Angela closed her eyes. The strength of his raw emotion must be the key to helping her to transform. She'd looked into Victor's mind and automatically rebuilt herself to match his fondest desires. Could she do the same with Dante's, even if she couldn't actually view his thoughts?

She waited but nothing happened.

Was there something she had to do to start the process? Some trigger?

"Think harder," she demanded.

After a long minute, she told herself that the sensations she felt must mean some sort of transformation was taking place. She was concentrating so hard she barely heard Dante when he spoke.

"Angela? Stop it."

She felt him shaking her shoulder.

"Stop before you hurt yourself."

"What?"

When she opened her eyes, all she could see was his face, creased with concern.

"Did it work?" Did her voice sound different?

He gently turned her around toward the mirror where she saw Angela Sands staring back, tears streaking her cheeks. Dante stood behind her, his sad smile reflecting in the mirror.

"Nothing happened. You don't look anything like Maggie. You're still you."

"Maggie? Oh. Her."

"Yes. Her. The woman I loved. The woman who loved me. Who made me." He abandoned his position beside Angela and walked over to the window where he looked into the courtyard below. After a moment, he turned away from the view and the memories that evidently had had a temporary hold on him. "I'm not sure what you were trying to prove with all that. Was that supposed to be a test of your abilities or were you testing me?"

"I suppose both."

"Did I fail?"

Did he? The answer came quickly from her heart. "No. You won."

He stared at her without comprehension. "Come again?"

"Whatever I feel for you, it appears to be an honest emotion. My own emotion."

He caught her in a dark gaze that rocked her to her shoes. "What do you feel for me?"

"I'm not sure."

"Will you tell me when you figure it out?" he said softly.

She nodded, unable to trust her voice.

"Good. I'm going to leave now. I think it's the best thing to do."

She reached up and grabbed his arm. "Don't go."

He patted her hand and then with great deliberation and even greater care, he pulled his arm out of her grip. "I'm not sure this is a complication that either of us need right now," he said in a hoarse voice.

"But I want you," she said simply.

He swallowed hard. "I know, and I want you. But I'm not sure if it's my own idea or one coming from you. Let me go home and sort things out. And tomorrow, we'll talk about it again. Okay?"

Angela couldn't trust herself to speak, so she nodded. She remained in place when he closed the door after himself.

What if he was right? What if the desire he felt for her was simply forced on him, by these strange talents she possessed?

The answer was simple.

Either I learn to control my talents or they're going to ruin my life.

19

It took over an hour before Angela gathered enough courage to go downstairs to the lobby bar. Luckily, there were only a few patrons there and she was able to select a booth in the back corner of the room.

She had a mission.

The only way she'd learn how to control what she did would be to practice.

First, she limited her exposure to one man at a time. She didn't try to encounter them, just sit close enough to them to pick up on their desires. She'd purchased a small hand mirror in the hotel gift shop and surreptitiously monitored her appearance. At the first signs of any changes, she got up and moved away.

After a while, she didn't need the mirror to recognize the initial indicators of imminent change. Just prior to the first moments of transformation, she experienced a buzz in the back of her head and the sensation of something like a spiderweb brushing against her arms.

Each time she started to experience the feelings, she ducked into the women's restroom, putting the maximum amount of distance between her and the man whose desires she was reading.

After about a dozen encounters, she delayed her escape, allowing herself to change a bit more before she hightailed it to safety. The first three times she tried it, she managed to get away before the transformation got out of hand. But a fourth attempt went badly when someone blocked her escape route. She barely made it to safety in time.

I can't do this by myself.

There was only one person who could help her—Dante. But how could she call him for help after the way they parted only a few hours earlier?

She couldn't bring him into this, not until she established better control over her talents.

She heard the door scrape open and the female bartender walked into the restroom.

"You okay in here?"

Angela nodded. "I'm fine."

"It's just that you keep running in here. Like you're trying to hide from someone." The woman crossed her arms. "Like the cops. If so, get out. I don't tolerate stuff like that in my establishment."

"No one's looking for me. It's . . . it's hard to explain."

The woman uncrossed her arms long enough to consult her watch. "I have five minutes. Talk."

Angela ran through a dozen explanations in her head, settling on the one that sounded the least implausible. "You know how there are people who are afraid of heights and they try to overcome their fears by deliberately climbing to increasingly higher places?"

The bartender looked unimpressed. "It's called desensitization. It's a behavior modification technique." Before Angela could remark, the woman lifted one shoulder in a shrug. "I have a degree in psychology. So, what's your problem? Alcohol?"

"No. Men."

The woman relaxed and turned to the mirror to adjust her hair. "Join the club, sister. Men are the great mystery of life."

"Especially to a nymphomaniac."

The woman spun around to face Angela. "No shit? For real?"

"I love men," Angela said with a dramatic sigh. "I can't get enough of them. I'd gladly jump the bones of any man out there."

The bartender glanced toward the door. "I wouldn't touch half of those guys with a ten-foot pole much less want to screw them."

"I'm like an alcoholic. I see the man, I tell myself I don't need or want him, but then I suddenly find myself wanting him and asking him if he would like to go back to my place and have sex."

"So you're a nymphomaniac, trying to desensitize yourself?"

Angela nodded. "Exactly that. Every time I'm around a man and I don't proposition him, I figure I'm getting a little bit better. But I have to have a place I can retreat to if the temptation gets too hard to ignore."

"Temptation," the woman repeated. "Well, if it works for you, I'm cool with it. Good luck." She turned toward the door.

"Wait," Angela said, stepping in the woman's path. "I could really use your help."

The woman crossed her arms again, her sense of doubt reengaged. "Doing what?"

Angela reached into her pocket and pulled out three twenties. "Help me. Don't let me leave with anybody."

The woman stared at the money, but didn't reach for it. "Let me get this straight. You want to pay me sixty dollars to keep an eye on you and not let you leave the place with any man."

"Exactly."

"How am I supposed to stop you?"

Angela held out her hand, indicating the room. "Get me in here. Push, pull, or threaten me. Whatever it takes. Just get me in here even for a moment. That's all it'll take and I'll snap out of it."

"Seriously?"

"Seriously."

The woman stared at the proffered money for several seconds, then shrugged and plucked the bills from Angela's hand. "You got a deal. But I get off at midnight. That's four hours from now." She paused before heading out the door. "By the way, I'm Jenna."

"I'm Angela. Thanks."

During the rest of the night, Angela managed to retain enough control to remove herself from harm's way all but three times. In two of those encounters, she was vaguely aware of Jenna hauling her into the bathroom. Each time, the more distance between Angela and her quarry, the more control she retained.

But it was during the last incident that things came close to going terribly wrong.

A nearby theater had let out and the empty bar filled up quickly with couples. Up to that point, there had been plenty of single guys but plenty of space. But now, every inch of the bar was filled with humans. She couldn't even walk to the restroom without bumping into people. Every time she made inadvertent physical contact with any man, her libido went crazy.

Although she thought she'd made progress in terms of how long she could be in the presence of a man before starting to transform, a crowded bar was more than she could take.

As her control began to weaken, she tried to flag down Jenna, but the bartender was busy taking orders and serving customers.

Angela headed for the restroom, only to see a line of women waiting to use the facilities. Cut off from that avenue of escape, her only other choice was to open the door that was marked "Employees Only." Although the room was empty, it also had no other doors.

Angela shoved a chair under the doorknob and then pushed herself into the corner farthest from the door. There, she contemplated her options; she was stuck there until the bar cleared.

Or a man walked in on her.

Or . . . she got help.

As much as she didn't want to do it, she pulled out her cell and dialed the only number she knew.

Fifteen minutes later, she heard a knock on the door.

"Angela?"

It was Dante. She uncurled herself from her hiding place, tugged the chair free, and slid back into her hiding place. The door opened inward and a wedge of light sliced the room.

"Angela? You okay?"

"Close the door," she whispered. Once he complied, she scrambled out and threw her arms around him. To her relief, nothing happened. No buzz, no spiderwebs. Instead, she felt comfort and strength.

"What happened?"

"I figured that the best way to get control of my talents was to practice."

He stepped back in order to see her eye to eye. "Here? Are you crazy?"

So much for comfort. She wriggled free of his embrace. "Nice thing to say to a woman who checked herself out of the nut ward. For your information, the bar wasn't busy for most of the evening. It wasn't until eleven-thirty or so when a bunch of people came in and it got suddenly crowded."

"Bars tend to do that."

She punched him in the arm. "You're supposed to be impressed with my initiative."

"I'd be more impressed if it wasn't after midnight." His voice softened. "You didn't have to do this by yourself. You know I would have helped you."

"I know. I just needed to prove something to myself." She felt her stomach twist. "That I'm not a freak."

He pulled her into his arms again for another embrace. "You're not a freak. You're a miracle. You're a superwoman. Wonder Woman, even. All you lack is that outfit. You know? The gravity-defying bustier with the eagle on it and the striped cheerleader short-shorts? Don't forget the hair. That raven-black flip and the golden tiara."

She leaned into his strength and warmth. "You spend entirely too much time fantasizing about comic-book women."

She felt his body shake as he laughed. "It's a logical step in a young boy's sexual awakening. First, you lust over impossibly drawn women in comic books, then you switch to impossibly airbrushed women in your dad's *Playboy*s." He squeezed her and then released her, to her regret.

"So . . . you're still horny for Wonder Woman?"

He nodded. "Ever since I was nine and inherited my cousin Dennis's comic-book collection."

"She's your heart's desire? A secret passion for you?"

His nostalgic expression faded. "Yes, and why are you so interested in my taste in reading material?"

"I'm more interested in your taste in women." She pointed to her face. "I'm still me. Right?"

He nodded.

"Even though you're thinking about Wonder Woman, recalling her with fondness, maybe even desire, I'm not changing, right?" She reached up and pulled at a strand of her own hair. "No change in my hair color, right?" She tapped her forehead. "My eyes are still blue, right?"

"Wonder Woman has blue eyes. But the point is—she's not real."

"She is to the nine-year-old boy inside of you. Your memories of her are just as real as those of your Dr. Taylor." As soon as she said the name, she saw his eyes shutter and his lips tighten. It was a name she shouldn't have used.

"I'm sorry," she said quickly. "I shouldn't have said that. One was a dream, the other was reality. I didn't mean to equate the two."

He drew a deep breath and his shoulders dropped perceptibly. "It's okay. I understand what you're getting at. Real or not, both are desires of the heart."

Relieved, she continued. "Exactly. And that's what I seem to pick up. Desires of the heart. But nothing's happening to me. I'm not turning into Wonder Woman, even though for a moment there, you were filled with desire for her. I didn't change. What you think doesn't affect me so I'm pretty sure that the reverse is true, too."

"Meaning . . ."

"What I feel for you, what you feel for me, are honest emotions, not the effect of some supernatural emotional boomerang."

He studied her quietly.

Evidently, she hadn't made her case quite yet. "If I could control or at least influence you, I'd have you pull me into your arms and kiss me like they do in the movies."

His smile formed slowly. "Like this?" He swept her up, and with perfect cinematic staging, dipped her into a classic hero-wins-the-girl position.

"I want it on the record that this is all your doing," she said, leaning backward, suspended in his arms.

"Duly noted."

"And I was thinking about a position a little less . . . precarious."

He pulled her more upright and closer. "This better?"

"Yes."

He stared deeply into her eyes. "Now what?"

"You kiss me."

"I think I can do that." He leaned down slowly, his lips brushing hers, then he—

The door burst open and Jenna the bartender appeared as a silhouette in the doorway. She slapped the small Billy club she held against the wooden door frame. It made a walloping sound that neither marauding attacker nor amorous lover could ignore.

"Step away from the lady," she growled.

Dante's muscles tightened and he swung Angela behind him, raising his palms as a gesture of peace. "Everything's okay, ma'am."

Angela peered from around Dante. "It's okay, Jenna. I know him."

"Sure you do. I've been watching you all night. You've not met a stranger yet." She used the club as an instrument of direction. "Step out from around him and come to me." The bartender almost snarled at Dante. "Touch her and I'll beat the holy crap out of you."

Dante raised his hands higher and stepped aside, giving Angela a clear pathway to the door. "What'd you do? Hire a bodyguard?"

"Sorta." She turned to her self-proclaimed rescuer. "Jenna, really! It's okay. He's not like the others."

"Sure he's not. C'mon, Angela," the bartender demanded. Once Angela moved closer, the woman shifted so that she stood between Angela and Dante and he had a clear path to the door. "Get out. And don't come back."

Dante appeared somewhat amused about the situation because he wore a broad smile as he kept his hands up and sidestepped to the door. Before he left, he paused and winked at Angela. "You sure your talent doesn't work on some women, too?"

Angela opened her mouth to answer, then clamped it shut. Did it? She hadn't anticipated that. Had sixty dollars bought Jenna's elevated sense of protection or had Angela influenced her somehow?

Dante's expression turned into a full-blown grin. "Food for thought, eh?" He stepped out and then appeared in the open doorway. "Oh, by the way, I'll pick you up in the morning at eight. You just became my new assistant. Good night."

Jenna remained in place for a full ten seconds before relaxing. "Do you actually know that asshole?"

Angela nodded, still trying to cling to the glorious haze surrounding their interrupted kiss.

"Who is he?"

"Evidently, my new boss."

20

By ten o'clock, Dante was comfortably situated in his new office, poring over employee files in order to assemble his own reporting team. Rose, the Old Man's secretary, had provided him with a temporary secretary named Selma Todd, who knew almost as much as Rose did when it came to slicing through red tape. Not only did she know where the bodies were buried, but Dante had a sneaking suspicion that she had had a hand in digging the graves.

However alike the two women were in their knowledge, they differed in looks. Rose had a sense of quiet gentility about her and Selma looked like she'd be far more comfortable singing karaoke in a biker bar.

Selma didn't even bat an eye when he introduced Angela as his new production assistant. "You're that chick who survived the Hudson crash, right?"

"Yes."

Selma cracked a small smile. "Good going, saving the kid and all that. Guess that's where the two of you met." The smile faded. "So, can you type?"

"I don't know. I've never tried."

Selma showed no reaction. "Know anything about editing?"

"No. I can read and write, though."

"I'm thrilled," Selma deadpanned. "Ever use a video camera before?"

"No, but I'm willing to learn."

Selma looked at Dante and shrugged. "Eh . . . I've done more with less." She turned back to Angela. "At least you don't overestimate your skills. You'll be okay. But we gotta do something about your clothes."

When Dante started to protest, Selma held up one acrylic-tipped forefinger. "Hang on." She used the other forefinger to tap out a telephone number. "Don't worry, boss. I'll take care of it."

Five minutes later, Francisco No-last-name-because-those-are-so-very-bourgeois circled around Angela, taking notes and spouting words like *prêt-à-porter, haute couture,* and *fashion tribes.*

When the man began touching Angela under the guise of measuring her, Dante cringed. Would Francisco's proximity have the usual detrimental effect on her? Dante watched her face carefully as Francisco made physical contact. At the first sign of any erosion in her self-control, he planned to grab her and pull her into his private office.

But her pinched look of fear faded quickly away without any other visible transformation. She began to relax and even smiled when responding to Francisco's suggestions and answering his questions about color and style preferences.

After the man finished reviewing her measurements and answers, Selma and he huddled in deep discussion, leaving Angela and Dante free for a moment.

"I guess that answers one important question," Angela whispered to Dante.

"Gay guys don't affect you?"

"Evidently not. And that makes sense. I can't become their heart's desire or the object of their lust."

"Good to know."

"On the other hand, I can still read his desires and I'm pleased to say he's extremely attracted to you."

"I think that was fairly obvious." Dante had been trying to ignore the occasional come-hither eye contact from Francisco.

"True."

The young man broke off from his heated discussion with Selma and turned to Dante. "Mr. Kearns, sir, Selma and I are at an impasse. She insists that I select off-the-rack for Miss Sands whereas I believe she'd look scrumptious in Valentino or Lagerfeld. She's got the right figure, the right look—"

Selma harrumphed. "Frankie, she's a working woman, not a dress-up doll. The only reason why you want to outfit her up like a model is because she looks like she hasn't had a decent meal in months." The older woman balanced her fists on her generous hips as she turned to Angela. "You gonna stay wafer-thin or are you going to put some meat on your bones?"

"I think she looks too thin," Dante offered.

"She's perfect the way she is!" Francisco said, his voice growing shriller.

"C'mon. She's practically emaciated," Selma countered.

"Stop. You're all acting as if I'm not here."

It was evident from Angela's tone of voice that she'd had enough of the discussion. Dante tried not to smile.

Now that she had their collective attention, she continued. "I'm thin because I'm poor. Food costs money." Then she turned to Dante. "Thanks to getting this job, I don't expect to remain destitute for long." She turned to Selma. "So yes, I'll probably gain some weight back. Not a lot, but enough to be healthy." She pivoted to face Francisco. "And all I need for a wardrobe are basics. Nothing fancy. I need to look professional and nice. I don't need designer clothes to do that, right?"

Francisco pouted. "I guess not."

"Get her one designer outfit," Dante suggested. "A really nice dress or something." He turned to Angela and held up his hands before she could protest. "Just one, in case you have to go anywhere special or highbrow or something like that. As a part of the job," he added quickly.

She shrugged in defeat. "Okay. One."

Francisco brightened. "Excellent! Then I'll be back before lunch with a new wardrobe for you. Ta-da!" He sprinted for the door and disappeared.

Dante turned to Selma. "Does he work for us?"

Selma nodded. "He's in charge of wardrobe for the television division."

"Did you . . . er . . . we give him a budget or something?"

She plopped down at her desk. "Don't need to. He manages the wardrobe for all the on-air talent and can pull from their collections. They'll never miss it." She consulted the computer on her desk. "What next, boss? You finished reviewing the employee records, yet?"

"Let me go over them one last time." He motioned for Angela to accompany him into the inner office. Once she stepped inside, he closed the door behind her. "God only knows what Selma thinks we're doing in here."

Angela dropped into the chair across from his desk. "Yeah, between my lack of skills and lack of wardrobe, I'm coming across as the ultimate gold digger. But she's much too polite to say anything."

"Then let's change her mind." He sat down at the desk and

pushed a pile of folders toward her. "These are the people I'm going to tap for my team."

Angela thumbed through the folders, seeing an early pattern in the first few selections. She checked the rest of them, seeing the pattern hold strong. "Interesting," she observed. "They're all women."

He grinned. "You noticed."

"Who could miss that? If Selma doesn't think you're a playboy now, she sure will when you assemble this team. And she won't be the only one who thinks this."

"I don't care what people think. I'm choosing these women because they're extraordinarily good at what they do."

"And they're all women," Angela prompted.

"And they just happen to be women. And right now, it's the right team dynamic. You can work closely with them with absolutely no complications. My only problem is that I don't have a camera operator. But I think I might know someone right for the job. She's coming in for an interview at eleven."

"So, once you get your team put together, what's going to be our first story?"

He reached into the middle drawer and pulled out another folder which he slid across to her. "The unfortunate death of Chloe Mason."

"I don't understand," the young woman said, shifting the video camera from her shoulder. "If it's not a live broadcast, why are we using a remote truck?"

Luckily, Dante had anticipated the question. During his interview, he'd realized how incredibly sharp Ivy Grant was. "Practice. We're a new team and I want to make sure that when it comes time for a live shoot, we can do it error-free. This way, we get used to the equipment."

In reality, he'd devised the plan so that Angela could see and hear what was going on while sitting in safe isolation in the remote truck.

"I'll be your eyes and ears," he'd explained to her. At her protest, he held up his hands. "Temporarily. Until you feel like you're in control of your talents."

She'd grumbled then and was still grumbling, but he knew she was safe, sitting next to Althea Canton, learning the ins and outs of on-site editing and remote uplinks. Althea was the best in the business and had seemed intrigued by the idea of working with Dante and his all-female crew.

He adjusted his IFB. "Test. Test. Angela, can you hear me?"

"*Roger. I mean, yes,*" she said in his earpiece.

"Keep it rolling, this first time out," Dante instructed Ivy. "Then when you see our edited version, you'll get a better idea of what sort of shots Althea and I prefer."

"You got it, boss." Ivy had quickly picked up the nickname from Selma, who had already petitioned to move from temporary status to permanent. Ivy swung the camera up and took some establishing shots of the museum entrance and signs.

The head docent, a Ms. Hale, met them just inside the entrance, quickly closing the door behind them.

"Come in, please. Sunlight is bad for our displays," she explained. She turned to Ivy. "You won't use any harsh lights, will you?"

"No, ma'am," Ivy answered promptly. "I can adjust the camera to shoot using the existing light."

"Good." She turned to Dante. "I'm Thomasina Hale. I believe we spoke on the phone?"

Dante took one look at Ms. Hale and knew that he would accidentally call her Ms. Pale at least once. She had the ashen complexion of an academician who seldom pulled her nose out of her books long enough to see actual daylight.

"I don't remember the name," Angela offered in his ear.

"We appreciate the opportunity to talk to you and to see your museum."

"Not half as much as we appreciate the potential publicity. It's hard to run a place like this on donations alone. Upkeep and expenses eat up most of our funding, leaving very little for promotion."

"Hopefully we can help drum up some business for you. How about a tour?"

Dante and Ivy trailed the woman as she led them through the museum devoted to re-creating the look of an early-twentieth-century tenement house with each apartment reflecting immigrants from different countries.

"My great-grandparents lived in a place like this," Ivy commented. "I've seen pictures of it."

Ms. Hale smiled. "How many children did they have?"

"Six." Ivy looked around and her mouth dropped open. "I never realized these places were so small. Can you imagine? Six kids in a one-bedroom flat?"

"The family that originally lived here had eight children. Luckily, the father had a camera and we've been able to rely on the photos he took to reconstruct their whole house. Everything you see is either an antique, matching their original furnishings, or a faithful reproduction." She opened a kitchen cabinet, indicating the various vintage-labeled foodstuffs, some old and faded and others bright and clean. "In the case of the other three apartments, they reflect likely furnishings of the time period, country of origin, and ethnicity. We don't have pictures or written accounts from the previous occupants."

"Irish. Ask her if the people who lived there were Irish."

"So, this apartment reflects what nationality?"

"Irish. The O'Flannery family lived here for forty years." The woman continued her spiel as she led them through the rest of the museum. They finally ended up in her office. Ivy stationed herself in a corner and kept the camera rolling. Dante sat across from the woman and consulted his notebook as if reminding himself of questions to ask. In reality, he knew exactly how and where to steer the conversation.

"I understand that the museum might be receiving an endowment from a former docent, a Chloe Mason?"

What little color the woman's face possessed drained out.

"Talk about a physical reaction," Angela exclaimed, a bit too loudly. *"Is that regret or guilt?"*

Dante reached for his control pack at his waist and turned down the volume a bit.

Ms. Pale . . . er . . . Hale continued. "I know she intended to put us in her will, but it appears that she never had a chance. We're hoping her husband will respect her wishes, but at this point, there's no guarantee."

"I understand she was murdered. It occurred in this general vicinity, correct?"

Ms. Hale stiffened. "Please. I want to assure you and anyone watching that this is an extremely safe neighborhood. The police described the attack on Mrs. Mason as completely random. Plus, it happened in mid-morning on a day she was supposed to be off. No one even knows why she was here in the first place."

"It's never a good idea to take a shortcut through an alley, even in the middle of the day."

Dante closed his notebook. "We won't go into the circumstances around her unfortunate death, but I would like to discuss the impact of her death on your organization. She was more than a benefactor. She was also one of your volunteers."

"A very dedicated volunteer—one of our favorites. Chloe worked here three days a week, giving tours, researching our displays. She acted as a bridge between the museum and some very wealthy patrons. Now, with her gone, we'll probably lose half of our donation base. And we've even noticed a drop-off in our numbers because people have become wary of the neighborhood."

"Sounds like she misses the money more than the person."

Dante turned the volume down even more, now debating the logic of giving Angela the ability to be a persistent little voice in his ear while he was trying to talk to others. "Then that makes this story that much important; the human-interest angle. What happens when a worthy organization like yours loses a key volunteer? How do you adjust? What repercussions are there? And what about the unfair assumptions that it's not safe here thanks to one unfortunate incident. Your museum represents a living snapshot of history that needs to be protected and cherished."

The woman clapped her hands. "Exactly. You get it! And you don't know how much I appreciate that."

"Excellent. Let's start with Ms. Mason. Tell me about her."

The woman launched into a description of Chloe Mason, painting her as both a saint and a savior. "She is . . . er . . . was a real lover of history and of the city. Chloe not only researched what items should be on display in the museum but she often hunted them down in antique shops and acquired them on our behalf."

Angela's voice was faint in Dante's ear. *"She liked to shop. So that's a reason to canonize her?"*

Ms. Hale stared off in the distance, a smile tugging at her lips. "Chloe really knew how to wring the most out of a buck, too. She could bargain with the best of them. I can remember an excursion we took together and I saw firsthand how well she wheeled and dealed. She talked one dealer into giving us some key furniture pieces on 'permanent loan.' It's not often you find someone so wealthy with such an everyday sense of money."

"So you'd call her a penny-pincher?"

"Oh, no." Ms. Hale shook her head as if shaking away the

memories. "On the contrary, you'd never meet a more generous woman. When we had a problem with our furnace last winter? Chloe was the one who called out a repairman on a holiday and covered the extra cost. It was easy to forget she was extraordinarily wealthy until something like that happened."

"Sounds like she was one of a kind. Her family must be devastated by her death."

A guarded look dropped over Ms. Hale's face. "I'm sure they must. I can't say I ever met her husband. I do know they had no children." She leaned forward and lowered her voice in an air of conspiracy. "I suspect that's why she devoted so much time to the museum. Chloe especially loved leading the school tours. She was so great with kids."

"And yet her husband never came around to see what occupied so much of his wife's time?"

Ms. Hale made a dismissive gesture. "I'm sure he's a very busy man with a lot of important business. I've been trying to contact him about some of Chloe's personal possessions that she kept here, but he hasn't returned my calls. I suppose I'll just box them up and send them to him."

"What sort of personal belongings? Could I see them?" Angela's voice rang in Dante's ear.

"Could we be permitted to film them?" he said. "They'd make a poignant counterpoint to the museum's story, and to Chloe's story."

"I'm not sure," Ms. Hale said.

"When my aunt died, my uncle couldn't bear to deal with her personal effects for over a year. Mr. Mason is probably still mourning his wife. But it seems a shame for our viewers to lose the opportunity to see what this museum meant to her."

Angela remained a persistent buzz in his ear. *"Make her show them to you. And while you're at it, ask her—"*

He reached around to the control box and thumbed the volume

control down yet again. With Angela sufficiently muted, Dante asked Ms. Hale a half-dozen other questions about the museum in general. The woman's answers were as enthusiastic as they were long-winded. After twenty minutes of minutiae in which he had little interest, he sprung his trap. "Could we have just a look at Chloe Mason's box? It makes such a lovely visual to end the piece with. You've made Chloe Mason come alive in this interview."

Ms. Hale hesitated, then nodded. She retrieved a battered cardboard box from the credenza in her office, set it on her desk, and opened it.

Dante gestured Ivy forward to film it, but he couldn't resist taking a peek in the box himself.

It was sad, looking at the detritus of a dead woman's life. He saw a docent's badge with Chloe's picture on it, a few pretty bits of art that had probably adorned the dead woman's cubby, and a snapshot of Chloe standing in front of the museum with a small group of well-heeled people, probably fellow donors. She looked so happy, but in the background was the entry to the alley where she'd lost her life. It was like seeing into the future, where her existance would be cut brutally short. In his earpiece, he could hear the muted sound of Angela sobbing. The sound wrenched at his guts until it felt like he was tearing apart.

To take his mind off Angela's pain for the moment, he focused on the artifacts in front of him. Notably absent was any picture of Chloe with her husband. Dante thought that spoke volumes about her relationship with the man. He'd cut her out of his life long before her life had ended.

"I hate to leave you, Ms. Hale, but I'm afraid we have another appointment we must make. However, I do want to run with this story. Can we come back and do a more formal interview, say, next week? Maybe we can arrange to be here during a school tour and we can show how important it is to protect this special segment of New York City history."

Her face brightened. "That would be wonderful."

"What say I call you the beginning of next week and we can set things up then?"

She rose and shook his hand with more energy than he expected. "Thank you so much, Mr. Kearns. I'm looking forward to it."

As soon as they hit the stoop and the museum doors closed behind them, Ivy turned to Dante.

"What in the hell was that? You're not interested in the museum. You're chasing the story about the murdered woman."

He pulled the IFB out of his ear and the battery pack out of his waistband and pocketed both. Angela's sobs were going to make him lose focus if he wasn't careful. He needed to get back to her. But he had a job to do first. "Was I that obvious?"

Ivy pursed her lips in thought. "Not that Ms. Pale Hale would notice. But I did. What gives?"

He crooked a finger. "Follow me."

Dante had studied the police reports including photos and a CAD drawing of the crime scene. He led her straight to the alley.

"Get this from every angle."

She complied, hoisting up the camera and starting to shoot.

He went to the alley entrance and then turned left into a small setback in the back wall of the museum. It had once been a doorway, but was now bricked up. There was another active entrance that appeared to be the museum's back door.

"The body was found here, tucked back in this alcove, completely out of sight from all angles. She'd come by cab and had been dropped off at the corner because the museum is on a one-way street. The cabbie didn't see anything. The police believe the assailant might have been hiding here, next to the garbage cans."

Ivy aimed at the cans. "Not much room to hide there. He had to be small."

"That's because there's no garbage there right now. The businesses in the area had set out their trash for pickup. So there were a lot of bags and boxes there at mid-morning, creating plenty of places for an attacker to hide. The cab left her at nine-fifty but she wasn't discovered until almost ten-twenty by a sanitation crew. EMS responded, treated her on the scene, and were in transit to St. James when she expired. COD was gunshot trauma."

"You sound like a cop."

"It helps to think like one when you're doing a crime story. Get acquainted with the facts, first. There will be room for speculation and supposition after that. For instance, stand here." He indicated the spot where the EMS said they found the body. "Shoot up and tell me why there weren't any witnesses."

Ivy complied. "No direct line of sight from any window." She continued to scan the area. "What about security cameras? On TV, there's always a convenient ATM or traffic camera."

Dante shook his head. "That's only on television. We're not that lucky here. In reality, the only two people who know what really happened appear to be the victim and her assailant."

Ivy continued to shoot the area. "And the victim's dead. Too bad you can't bring in a sensitive to read the scene."

A chill danced down his spine. He wondered what Angela had read in the information they were recording. "A sensitive?"

Ivy nodded. "Someone attuned to ghosts and the spirit world. My dad says it's all bunkum, but I have a cousin Winona who can walk into almost any place and find ghosts lurking there. It's really creepy."

"You believe in stuff like that?"

"Only because I've seen her in action. When she describes what or who she sees, you oughta see the reactions of the people who live or work there. She's always right on the nose. That's why I believe in her. I know it's not a scam. I'm not too sure about other so-called psychics."

"I'll keep your cousin in mind in case we decide to go that route." He thumbed toward the truck. "Let's head back and see what Althea's done with your test footage."

When they arrived at the panel truck, Angela jumped out to greet them. Dante could tell she was still very upset. He made an excuse to send Ivy into the truck and for him and Angela to remain outside.

"I'm sorry I had to put you through that," he said.

"It was like staring back into Chloe's mind. I remembered what it was like to be there in that museum. I remembered bits from the day I died, even if it's not completely clear to me." She sniffed, pulled out a tissue, and wiped her eyes. "You realize that Althea now thinks I'm an emotional wreck." Then she squared her shoulders. Dante could almost see the switch from the vulnerable Chloe to the angry Angela Sands. "I know enough now to put the fear of God into Lars Mason. Ivy's idea is the perfect solution," she whispered.

"Which idea?"

"About her cousin the psychic. Only I can pretend to be one, instead. That way I can appear to be talking to the ghost of Chloe Mason and letting 'her' describe how she died. But in reality, I'll be describing what I remember."

"But you're not all that clear on the details, yourself."

"I'm a lot clearer now. And I want Lars to pay for what he did to Chloe. If he is guilty, he won't be able to correct me without tipping his hand. If he's innocent, then he won't know when I'm right and when I'm wrong. Best of all, I'll be able to read his mind and tell one from the other."

"That might work, but do you really want to risk being in the same room as the man who may have killed you? What if he buys your act and decides that you know too much? If he got rid of his wife, I doubt he'd think twice about getting rid of a possible witness."

The excitement in her eyes drained out. "I . . . I didn't think about that."

"What we have to do is play it safe. That's the only way I'm willing to run this." A pair of men walked toward them in deep conversation. It was an automatic reflex for Dante to shift so that he stood between them and Angela.

She noticed the men and shot them a smile as they walked by. Had she been any other woman, Dante would have considered the action to be nothing more than an innocent gesture, maybe more appropriate to middle America than midtown Manhattan. But given Angela's abilities, such a smile might be an overture to something complicated.

The men both smiled back.

Far more complicated.

Dante shifted again, breaking her line of sight with her new quarry. "I'm still concerned about your talents taking you over," he said in a low voice.

At first, she arched to see around him, then she snapped back, physically and mentally. Whatever attraction she'd felt toward the men, she'd conquered it.

For the moment.

"You know what it's going to take for me to get more control, don't you?"

The word soured his stomach.

Practice.

21

Dante and Angela spent the next four days and nights trying to experiment with her talents with as much scientific detachment as possible. But all the research they did during the day didn't blunt the unsettling feelings Dante experienced each time he witnessed Angela's actions and reactions around various men. It was damn hard to retain his objectivity when watching her various personalities emerge.

They started in the most controlled environment Dante could create—his own office. Under the guise of interviewing potential teammates, they brought in a variety of men, one at a time, seating them in the outer waiting room with Angela acting as secretary. Dante sat in his inner office, monitoring everything via several hidden cameras and microphones.

When each man walked in, Angela would shake their hand,

thereby making brief physical contact, and then she'd offer them a seat near her desk. Then as they waited, she would type up her impressions of the man and instant message them to Dante.

Carlton North. Chair at 10 ft. Ambitious. Wants to make good impression. Overspends. Dating 3 women. Likes blondes. Really likes blondes. Thinks I'm too short.

Feeling anything? he typed back.

Not getting taller.<g>

Good. Wait 3 more mins & send him in.

They continued like this all day, randomly varying the amount of contact and the distance between the man and Angela. Dante had described it as the discovery phase—determining the strength of her reactions at varying distances. Dante only had to intercede four times out of the twenty or so encounters, when Angela's control slipped due to proximity. On the second day, they worked systematically on desensitization, trying to lengthen her exposure and shorten the distance.

By the end of the day, she'd been able to read the thoughts of any man standing two feet away without transforming, as long as there was no contact. However, if he touched her, the only way she could stop the transformation process was to exit the room and put at least one wall between them.

Touching Dante also seemed to help break the connection and she returned to "normal" faster.

During the entire day, Angela only had one situation where she didn't retreat fast enough. Her transformation unfortunately progressed from physical to mental as well. Dante hadn't responded fast enough, thanks to a phone call that had diverted his attention.

As soon as he realized what was happening, Dante charged out of his office. He found Angela, sitting on the desk, her skirt hiked up to reveal some leg. A *lot* of leg. She had already undone the top button of her blouse and was dipping down for a second fastener when he stepped between her and the young intern ogling her.

"Step into my office, please, Mister . . . ?"

The young man tried to tear his gaze from Angela's burgeoning cleavage. "Eastwood. S-Sid Eastwood, sir."

"Just go have a seat while I have a word with my assistant."

When the young man stepped away from Angela, she hopped off the desk as if to follow him.

"Angela, if I may have a word?"

She looked torn as if something in her was commanding her to follow the young man and to complete her transformation based on his fondest dreams. When Dante placed a hand on her shoulder, she pushed it aside and tried to sidestep him.

"Angela, stop." He turned to Sid. "You can close that door behind you. I'll just be a minute."

Sid gulped and nodded, shifting so that he could see the last few tantalizing seconds of the magnificent sight of his ideal woman.

As soon as the door closed, Dante grabbed both her shoulders and shook her lightly. "Angela, get control of yourself."

She glared at him, her eyes filled with anger and confusion, as if she didn't understand why he'd come between her and her chosen man. Then the confusion faded and her expression sharpened. Her posture changed and something snapped back into place.

"Oh, shit. It happened, didn't it?"

He nodded. "If I hadn't stepped in, I'm pretty sure you would have jumped his virginal bones."

"But why him? Why now? I've been closer to other men for longer. What's so special about him that he triggered a change in me? By the time I felt the signs, it was too late. I was already starting to change."

"That's what we have to figure out. There's got to be a pattern we just don't see." He glanced back at the door leading to his office.

"Why don't you go upstairs and let me talk to him." His face darkened. "You definitely don't need to be out here when he leaves."

Angela was trudging toward the stairs when it hit her. "Dante? We did learn one thing, though."

He paused by the door. "What?"

"When you touched me, it stopped my transformation. I began to revert immediately after that."

Dante stared across the room, as if replaying the incident in his mind. "What makes you sure it was me rather than the fact I made him leave the room?"

"I don't know. I just felt it."

He shook his head. "It can't be that easy of an answer, Angela."

"Why not?"

That evening they tested their new theory at a series of crowded public venues: a bar, a restaurant, and an outdoor concert in Central Park. While at the bar, Angela learned that when she and Dante maintained contact, she could keep herself from transforming.

As much of a relief as that was, she quickly learned that the contact didn't help her sort through the dozens of thoughts that bombarded her mind whenever she came within proximity of men.

The more men, the more thoughts assailed her, making her brain swirl.

Dante pulled her out of the bar when she finally admitted that she felt as if her head was about to split open. Once they were on the sidewalk, he pulled her closer, shielding her from the people walking by. "Why didn't you say anything earlier?"

She relaxed as the noises in her head faded away. "How can I get better if I don't keep pushing past the safety zone?"

"I thought we agreed to take this slowly," he said softly, his face a mixture of admiration and concern.

A dam of emotion broke inside of her. Whether it was the result of too many borrowed emotions or thanks to her own feelings, it didn't really matter. The cathartic act of crying and releasing everything she'd held inside was as freeing as it was embarrassing.

To his credit, Dante didn't say, "Don't cry." Instead, he held her, patting her until her gulps subsided. Finally, she drew a deep breath and felt moderately better, as if the pressure inside her had been bled off by her crying jag.

"You okay?"

She nodded, daubing her eyes with her shirtsleeve. "Better." She sniffed and straightened, trying to recover some poise. "Where now?"

He stared at her as if she'd grown a pink sequined horn in the middle of her forehead. "Don't you think it's time to stop for the night?"

"No. Look how far we've gotten. I've learned that with your help, I can keep myself from transforming. I honestly believe the only reason why I had a meltdown was because I got overwhelmed by the number of men in a small space."

"That's why I don't think it's wise to keep pushing." He shot her his most charming smile. "Why don't we call it a night?"

"You can go home if you want"—she pulled out of his loose grasp—"but I'm not finished."

"C'mon, Angela, don't do this." He reached for her again, but she shifted away. His smile faded. "It's not safe for you to be alone."

"I can take care of myself," she retorted, realizing exactly how juvenile she sounded. Glancing through the back into the bar from which she'd just fled, she backpedaled quickly. "Okay, maybe not in there. But I'm not ready to give up for the night. I feel like we're on the verge of figuring this out."

Dante plowed his hand through his hair and then released a deep sigh. "Okay, we'll keep going. Where to next?"

"Central Park."

He winced. "The concert?"

She nodded.

Dante squeezed his eyes closed for a moment. "I know I'm going to regret this." He opened them and stuck out his hand. "Let's go now before I change my mind."

The sun had set about a half hour ago and they could hear strains of music and see a faint glow of lights from the Great Lawn.

The concert was in full swing, the lawn a sea of people seated on blankets or folding chairs. Angela and Dante skirted the edges of the mass of concert-goers and staked out a spot under a stand of trees away from the crowd and on a small rise.

Dante leaned back against the tree trunk. "Now what?"

Angela closed her eyes and listened to the murmur of voices in her head. No single voice stood out. "I don't hear anybody in particular. It's so many thoughts out there that they're all blending into white noise."

"That's a good thing, right?"

"It's easier on my sanity, but it's a poor way to test my talents." She kept her eyes closed, trying to reach out and select one voice, any voice, and listen in. Finally, one voice began to emerge. She imagined it like a fishing line so she reached out mentally and began to reel it in.

The words coalesced in her mind. "*. . . when she said concert, I thought she meant Springsteen or someone like that. I hate this high-brow stuff. I wonder if there's any more beer.*"

Angela couldn't help but grin at her success and her catch.

"You're smiling. Why?"

"Caught one. One of the gentlemen out there prefers rock to Rachmaninoff."

"It's Beethoven."

She cracked open one eye. "I know, but I couldn't figure out a joke using Beethoven."

Dante nodded toward the crowd. "The question is, Which male out there is thinking that?"

Angela opened both eyes and stared at the carpet of people. There were no neon arrows pointing at a specific man. Not a single person was highlighted by an unearthly glow. "Judging by some of the glazed faces I see, a lot of them. But I don't think I can identify the one specific man whose thoughts I'm hearing."

"Try again with someone else."

She kept her eyes open as she tuned into the voices, again picking the strongest one and listening in. This time, she was able to match face and thoughts together.

"Don't turn around. Don't notice me. Don't turn around."

She watched the thief deftly reach into the woman's purse and extract her wallet.

"Pickpocket. Green hoodie. Just lifted the wallet from the lady in pink. Headed this way."

Dante pushed away from the tree. "Damn. Do you want me to go tackle the guy or something?"

"No need. Watch."

She'd picked up a second set of thoughts, this time from an off-duty cop observing the crime in progress. She and Dante watched the officer spring forward and intercept the pickpocket.

"Sweet." Dante turned to her. "Did you do that?"

"Do what?"

"Tell him to jump the pickpocket?"

She hesitated. Her first reaction was to say, "Of course not," but she stopped to think. Had she actually heard the cop's thoughts as he observed the crime? Or had she simply called it to his attention? Pointed him in the right direction?

Made him notice and capture the thief?

"I'm not sure. Maybe."

"Let's test it." He scanned the crowd, then pointed to a nearby knot of people sitting on a blanket, playing cards while listening to the concert. "See the guy in the Yankees cap? Can you make him do something?"

"Like what?"

"I don't know. Stand up and sing. Or—"

A new set of thoughts suddenly thrust themselves into her mind, intrusive and demanding her attention. Instead of words, they were mostly still images, both crude and cruel, of a woman, frozen in mid-scream and begging for release. The man who entertained those thoughts was enjoying the images far too much, finding great pleasure in her pain.

Angela grabbed Dante's arm for balance and in hopes the contact would help her push the intrusive thoughts away. But the degrading images persisted, each frozen image freezing her heart.

Dante braced her, helping her lean against the tree. "What's wrong? What are you hearing?"

Her teeth clenched in sympathetic pain for the female victim. "It's awful," she managed to say. "Awful." In the next image, the man stood over the woman and she cowered in fear.

Angela felt herself shaking, too.

Dante pushed into her face. "Look at me, Angela. Concentrate on me. Whatever is happening, it's not happening to you. You're safe. You're here with me. No one can hurt you."

She took his words and tried to picture them as a transparent shield surrounding her, one that protected and distanced her from the physical horror of what she saw. Slowly, the pain subsided and instead of experiencing the horrific images, they transformed into grainy pictures, projected on a distant screen.

At any time, she could turn on the lights, ending the slide show of terror.

But she watched, mostly out of a deadly sense of curiosity and in hopes of uncovering enough clues to identify the culprit and rescue his victim. If she could just figure out who he was . . .

Dante held her hand tightly. "Tell me what you're seeing," he whispered.

"I think maybe he's looking at pictures, not actual women, but his thoughts are still . . . really raw. He's getting off on their pain, their fear." The image changed to another woman, strung by chains and suspended in a near-impossible position. The image wavered for a bit. "Something's happening. It faded for a moment." The picture reformed. "It's back to a different woman."

Dante continued to hold her hand but his attention was on the crowd.

The image changed rapidly to yet another kneeling woman, bound by over a dozen silk scarves and ball-gagged.

The sudden thunder of applause caused her to jump when the orchestra ended their song. When they started the next tune, the frozen image of the terrified woman folded in on itself.

Angela pulled her hand from Dante's. "The applause caused the images to . . . fold up in the middle like this." She demonstrated with her two palms held out, then closing them together.

"Like the way you'd close up a magazine if you didn't want your dad to see what you were reading?"

"A magazine?" Her knees grew weak in relief

"Yeah. A porno mag." He pointed into the crowd. "See the family in the semicircle of chairs? There? Just behind them is a boy sitting on green plaid blanket. He's reading something. Just a second ago, he was so into his magazine that he was startled by the applause. He stuffed the magazine under the blanket."

She searched the sea of people and spotted the blanket and its lone occupant.

Dante reached over and hugged her. "It's just a teenager, looking at porn. It's not real."

She stared at the young man who couldn't have been more than thirteen. This was no street thug, but a middle-class kid, apparently on a family outing with his two parents and several stair-step siblings.

And what he was looking at wasn't a purloined *Playboy,* stolen from his father's underwear drawer. It was hardcore bondage and submission porn, and this wasn't the first time he'd looked at it.

The thoughts that filtered from his mind to hers revealed the unvarnished truth.

"It's real to him." She turned and grabbed Dante's sleeves. "We have to stop him. We have to let his family know what he's thinking, that he's enjoying what he's seeing."

Dante plowed his hand through his hair for the second time that night. After a moment's hesitation, he finally spoke. "We can't," he said softly.

"But he's dangerous." Why did she have to explain this? Didn't Dante understand? "He might be only reading about it now, but someday, he's going to act on his desires and he's going to hurt someone."

"Angela, we can't become the thought police. People think horrible thoughts every day, but only a few act on them. He's only a teenage boy learning about his sexuality. He's not hurting anyone at the moment and there's no real statistics that suggest he's going to become a monster because he's looking at porn."

"But I know. I can see what's in his heart. I can see how much he enjoys the pain."

"But will he ever transition from thinking about it to doing it?

That we don't know. And until he starts to make that transformation, there's nothing you and I can do."

She pulled away from Dante's grasp and turned away from the concert field, unable to look at the teenager any longer.

"This really sucks," she said, kicking at a discarded paper cup. The remaining ice and drink exploded out, leaving a trail of red liquid across the sidewalk. She shivered when her mind equated the sight to the blood of the young man's first victim, some day in the future.

"What good is this talent if I can't use it to help people?"

Dante reached down and retrieved the cup, tossing it into a trash can. "You can still help people. But not everyone. You just have to choose wisely. Catch them red-handed but before anyone is hurt. But you can't put yourself in the position of judge and jury."

"I can when it comes to Lars Mason. I know he killed me. I don't see why I can't return the favor."

Dante scanned the area, as if afraid of being overheard. Angela didn't care if everyone heard her. She'd shout it from the mountaintops if she thought it'd help.

Dante shifted closer and lowered his voice. "That's exactly what I'm talking about. You can't become his judge and jury. If you kill him, it's murder. But if you want to see him punished for what he did, you have to prove he did it."

"I know he did. I'm living proof."

Dante didn't move a muscle, but continued to stare at her with an eerie sense of serenity. His silent treatment bothered her at first, but she finally calmed down, realizing the absurdity of her words.

She even managed a little laugh. "Living proof. I guess that's the ultimate oxymoron in this case."

He nodded. "I'm all for bringing the asshole to justice, but we have to do it the right way."

"Define 'the right way.'"

"Just like we did Victor. We set him up and wring a confession out of him. He hangs himself and our hands stay clean. Agreed?"

She stuck out her hand. "Agreed."

Too bad she wasn't sure if she was telling the truth or lying. . . .

22

One of the great advantages of Dante's new position was that Selma seemed to not only cut through interoffice red tape but she was able to slice through a lot of the bureaucracy that existed beyond the domain of TwentyFourSeven.

Dante knew that as a reporter, he had a one out of ten shot of getting past the administrative fortress that surrounded a high-profile Wall Street executive like Lars Mason. But Selma didn't even have to storm the moat. All she did was pick up the phone and make one call to arrange an interview.

She didn't even raise an eyebrow when Dante announced that he wanted to hold a meeting at one o'clock with Angela, Selma, Ivy, and Althea—the inner circle. It hadn't gone unnoticed by other employees that Dante had hired only females. Rumors abound and their offices had already received the unfortunate nickname of "the

Harem." Dante found being called "The Sultan" almost as annoying as answering to "Hellboy."

But he and Angela had agreed that in order to pull off their plan to reveal Mason's guilt, they had to bring the three women into their confidence. How else would they be able to explain Angela's role and what strange occurrences that they might witness?

The three women sat around the conference table, Selma and Althea nursing cups of coffee and Ivy drinking a Coke. Dante cleared his throat and began.

At least he tried to.

"I know you've all wondered why I chose to include Angela as part of our team. I have a very good reason, and I'm going to tell you, but it's going to be hard to explain. First, you really need to keep an open mind. Okay?"

He received three blank stares in return.

"It all started during the Hudson crash." He stopped and corrected himself. "Actually, shortly before the Hudson crash." He searched for the right words, finding them strangely absent from his mind. "When Angela got on the plane, we think she was still Angela. But shortly before the plane crashed, we think Angela died."

"She looks alive to me," Selma quipped.

"I am," Angela responded. She looked at Dante and shook her head. "You're making a mess of this."

"You wanna try? Be my guest." He stepped back and waved for Angela to stand front and center.

She took his position and looked at the other women. "You know Dante's not stupid or crazy, right?"

They all nodded.

"But you all wonder why he's insisted on making me his assistant. It's obvious I don't know anything about reporting or editing or anything like that. But you're not ready to call me a gold digger or a bimbo because you're pretty sure I'm not one of those. Right?"

This time, the trio hesitated before answering, consulting each other with brief glances.

"You're okay," Selma pronounced. "I'm not sure what your role is or will be, but you've been carrying your own canteen."

Angela smiled her thanks. "I hope you'll be as understanding about this next part." She turned to Ivy. "You told Dante that you believed in ghosts. I don't know if I'm a ghost or what, but I think I'm being haunted, or possessed, or whatever you want to call it . . . by Chloe Mason."

Neither Selma nor Althea reacted, probably having heard everything at least once in their lives.

But Ivy grinned with enthusiasm. "For real?"

"It's the only explanation that seems to fit. I still don't remember anything about my life as Angela Sands. And nobody seems to remember me, either. It's like I never existed. But what little I do remember is centered on Chloe Mason. Not her life, but her death."

"Police say she was murdered by persons unknown," Selma offered.

"And they're wrong. I know exactly who killed Chloe Mason. Her husband. He shot her while she was in his office. Then either he or someone else dumped her body in that alley."

"She's told you this?" Althea's doubt began to show on her face.

"It's probably not fair to describe this as a haunting. I'm not getting ghostly visits or messages from beyond. I simply . . . know things that only Chloe Mason would know. From best we can determine, I woke up on the plane as the person I am now within seconds of her reported death. The plane may have been close if not directly overhead at the moment of her death."

Ivy boiled over with zeal. "I can just see it. Mason shoots Chloe but she doesn't actually die until after he dumps her in the alley." Her avenging spirit soars up from her body and *BAM!* She bangs into the airplane, spots you sleeping, and pushes your soul aside because she wants to exact retribution for her death."

"Uh . . . something like that."

Selma crossed her arms. "So what are you planning to do? Kill her husband in punishment for his crimes?"

Yes. "No. All I want to do is bring him to justice. We think that because of the details I know about Chloe's death, we can get him to confess. I'm willing to let a court of law take care of meting out the punishment."

As usual, the ever-practical Althea was the one who cut to the chase. "So how does this involve us?"

Dante stepped forward. "We've contacted him with the request to do a piece on his success on Wall Street despite the downturn in the economy. We're appealing to his sense of vanity as a hotshot doing well while everyone around him tanks."

"The only people doing well are the crooks," Selma observed.

"And we're giving him a chance to prove he's not a crook but rather, an extremely savvy investor who anticipated problems and protected himself and his handful of clients from economic ruin."

Selma's dispassionate face began to warm with feeling. "The rich get richer and the poor get poorer. I wouldn't mind helping stick it to someone like him."

Althea still looked dubious. "How are you going to make him confess?"

"I don't care. I'm in," Ivy said, leaning back in her chair.

Selma and Althea, the older and wiser members, threw one another wordless glances. Finally, Selma nodded. "I may or may not believe in ghosts and stuff, but I've seen far too many things in my life that I couldn't explain. As long as we're not talking about using violence, I'm in."

Althea nodded. "Me, too. I mean, the bit about not being able to explain things and the part about being in."

"Good. But that's not all." Dante sat down and glanced at Angela for reassurance and she gave him a nod. He launched into the shortest description he could manage about her abilities to read minds.

They watched both Selma and Althea reach the limits of their willingness to accept the impossible. Ivy looked dubious, but they hadn't lost her. Yet.

Selma broke the unearthly silence that followed his explanation. "You're kidding, right?" She turned to Angela. "If what he says is true, then read my mind."

"It doesn't work that way," Angela said quietly. "I can only read the minds of men."

Selma pointed to Dante. "Then read his mind."

"Except for his."

Even Ivy appeared to surrender to disbelief. Althea stood, apparently ready to leave, but Selma held up her hand. "No, don't. We owe them one chance to prove what they're saying. I think I'm a good judge of character and neither of them has struck me as being crackpots or even deluded. Let's test this out." She reached into her jacket pocket and pulled out a cell, punching a few keys.

"Hey, it's Selma. Can you come up to 2507 for a moment? I'm having a problem with the phone system. Yeah. Thanks." She turned to the group. "One male test subject on his way."

She reached under the conference table and gave something a sharp pull. "And now there's a problem with the phone."

There was a knock on the conference room door a few minutes later, interrupting the eerie silence that had befallen the room.

"Thanks, Perry. We were on a conference call when suddenly the phone went dead."

The technician wadded himself under the table and only a few moments later, emerged with a smile. "Someone kicked the plug out. Simple fix. I can requisition a cover to put over it so that it's better protected, if you like. It's in a pretty vulnerable place."

"That'd be great. I appreciate the quick response and even

quicker fix." Selma walked with him to the door, and stopped him for a quiet conversation. He nodded a few times in response to her questions, and then gestured with a wave. Once the door closed behind her, Selma turned to face Angela. "Well?"

Angela winked at Dante. "At first he was confused about why you brought him up here, considering it was just a loose plug. But when he spotted Ivy, he thought you were one great aunt because he figured you engineered a reason why he could meet her. He's hoping you'll follow through on a matchup. He really thinks she's cute."

The three women registered varying amounts of shock. Selma sat down to deal with her feelings. Althea stood, gripping the back of her chair with a white-knuckled grip. Ivy simply glared at Selma.

"A date? With him?"

Selma seemed relieved to have something else to discuss for the moment. "Hey, he's a nice guy. A little nerdy, but still nice." She swallowed hard and turned to Angela. "Here's what I know: you don't have supersonic hearing or something. I was whispering and I never even said Ivy's name. Plus, I was facing away from you so you weren't reading my lips. That leaves only one other explanation."

Angela nodded. "Now, will you help us trap Lars Mason? Maybe if Chloe Mason decides her murder has been avenged, she'll release whatever hold she has on me and I can start to remember my own life."

The trio of women shared a few glances, then all nodded.

Selma gave them voice.

"We're in."

23

Dante knew it would take just the right story pitch to gain entrance to the world of Lawrence "Lars" Mason. Everyone on the team had joined in the research efforts. By noon the next day, they had a comprehensive background study on a man who had eerily survived several Wall Street debacles that had pulverized the careers and psyches of so many other investors.

However, Lars Mason had not only survived, he'd prospered with a series of some suspiciously timed divestitures of a great deal of stock. Essentially, he'd gotten out early enough to protect his fortunes. Then, when stock prices dipped to subterranean values, he made judicious purchases, profiting off the misfortunes of others. Whereas other Wall Street investors were trying to live on crumbs, he enjoyed a nightly feast.

But Dante knew that he couldn't set up the interview under the guise of a piece on business and then suddenly turn the topic to Lars's lately lamented wife. The crew would be thrown out on their collective ears in seconds. The transition of subject matter had to be subtle and, more importantly, a topic broached by Mason, himself.

Mason's own secretary gave them the perfect opening when she mentioned that Lars was selling his South Hampton mansion and moving into something smaller. The excuse was that his home reminded him so much of his deceased wife. However, wasn't it too bad that the lousy housing market had put his escape plans on hold?

Dante immediately dropped the business-profile interview idea and the fake "Leaving Home" television concept was born, complete with a snazzy LH logo. The premise of the "show" was to feature one particular home for sale while examining the homeowner's reluctance to leave behind so many memories.

Dante couldn't imagine anyone wanting to watch something so potentially maudlin but in their case, it didn't matter. Just as long as Lars Mason bit on the concept of getting his hard-to-sell mansion some free public exposure. Althea was the one to come up with statistics that showed that homes for sale that received national exposure on the various home improvement and design networks sold faster and for higher prices than those limited to traditional sales venues.

"Is that true?" Ivy asked.

Althea laughed. "Doesn't matter whether it is or not, it sounds good, don't you think?"

Once they threw out the baited offer, they all waited to reel it in. Mason took an entire day to consider it. Finally, his personal assistant rang back the next morning with the acceptance.

"I told you he'd jump at the chance." Selma distributed several pages of biographical data to the team as well as pictures of Mason's house purloined from the real estate agent's website featuring the house.

Angela showed no recognition as she studied the photos until she got to his private study. The sheet of paper began to shake in her hands and her face paled.

Dante noticed first. "Angela? You okay?"

She pushed the page away as if the paper was burning her fingers. "That room. His room. That's where I was when he shot me."

No one spoke.

She stared at the picture. "I'd hired a private investigator to follow Lars and take pictures of him with other women. But he found out about it and paid an obscene amount of money to the investigator to get the pictures. That's when he decided I was a liability and he was going to divorce me. But then he realized I'd never signed the prenup." Emotion choked out her voice and Dante continued her story.

"So he decided a messy death would be far less of an interruption than a messy divorce. A real prince of a guy." He turned to the team. "Take note of that. He's ruthless. If he catches a whiff of anything that suggests there's no real show, we could be in danger. Understand?"

The four women, Angela included, all nodded.

Dante tapped the papers stacked in front of him. "So let's go over the plan one more time."

The next morning, they left Manhattan at an obscenely early hour in order to make the two-and-a-half-hour trip to Water Mill, where Mason lived. When they pulled up to the gates, Dante reached over and grabbed Angela's cold hand.

"You okay?" he whispered. "Ready to do this?"

She nodded. "Ready."

Once he identified himself, someone buzzed open the gates and they headed up the long tree-lined driveway. Once they'd parked, he, Angela, and Ivy climbed out of the truck and Selma and Althea shifted into the back to start setting up the equipment.

Ivy carried along a small video camera, supposedly to take visual notes of angles and details they would need to capture. In reality, she had been instructed to get as much footage of Lars Mason and his office as possible without appearing obvious. Thankfully, Angela had a clipboard to clutch to her chest. Otherwise, Dante was afraid her case of nerves would reveal their subterfuge.

They were met at the door by a stern-faced housekeeper who apparently had been expecting them.

"This way."

As they trailed her, Dante shot Angela a questioning look and nodded toward the woman. *Familiar?* he mouthed.

Angela shrugged and shook her head. *No.*

"You must be sad to see Mr. Mason selling his house," Dante offered as a conversation starter.

"Makes no mattah to me," she said with a broad New Englander accent. "I wohk wheyah they send me."

She led them to a set of double doors. "Mistah Mason is waiting for you." Rather than knock or open the doors, she waddled off.

"Here goes," Dante said under his breath. He knocked on the door and heard a voice inside call out. "Come on in."

He held the door open for Angela and Ivy, then stepped in himself. "Mr. Mason? I'm Dante Kearns with TwentyFourSeven." *Shit, mistake number one.* "And *Leaving Home.*"

The smiling man strode across the room, hand outstretched. "Lars Mason. Please call me Lars. I can't tell you how pleased I am to be the first home featured on your show."

"We appreciate your cooperation, sir." He turned to Angela and

Ivy. "These are my associates: Ms. Grant, our camera operator, and Ms. Sands, my production assistant. The rest of our crew is in the truck setting up the video equipment."

"If there's anything they need, please don't hesitate to ask me or any of my staff. To be frank, I'm thankful for the added exposure your show will give my house." He gave them a rueful grin. "You know how slow the housing market has been."

"Can we sit and talk about your house for a moment?"

"Certainly." Mason led them to a seating area formed by a long leather couch and two matching leather chairs. This was definitely the ultimate home office: rich paneled walls lined with book-shelves, a discreet but well-stocked wet bar in the corner, and a credenza that probably hid a fifty-inch flat-screen TV.

When Dante sat down, he couldn't help but admire the view through the window behind him—a wide expanse of lawn ending in shoreline.

"That's Hayground Cove," Mason said. "We're sitting on a little over eight acres with about three hundred feet of shore. Prime real estate in any market."

"Indeed. If I may ask, why are you selling?"

The man was a decent actor. He went from jovial host to dis-traught mourner in a split second. "It's been hard living here, ever since my wife was murdered. Everywhere I look, I see reminders of her and if I can be honest, Mr. Kearns, it hurts to be reminded of her tragic death."

"Please, call me Dante. And I can certainly understand. What we'd like to do is touch on that in the show. We don't want to be maudlin or appear to be playing the sympathy card, but people do care about the backstory of a house."

"You don't think they'll be put off by the circumstances around her death?"

"Not at all," Dante said with as much assurance as he dared

offer. "It's a love story, too. And the American public will see it like that."

A shrewd light pushed away Mason's artful sadness. "I like how you think, Dante. It's a good hook for your show and I suspect I'll benefit from the approach if I can sell the place." He rose from his chair. "Can I take you and your ladies on a tour?"

Angela reached over and touched Dante's arm. "I'm going to head back to the truck and confer with the others. Okay, boss?"

Dante read the first signs of panic building in her eyes. He reached over and placed his hand on top of hers, giving her a little squeeze to indicate he understood. Earlier, they'd discussed a few signals and key phrases she could use if she felt changes coming and wanted to retreat. Using the word "boss" was one of them. But he simply didn't expect her to need rescue quite this soon.

"Sure thing, Ange. Ivy and I will take the tour and will get back to you with our notes."

Angela headed for the door, managing to smoothly sidestep Mason, her actions not appearing to be a deliberate attempt to avoid any contact with him.

However, Dante spotted a look of interest on the man's face as he watched her departure. But whatever awareness Mason had of her was pushed aside as he turned and smiled at Ivy and Dante.

"Shall we start the tour?"

They trooped all over the house, starting with a living room that was bigger than Dante's entire apartment. Mason proudly pointed out the custom wall murals, painted by some artist whose name Dante guessed he was supposed to know. At the end of the room sat a fireplace big enough to roast an entire cow on a spit. Then they hiked across the vast expanse of the living room and entered the dining room. The table that stretched the room's length was set with a full complement of china and sterling as if being prepped for a formal dinner party. Dante counted at least nine pieces of flatware at each setting.

Conspicuous consumption at its best, he thought.

Next, they headed upstairs to view the ten bedrooms, including the master suite. For a man who was still in mourning, Mason had no problem strutting around and proudly showing off his bedroom including the astonishing three-room closet that left Ivy both motionless and speechless.

"Your camera operator seems a bit . . . in shock," Mason remarked as Dante nudged her back to life. She gulped and took more shots.

"She's not the only one. I've been around my share of big homes but I have to admit that I'm taken aback by the sheer elegance and size of your home. It's really stunning."

The compliments seemed to play to Mason's sense of authority and elevation. "Thank you very much." His face fell as if he suddenly remembered to be sad. "That's one of the reasons why I want to sell. My late wife had quite a hand in decorating the place. Everywhere I turn, I see her handiwork—something she purchased for a special corner of the room, a piece of art she had to have. I won't say she was extravagant, but my Chloe earned a Ph.D. in shopping." He brushed away an imaginary tear. "Perhaps I indulged her too much, but isn't that the responsibility and privilege of a happily married man? To make sure that his wife is deliriously happy?" The sigh he released had just the right amount of pathos and nostalgia to sway anyone who didn't know better.

Dante elbowed Ivy again, not because she was in shock but because she was glaring daggers at the man. She raised her camera to her eye, sufficiently camouflaging her expression. However, she did note his silent command to film the closet contents, including the remarkably small amount of women's clothing.

He turned to Mason. "Rather than dwell on your wife's untimely death, we should instead celebrate the remarkable life she lived, featuring all the special touches she added to this place to turn an elegant house into a warm and inviting home."

Mason's facade of grief cracked momentarily, releasing a brief gleam of greed. Then the mask mended itself. "That would be a very fitting memorial to my Chloe. That she lives on, in this house."

"Exactly!" Now, if Dante could only feel as triumphant as he sounded. Problem was, there was no way they could pull off their plan with Angela hiding in the truck. . . .

She was the key to everything.

"Let me show you the grounds."

The tour continued outside to the backyard with Mason showing off the saltwater pool with its retractable roof, the staff apartment above the six-car garage, the gym, the impressively large and well-stocked wine cellar, and, of course, the tennis courts.

All the comforts . . .

"The house itself was designed by Dwight Krause to resemble some of the older mansions in the area, but it was only built six years ago. Old-school charm and class but with new construction techniques and technologies."

They ended their tour by the front door, where the truck was parked. While they were gone, Althea had tapped into the house's power grid, saving them from running the generator. As they passed by, Angela leaned out of the truck's door and motioned to Dante. He excused himself but before he made a couple steps toward the truck, he watched Mason turn his attention to Ivy, insisting that she join him for a quick tour of the orchard. Ivy didn't seem thrilled, but begrudgingly took one for the team and walked off with the man, keeping herself at arm's length.

Once Dante was inside the truck, Angela shut the door quickly. "It's taking everything I have to not scream at him."

Selma glared at them both. "If you gotta do something, do it soon. I think the girl's going to explode."

Dante turned to Angela. "We can push the timetable up. There's no need to sell him on our plan; he's ready to make this the Chloe Mason Memorial."

"The cameras are in place," Althea said from the main editing position. She punched up the five feeds, three from the study: camera one, focused on the couch; camera two, pointed toward the desk; and camera three, a wide shot from the corner, capturing the entire room. "I also set up two in the bedroom." She pulled up the feeds on the monitors. "Camera four goes wide to get the bed, and covers the doors to the hallway and the closet suite. Camera five reverses the angle, getting the bed and also covering the bathroom door."

"Excellent work. What about sound?"

"I placed wireless mics so that we should pick up anything above a whisper in either room." She leveled Dante with a dark-eyed stare. "You know that nothing we get will be admissible in court if you don't get the releases signed."

"Next on the agenda." He turned to Angela. "That's a good place for you to start."

She swallowed hard. "Okay."

When they stepped out of the truck, Ivy and Mason were returning to the front door. Ivy excused herself and almost ran into the truck, leaving Dante and Angela to follow Mason back to his office.

Angela stepped into her role nicely. "Mr. Mason, we have standard releases we need you to sign. Basically, it says that you give us permission to record you and we promise that during editing we will not take any of your comments or remarks out of context. It gives us permission to use your image or words in the show itself as well as in any promotion of the show. The second form describes the limits of our liability. The usual stuff. We'll take ordinary precautions while filming in your home and in the case of damages, the company will return the home and its furnishings to their original condition."

Dante watched her step closer to Mason, an action he knew pained her in many ways. Her smile wavered, then grew stronger. Was it self-control or was she already picking up on his desires?

"I'm sure you'll want a lawyer to look over these before signing them."

When Mason took the papers and scanned them quickly, the message on his face was clear. *No way in hell am I signing those.* But a moment later, his resolve seemed to weaken. He leaned forward slightly as if trying to get closer to her. To her credit, she didn't lean away.

"For you, beautiful? Anything."

Dante was torn. He'd battled his protective instincts earlier when they first discussed how to coerce a confession out of Lars Mason. Now, he discovered that executing the plan was far harder than he'd ever imagined.

But he excused himself and stepped out, trying not to be obvious as he raced back to the truck in order to monitor Angela's controlled seduction.

By the time he jumped into the truck, Mason was standing at his desk signing the release forms as Angela stood next to him. Dante knew it wasn't his imagination running wild when he realized her hair had darkened to honey gold and her torso had lengthened, causing her short skirt to appear even shorter.

Her otherwise loose blouse appeared to be growing tighter, too.

"Tell me what the hell is going on," Selma demanded. "Either I'm crazy or Angela's . . . getting taller. Bustier."

Dante stared at the monitor, looking for the secret signs that Angela had agreed to give to assure Dante she was still in control. "I can't begin to explain, but call it a side effect of being possessed by a dead woman."

Althea zoomed in on Angela in time to see her lick her lips and use her pen to tap on the clipboard.

The sign! Dante released the breath he didn't realize he was holding. So far, so good.

"I'm so sorry I missed the tour of your home, Mr. Mason," she purred, shifting closer to him. "Your home is spectacular."

He turned to hand her the papers, somewhat startled by her close proximity, but quickly accepting it. "Not nearly as spectacular as you, my dear."

Ivy snorted. "He pulled that one on me, too. You don't know how hard it was to resist the urge to slap him."

Dante hushed her and asked Althea to turn up the sound.

Mason reached over and touched Angela's cheek with the tip of his forefinger. "Just a moment. You have a loose eyelash." He held his finger out for her inspection. She pulled his hand closer to her mouth, paused, then softly blew the lash away, holding on to his hand far too long for Dante's comfort.

Then she bent down and bussed it with her lips. "Thank you, Mr. Mason."

He seemed both shocked and pleased by her overt gesture. "It's Lars."

"Lars," she repeated, shooting him a shy smile. "I'm Angela."

"A heavenly name for an angelic woman. I find it hard to believe that you're kept behind the cameras, a beauty like you."

Angela had indeed morphed into a long-legged beauty, her hair darkening to a rich chestnut brown and her fair skin gaining an exotic olive cast.

"Got to be a problem with the color," Althea explained, twisting several dials. "Give me a minute and I'll get it back to normal."

Dante reached out and pushed her hand away from the controls. "Nothing's wrong with the equipment. It's Angela. It's one of her talents—to change. She's reading his mind and transforming into the girl of his dreams."

"That's the girl of his dreams," Ivy said, pointing to another monitor. She'd patched her footage she'd taken from her small video camera into the system, fast-forwarding through it until she reached the shots taken in the bedroom. She paused the picture on a series of magazines scattered across an occasional table in the bedroom. Every magazine was turned to a particular page, each one containing a print ad featuring one particular face: a dark-haired, exotic, long-legged beauty who looked eerily like Angela looked now.

"Angela looks like her. Does that mean this woman is his dream girl?"

Selma leaned back in her chair. "Not anymore. Look. Our Angela is certainly a fast worker."

Mason and Angela were kissing and Dante decided that if she was playacting, then she was ready for an Oscar nomination.

To their collective surprise, Mason was the one to break away, first. "D-don't you worry about your colleagues finding us like this?"

The laughter still sounded like Angela, even if the voice didn't. "No. Now that I've brought up the subject of the releases and waivers, they won't . . . they can't step a foot back in here until I come out with signed papers. Our lawyers would have a fit. I can keep them outside for hours, if necessary."

"It wouldn't take hours." He reached out and toyed with the button straining against the buttonhole.

Angela obediently undid the button, giving them all an unobstructed view of the tops of her breasts, threatening to spill out of her bra.

"Man," Ivy said in a hushed voice. "I wish mine could do that on command."

Althea and Selma glared at her for a brief moment, then turned their gazes back to the monitor.

Dante searched her dark eyes, hoping to see some signs of Angela being still in control. He worried that she was already lost in the transformation, even though she'd assured him she would retain her hold on herself.

We should have practiced more. I should have never agreed to let her do this. I'm such an idio—

"God, they're perfect." After unbuttoning the rest of her shirt, Mason had released her bra, allowing her new abundance of breast to explode forward. He bent down and buried his face in her cleavage.

Dante pushed up from the chair, but sat down hard when Angela looked up into the camera, smiled with her new face, and held her hand behind Mason's back where he couldn't see her gesture.

Thumbs-up.

24

All Angela could figure was that her extreme hatred for Lars Mason protected her from falling completely under his control.

She felt as if she were working outside of her body, orchestrating every movement, every word with complete and total detached control. She controlled not only herself but him, too, anticipating his every reaction to her action.

She would be the puppet master, pulling his strings. First, she would have fun at his expense, making him dance for a while. Then once she tired of that, she'd wring a confession out of Lars, a total and damning accounting of the crimes he'd committed against her. Maybe she'd force him to go to the police and confess there. What a delicious revenge that would be.

"I want you. Now. Here," he said between clenched teeth.

Although his desire was mounting, it failed to penetrate her mental defenses. Angela remained strong. Remained herself. He groped and panted and led her to the rug in front of the fireplace. She'd made love to Lars on that spot right after they'd returned from their honeymoon. It was the first time she witnessed his cruel streak.

So she was ready when he hauled back and slapped her now.

"Slut," he growled in challenge.

Rather than cower in shock as she had the first time, she leaned up, turning the other check. "Do it again, baby."

A new light filled his eyes. And he hit her again with more noise and shock than actual damage. Why hadn't she figured this out the first time? Had Chloe Mason been so very naïve?

She reared back and returned the favor, obviously shocking him with her challenging slap. Reaching into his mind, she tickled his reaction, turning his momentary anger at being hit into an intense pleasure.

"Again," Lars moaned.

She debated using a closed fist and catching him in the jaw. But instead, she used her open palm to leave a red welt on his face.

His excitement mounted and suddenly, they were a fury of passion. Halfway through, her conscience sprung to life. Her control had slipped. For a few moments, she'd forgotten who she was, who he was. Her all-consuming anger had momentarily become an all-consuming passion. If she didn't give Dante a signal, she knew he'd be bursting through the door any moment now, playing White Knight.

"We better hurry before my boss gets too curious."

"Fuck-your-boss." Lars said the words in rhythm of his thrusts. Evidently, the physical abuse had constituted foreplay and now they were fully embroiled in the sexual act. Somehow, they'd shifted from the rug to hanging off the end of a zebra-print settee.

She bit his shoulder, drawing blood. He twisted her breast with a savage glee. When her moans got too loud, he slapped her in the mouth, then muffled her screams with his hand.

And God help her, she liked it.

She tried not to think about the audience, observing her little act. Then again, maybe they were enjoying the show.

Suddenly her conscience broke free, escaping from the hold of her overpowering desire. Shame filled her as she realized that only moments before, she had been willing to perform any and every sexual act that Chloe Mason couldn't bring herself to try.

This wasn't her lover, she reminded herself.

He was the enemy.

She heard a noise at the door and knew it must be Dante, come to rescue her. Maybe she could salvage the plan, redeem herself. But she only had moments to do so.

Mason had released her, his energies momentarily spent. He was sitting on the floor, panting in exertion. "What do you want?" he called to the door.

She wondered if he'd locked it. She didn't remember.

"Mr. Mason, it's Parker. I heard a noise. Is everything all right?"

Exhaustion had gotten the best of Lars and his voice was little more than a whisper. "I'm fine."

Evidently, the door wasn't locked, because it opened and a man leaned inside. "Mr. Mason, sir?" He spotted Angela and his innermost desire slammed into the room, pushing Mason's aside.

The man smirked. "Did I miss something?"

"Get out, you asshole. Can't you see I'm busy?" Lars turned to Angela. "It's just one of my employees." He turned back toward the door. "Shut the door."

"Gladly." But instead of stepping outside, he stepped inside and locked the door behind him. "If you're tired, I'll be glad to stand in for you, Mr. Mason. After all, I am your bodyguard. But honestly? It's her body I'd much rather guard."

Mason stared dumbfounded at the man. "What part of 'get the hell out' do you not understand?"

The man strode across the room, dropping his coat and hat on the floor behind him. "I deserve to have a little fun, too."

His fondest desire slammed into Angela, hitting her hard enough to cause her to arch backward and almost lose her balance. She felt her body warring between the two desires, trying to decide which was the stronger of the two. Which man would be the superior mate . . .

"Make him go away," she managed between clenched teeth.

Mason struggled to his feet. "Take a hike, Parker. She's mine."

"The hell she is. I want her." The larger man advanced on them, the look in his eyes suggesting he had the strength and skill to back his declarations.

When Parker threw his meaty fist at Mason, Angela thought surely she was about to witness a slaughter. But Mason surprised her by dodging the blow and slamming his fist into the man's unprotected ribs. They danced around each other, throwing punches as if their desires had been temporarily redirected into a need to eliminate the competition.

The heat of battle meant that they both freed Angela from their innermost lust, allowing her to read their minds without any boomerang emotions in return.

Even though Parker was fighting hard, he was trying to figure out the repercussions of his rash actions. His biggest fear seemed to be incarceration. As a result of his ill-timed attack, he'd already come to the conclusion that he would have to kill his boss or risk being arrested for assault and battery and the larceny charge Lars had been holding over his head.

Kill his boss and maybe kill her, too. His thoughts sliced through her mind. *"After I get through fucking her."*

Then his mind took an odd turn, accompanied by some equally

odd images—a bloody Chloe Mason, lying in this very room. *"I should have fucked his wife, too."* Chloe's body shoved carelessly in a car's trunk. *"Before I dumped her. I wonder what it's like to fuck a dead body?"* Parker standing over Chloe's inert form, shooting a gun into the air.

"Maybe I can kill this one first, then fuck her . . ."

"Angela!"

She felt Dante's presence even before she heard him pounding on the door and calling her name. Spurred into action by his shouts, Angela rose to her feet, spread out her arms, and closed her eyes. Using every bit of concentration she could muster, she reached into Dante's mind and borrowed his strength and his focus.

"Tell me what you did to Chloe Mason," she thundered in two voices—hers and Chloe's—as she screamed the demand at Mason and Parker. Her will would not be denied.

"He did it," Parker said, throwing a sluggish haymaker at Lars who easily ducked the blow. "He killed her. Not me."

"Tell me why you killed her," she demanded.

Lars threw a series of blows in slow motion, speaking between his attempts to connect with Parker's face and stomach. "A divorce would have meant . . . I had to reveal . . . my finances to her lawyers . . . they'd have realized . . . how much I've been embezzling . . . from my investment clients."

He finally smacked a lucky punch into Parker's stomach, causing the man to double over in pain. Angela felt Parker's consciousness wink out. His brain shut down.

Mason shook his head like a man released from a spell. Then he grabbed Parker's head and smashed it down into the coffee table. The sleek piece of furniture exploded into a bunch of expensive splinters.

Parker collapsed into a limp pile of flesh.

Lars turned a clear-eyed sneer of triumph toward Angela. "No way I'd let that bitch ruin me. Just like I won't let you."

Angela felt Lars's desires tug at her, demanding and deadly. She fought against his lust, his invasive thoughts.

She'd kill herself before she'd let this monster turn her into some obedient sex slave, begging for him to rape her, pleading for a chance to please him.

Losing herself forever in his lust.

No, no. Don't kill yourself. Was it Angela or Chloe she heard? She couldn't tell.

Kill him.

She heard a horrific noise of breaking wood and the door burst open. Dante tumbled into the room, evidently having lost his balance after using his shoulder to smash through the door. When she saw Lars lunge toward the desk, she tried to tackle him, knowing he kept a loaded gun in the top drawer.

Probably the same gun he'd used to kill her.

She knew he would shoot Dante and then her.

But Lars pulled out of her grasp. He drove a brutal kick into Dante's unprotected midsection. When he turned to the desk, she hit him again with all her might. She rocked him back on his feet, but not enough to knock him down. She knew she had to keep him away from the drawer.

He broke free and grabbed for the gun.

She struggled with him for possession of the weapon.

Logic said that she was no match for him. He'd displayed some advanced skills when fighting and beating his own well-trained bodyguard.

But she had something he didn't . . .

Lars had become a slave to his libido years ago, measuring everything in terms of his carnal satisfaction. He had an unquenchable hunger for wealth, an unending lust for power, and an undeniable appetite for women.

Lars was nothing more than a captive of his desires.

The poor bastard . . .

Angela stepped toward Dante, who remained motionless on the floor. She reached down, touching him. His strength flowed into her like water soaking parched ground. She could have drained him dry, but she wasn't greedy; she only needed a jump start.

"Get away from him," Lars ordered.

"Gladly," she said, as if she was willing to obey him. But in reality, she was positioning herself.

All the better to see you, my dear . . .

She had seen a particularly vivid image of Chloe in his mind, one she knew would be perfect for her needs.

"Lars, look at me."

She'd become a picture-perfect Chloe Mason, just as he'd last seen her the night he'd killed her. "Put the gun down, Lars."

He froze at the sound of her voice. Chloe's voice.

"I said, put the gun down. You've done enough killing."

His hand shook. He blinked as if he couldn't believe his eyes. His aim wavered. "You're not real," he whispered.

"I'm as real as you are." She reached forward and picked up a silver frame from his desk. Once upon a time, it had held a picture of them on the deck of their yacht, *Chloe-Bateau*. It now sported a shot of Lars standing by the boat, his wife and first mate conspicuously absent.

"You can try to remove me from your life. Destroy the pictures of us. Rename the boat. Even sell the house. But you'll never be rid of me. No matter where you go, I'll be there. People will start to whisper. Rumors will follow you. No matter how fast you run from me, I will come back. I'll never let you be free." She lowered her voice to a whisper. "I'll always be here to remind you of what you did to me."

He raised the gun and aimed it at her.

She laughed. "Go ahead. Shoot. It doesn't matter. You can't kill me. I'm already dead."

He tried to steady the gun with his other hand.

"Give it up, Lars. There's not enough money in the world to buy you out of this. Your bimbo of the month won't have anything to do with you once I get through with her. No woman will. You may like them young and stupid, but you always forget that those kinds of girls are the easiest ones to scare. I'll haunt you to a cold and lonely death."

She laughed again, blowing him a kiss. "Kiss everything good-bye: your wealth, your position, your friends. You'll be alone forever. Alone except for me."

"G-go away." He stepped backward as if trying to get away from her.

"We're going to have so much fun, Lars. Forever and ever. Forever and ever . . ."

He raised the barrel of the gun to his temple.

She said nothing to stop him. Although she'd prefer for him to live a long time in a miserable cell, if he made the choice to kill himself, then so be it.

So be it, right?

"Stop him, Chloe." Angela spoke calmly but firmly. This Chloe was nothing more than a terrifying construct, an image built from Lars's deepest fears and guilt. But now it was time to regain control of the situation.

This Chloe was completely his construct. Her words were only echoing his own terror that he'd face justice.

Angela kept the appearance of Chloe on her face, but blocked out the avenging Chloe filling Lars's imagination.

"Put the gun down, Mason," Angela said in Chloe's voice. "Killing yourself is not the answer."

An explosion ripped through the study.

25

"I didn't realize that the other man, Parker, had a gun." Angela kept a tight grip on Dante's hand as much for comfort as for the control he helped her to keep while being around a half dozen male officers and detectives.

"I guess it makes sense he'd be armed if he was Mr. Mason's bodyguard. I just didn't think about it at the time."

The investigating officer took notes as she spoke.

"I thought surely he was dead after he hit the coffee table."

The detective looked up from his notebook. "Could you tell what they had been fighting over?"

"Not really. All I know was that Mr. Mason threatened him by saying he was going to tell the police about something that Mr. Parker had done. I had no idea what they were talking about, but both men were really upset." The shiver that coursed through her body was real even though everything else she said was a complete and total lie.

"He just panicked."

Randall Parker had admitted that he'd shot Lars Mason, but he had implicated the man in the murder of his wife, Chloe. Even as he'd confessed, he'd sent terrified looks at Angela. Apparently her appearance as the ghost of Chloe had shaken him enough that he felt the need to purge his soul by confession.

Parker blurted out his story as soon as the police arrived, as if afraid he wouldn't be able to remember the embellishments he'd made up while being held at bay by Selma.

Selma had arrived on scene moments after Parker shot Mason, killing him instantly. Evidently, when Parker woke up, he was still gripped by the same kill-or-be-killed mentality that had guided the earlier fight. All he noticed was that Mason had the gun, not that he was aiming it at his own head.

Parker pumped three shots into him.

It took several moments for the shock to fade away and the revelation of his actions to sink in. When Parker realized what he'd done, he dropped the gun and tried to run, only to be tackled by Dante who had been roused by the gunfire. Dante'd gotten a few punches in, but it was Angela who had him shaking in his boots. It was clear he'd do anything to avoid going up against her. Her performance as the dead Chloe had clearly been enough to scare him straight for the rest of his life.

Parker had used his time wisely while awaiting police custody, though, coming up with an inventive story. Supposedly, after killing his wife Chloe, his boss Lars Mason had coerced Parker into dumping her body in Manhattan, near the museum where she worked. The idea was to make everyone believe she was shot there. Mason knew that Parker was guilty of a string of small robberies committed as a young man. If Parker didn't help him, Mason threatened to tell the police about the crimes. Mason was also the one who arranged to have his mistress, dressed in Chloe's clothes, take the train into town and then a cab to the museum.

Mason had covered all the angles but one.

It wasn't until Parker was stashing Chloe's body in the alley that he realized she was still alive. Afraid to go against his boss, he devised a quick plan. He deposited her body, then fired a shot in the air hoping someone would investigate the noise and find her immediately. When he saw a couple of sanitation workers rush out of the alley, Parker left, assuming she'd now get medical attention.

It wasn't his fault that she died on the way to the hospital. He'd done everything he could. . . .

But while he may have been an unwilling accomplice to one murder, he'd refused to have any part of a second. When he saw his boss preparing to shoot another poor unfortunate woman, he'd snapped, protecting her as he should have protected poor Mrs. Mason. . . .

Angela didn't buy a word of it.

But as long as the cops did, it served its purpose.

After confiscating the footage that Althea had artfully edited with breakneck speed that removed all evidence of their involvement and taking statements from them all, the police released the team.

They waited until they were safely off the estate grounds and several miles down the road before Dante pulled into a parking lot.

"I think we need to talk."

The discussion started out roughly. Angela first confessed that instead of being possessed by Chloe Mason's ghost, she only possessed some of Chloe Mason's memories. Somehow, those memories had been carried along with her as she was reborn into the mysterious Angela Sands's body shortly before the airplane crash. Who Angela Sands was, nobody really knew.

Despite their collective looks of disbelief, Angela continued, explaining how she discovered her morphing talents and what appeared to be their range and limitations.

Dante jumped in a few times to offer clarification, but he left most of it up to Angela. Although the three women had witnessed the transformations via the video, he learned that that didn't mean they were quite ready to accept the impossible.

"Show us now," Ivy demanded. "Change into . . . me."

"I can't do it on command," Angela said, her white knuckles betraying her irritation. "I can only pick an image from the mind of a man I'm near."

Ivy pointed to Dante. "Behold. A man."

Dante held up both hands. "It won't work with me."

"Why not?"

It was the question he feared the most, only because he didn't know the answer. "We don't know why."

"But we intend to find out." Angela turned to Dante for support. "Right?"

"Right."

Althea, who had remained quiet during the discussion, looked up from her PDA. She finally spoke. "A succubus." She tapped the unit's screen. "I remembered hearing about it in school."

"A succu—what?" Ivy pivoted to face her. "Isn't that what a cactus is?"

Althea shook her head. "No, that's a succulent. A succu*bus* is a mythological creature, a demon who turns into an attractive woman in order to seduce and feed off of men, often killing them in the process by draining them."

Angela covered her mouth with her hand and stared at Dante. "Have I been feeding off of you?" she asked in a hushed voice.

"Absolutely not."

Ivy bounced up and down in her seat. "Sure she has. We watched her do it." She turned to Angela. "When you . . . turned yourself into Chloe . . . you tapped him when you needed to." She replayed the tape. "There."

The video slowed to normal speed.

Angela was walking by the downed Dante. She looked terrible, half-dead, but after she touched him she was once again radiant.

The camera captured a slight spark between them which could have been lens flare or a reflection or caused by a host of other reasonable explanations.

Dante had noticed the spark the moment he saw the footage and he hadn't been concerned. She knew exactly what she was doing.

A week before, he'd watched as she regained control of herself in the bar when touching him. The contact between them had started the same chain reaction, one more time. She wasn't stealing anything from him, just triggering her own control.

Selma had remained quiet during the discussion, keeping her arms crossed and wearing a blank expression. She'd kept her belief or disbelief to herself. When she finally spoke, there was none of her usual brusqueness.

"Why didn't she suck everything out of you?" she asked in an uncharacteristically soft voice.

Dante squeezed Angela's hand, in support and also to demonstrate to the others that he didn't fear her contact. On the contrary, he craved it. Something about the transfer of his energy to her was just as personal and satisfying as . . . making love. "She didn't. She never will. I guess you can say I have faith in her." He turned away, praying no one saw the flush he felt rising from his collar.

Althea jumped in. "In her. A possible demon?"

Angela sat up straight in the seat. "I'm not a demon."

Before Dante could Angela's denial, Selma raised her hand with a sense of finality, which effectively cut off all responses but her own. "I agree," Selma said with conviction. "If you were a demon, you wouldn't have cared who murdered Chloe Mason. You definitely wouldn't have tried to stop the guilty party from committing suicide. Demons thrive on chaos, but so far, you've tried to stop the chaos. I don't know *what* you are, but I do believe you were put here, given your abilities to do something good in this world."

An evident convert, Ivy picked up the thread. "My nana says that demons always prey on the innocent; they don't protect them. And you've protected them."

Althea looked up from her PDA. "What's the opposite of a demon?"

Ivy whistled. "An angel!" She held out both hands as if weighing the words. "Angel. Angela. Coincidence or not?"

"Don't be ridiculous, Ivy. Dante can tell you that I've done a whole host of unangelic things. I may not know who Angela Sands is, but I know she's no angel."

"It's getting dark," Ivy noted. "We'd better head back."

Dante started the truck and merged back into the growing traffic.

Everyone remained quiet for the next half hour or so. Dante figured that they were still pretty stunned by the revelations and were going over the details, trying to rationalize how to accept the impossible.

Finally someone spoke.

"What's next?" Selma inquired. "You've solved the murder of Chloe Mason. Where do you go from here?"

Angela shrugged. "I don't know."

"Haven't you asked yourself, who is Angela Sands?"

"A thousand times."

"Don't you think it's a little suspicious that there's no paper trail for her?"

"Suspicious?"

Ivy popped up over Selma's shoulder. "Sounds like a cover-up by the feds. You know—like she was in the witness protection program?"

Althea joined in as well. "Nah, the feds would have created a trail for her. There'd be documents, faked backgrounds, identification. They would never have left a big hole like this. Also, they would have shut you down, hard and fast."

"And thus says our resident conspiracy theorist."

"At least I'm not some curly-haired moppet whose sole videographer credits are on YouTube."

Selma joined in. "Now, children . . ."

Dante laughed at the good-natured bickering, a sign that not only were they a team but that they had come to grips and accepted Angela, unbelievable talents and all. Angela slipped into the passenger's seat.

"What should I do next?"

"You mean what should *we* do next?"

She smiled at the inclusion.

"I think they're right. We need to figure out who Angela Sands is. Did she . . . did you have these powers before the crash?"

"So where do we start looking?"

They passed by a highway sign, proclaiming that they were forty-five miles from JFK. Dante pointed to the sign.

"We track her back. To Los Angeles."

EPILOGUE

Dante had only flown in the corporate jet once before, just because the chief of programming was flying to Atlanta for a meeting and he was allowed to tag along to minimize expenses. He'd been on a different story about a missing woman, reportedly spotted in Georgia.

It'd been a bust.

But now the corporate jet was at his disposal, thanks to the very grateful Smithfield family whose biggest fear appeared to be the criminal outing of their black-sheep son.

At first, Dante believed that he'd won his new position solely thanks to his talent, his long-term employment, and the Smithfield family's genuine appreciation for confidentiality in the matter of their wayward son. However, it didn't take too long for him to realize they wanted to buy his silence and short-circuit any black-mail attempts. The world knew about Victor's plans to embezzle the money and escape to Rio with his Double-D mistress. But not about the attack on Dante, the plans to frame him, or most impor-tantly, the bomb that would have killed everyone on board the flight to China.

And yet blackmail had never crossed Dante's mind . . .

He made sure the team knew that he didn't believe in extortion and that they would all have to work very hard to earn their high-rent office space and generous expense account.

It'd never crossed his mind . . .

But he made sure the team knew that he didn't believe in extor-tion and that they would all have to work very hard to earn their high-rent office space and generous expense account.

Despite their fancy digs and their combined efforts—Althea's research abilities, Selma's contacts, and Ivy's ability to see outside of the box—they'd reached a dead end when it came to Angela Sands.

She remained a nonentity. A woman who didn't exist one month prior to the airplane crash. She didn't appear in a single govern-ment database. She didn't even have any credit cards; her Manhat-tan hotel was paid for with cash.

So now the two of them were winging their way to Los Angeles while the rest of the team stayed behind, continuing to find dead ends in the search for information on Angela Sands.

Angela was nervous, but considering the outcome of her most recent flight, Dante understood completely. It was one of the reasons why he opted to take the corporate jet rather than a commercial one.

One of the reasons.

She tapped the leather armrest of her seat, betraying frayed nerves. "How are we supposed to find a trail that went cold over a month ago?"

He unbuckled his seatbelt and stretched. "We just dig, harder than usual."

"It sounds impossible."

"You want something to drink? The plane comes completely stocked." He stepped over to the bar and pulled out a full-size bottle of vodka. "And not with those tiny little bottles, either."

"No, thanks."

"It'd calm your nerves a little."

She appeared to contemplate the idea, then shook her head. "I don't think so. I'm afraid I'd just get tipsy and nervous and that might be even worse."

He abandoned the bar and dropped into the chair next to her, picking up her hand. "Boy, your hands are like ice. Want a blanket or something?"

She nodded and he retrieved one from an overhead bin. Unfolding it, he tucked it around her and in what he considered an afterthought, he kissed her on the forehead.

Angela felt a spark flare inside of her. But she squelched it immediately. Since she couldn't read Dante's mind, it had to be a stray thought from someone else nearby. Maybe the pilot or copilot.

He sat next to her and picked up her hand again trying to warm it. "What's wrong?"

"Something's wrong," she confessed. "My hands are cold, but I feel all hot inside. My heart's beating fast like I'm having an adrenaline rush. I'm having a problem drawing in a deep breath. I . . . I feel something." She lowered her voice, almost embarrassed by how husky her whisper sounded. "As much as I hate to say it, I'm feeling . . . desire, from somebody."

He looked almost amused. "From who?"

She shivered. "I don't know. Maybe the pilot?"

"From Marianna?" He shook his head. "I seriously doubt it."

A woman? "What about the copilot? Maybe he's attracted to her."

"God, I hope not. I don't think copilot's husband would appreciate hearing that. He's quite a jealous man. That's one of the reasons why Marianna and Penny fly together as a team."

"The crew's all female?"

He grinned. "Yep, and you don't know how many strings I pulled to make that happen. I'm getting quite an undeserved reputation as a lady's man, surrounding myself only with women." He laughed. "Not that I'm complaining."

"Then whose desire did I just pick up?" She thought of an unsavory answer. "Could there be a stowaway?"

He laughed again. "No. No stowaways." He raised her cold fingers to his lips and kissed the back of her hand. "You're forgetting one person."

She stared at him. "You?" Had she finally broken through whatever barriers lay between them and forced her will onto him? If so, she'd lost everything—including her best friend.

"Not me. You," he whispered.

"I . . . don't have desires, not of my own," she whispered back.

"Why not? You're a woman. You're entitled to them, too."

"But I can't ever tell if they're mine or not. So, I just assume that they belong to someone else." It'd been such an ongoing struggle, pushing away all those invasive thoughts. But hadn't she been getting better at compartmentalizing them? Evidently she wasn't good enough yet.

He leaned over and kissed her. "You're at thirty thousand feet and I'm the only man around. We know you can't read my mind and I can't influence yours. What you're feeling are your very own desires."

She looked into his eyes, seeing a sense of intimacy that she knew was real, not borrowed, not forced.

When he pulled back, she felt a momentary panic, as if she was about to let a singular opportunity slip away. But she understood what he was saying—the decision had to be hers.

Mine.

She pushed away the blanket, unbuckled the safety belt, then moved over to sit in his lap. When she brushed her lips against his ear, she felt him shiver in response.

"Hope you have some stamina," she purred. "I have a feeling that once I get started, I'm not going to want to quit. How long does this flight take?"

He began to kiss her neck. "Five hours."

"Hmmm. That'll be a good start."